A MAN OF HIS WORD

D1248916

A MAN OF HIS WORD

IMMA MONSÓ

Translated from the Catalan
by Maruxa Relaño and Martha Tennent

Hispabooks Publishing, S. L.
Madrid, Spain
www.hispabooks.com

All rights reserved. No part of this book may be reproduced in any form or by any means without permission in writing by the publisher except in the case of brief quotations embodied in critical articles or reviews.

Copyright © Imma Monsó, 2006

Originally published in Spain as *Un home de paraula* by La Magrana
(RBA Libros), 2006
First published in English by Hispabooks, 2014
English translation copyright © by Maruxa Relaño and Martha Tennent
Design © simonpates - www.patesy.com

Cover image © Philipp Salzgeber. Photo of the comet Hale-Bopp taken in the vicinity of Pazin in Istria, Croatia, March 1997.

A CIP record for this book is available from the British Library

ISBN 978-84-942830-3-1 (trade paperback)
ISBN 978-84-942830-4-8 (ebook)
Legal Deposit: M-21567-2014

The translation of this work was supported by a grant from the Institut Ramon Llull

**institut
ramon llull**
Catalan Language and Culture

And other strains of woe, which now seem woe,
Compared with loss of thee will not seem so.

SHAKESPEARE, "Sonnet 90"

CONTENTS

A, B . . . A . . . ? B . . . ?

Introit

I don't remember what I was like before I met him. All I know is that I used to traipse around with my eggs, searching for a place to put them, a basket where I could keep them all together, for I hated the idea of splitting them up into separate containers. All in one place: I knew that was what I wanted. My first acquaintance with Cometa came after a very difficult sentimental apprenticeship, and when I met him I knew that in him I had accomplished my goal. The Great Goal. Intellectual stimulation, warmth, brains, tenderness, comfort, complicity, and heated debate. Passion and compassion, earthly fire and roller-coaster adventure all held in the same gaze. Deep friendship and wild Eros all in the same nest. Starry, ardent nights and reading on the sofa with a smoking pipe nearby, all on the same stage. Summer storms and friendly fog all in the same landscape. I didn't need to move, I didn't need to. There was no reason to. There was no place to go. Everything was right there, within a small, circumscribed area, within reach.

I mention the eggs because my lyrical imagination has always tended toward the homespun. I've kept this atavistic longing for solid ground, and the cosmopolitan fumes of the large city haven't refined me. Even less so after living with Cometa for sixteen years. The image of someone strolling about with eggs in her skirt, searching for a basket to hold them is certainly arcadian. And very much me. I distinctly remember the origin of this image. I must have been about ten years old and mother's daily homecomings were never routine or dull—which is not to say that the woman experienced many momentous events, but she placed great importance on the things that did happen to her. That is what transformed her into a lively narrator who would sweep triumphantly into the house, her arrival generally prefaced by an opening statement that I immediately visualized in a vivid way. "Never put all your eggs in one basket," she proclaimed one evening when she returned from work. Apparently, that morning she'd discussed with the manager of her bank (or, rather, with her bank manager) how to invest her savings. He'd advised her to diversify. This was of course not a novel idea to her, nor especially original, but the man had used this intelligible, barnyard cliché, and it had instantly clarified matters. Much the way bewildering things can suddenly be illuminated when someone sums them up with the right turn of phrase.

The phrase had completely convinced her, and she was attempting to convey this conviction to me. It wasn't easy. She hurled the words with the forcefulness of a lapidary statement invested with indisputable power, provoking me— with my contrarian instinct—to claim them immediately as my own and apply to them a logic contrary to the usage intended. I was hooked forever on the image her phrase had evoked. I pictured myself at the age of ten, singing and strolling through a magnificent meadow of wild flowers, eggs gathered in my skirt, searching for a place to store them—*all of them*. I have to admit that the words "bank," "savings," and "allocation of eggs" meant nothing to me. The farm scene with the hesitant child traversing woods and meadows, her skirt filled with priceless eggs, was much more appealing. I saw her as a version of the dreamy-eyed milkmaid with a pail on her head, but unlike the milkmaid—a shrewd businesswoman out to multiply her gains—my vision bore no relationship to money. No, no.

Inside each of my eggs was an entire universe made up solely of passion and yearning, each associated with love. Oh, yes, love. To succeed in love, the true key to happiness, was the only challenge that interested me. This was a time when having a career was the great challenge that the majority of the girls my age had set for themselves; they wanted to be NASA scientists or Supreme Court prosecutors or something comparable; and if finding a partner was a girl's goal, it wasn't to live out some everlasting passion, but rather to set up the home-and-children business (which implied living with a man) only to subsequently forget about him and devote herself to house and offspring, or to physics and chemistry. What I wanted, however, was to experience Absolute Love, a love that would be sufficient in itself, difficult, rich, complex, a love beyond which nothing else would be needed. Because everything would be contained therein. In the same basket: physics and chemistry, music and logic, transcendence and descendants. None of that shrewd distribution of my affective assets: I had to satisfy all my many demanding appetites in the same person, and everything would be for that person. I wanted it all in one sole individual, everything in the same sanctuary, everything safely harbored. It was either all or nothing.

In the spring of 1987 I found that basket, and in the autumn of 2003 it burst into a thousand pieces. No one can ever be prepared for a sudden explosion of *all the eggs*, unless there's been a countdown. Nor, on the other hand, is it that usual to have them all in the same place: Many prudent people apply the investment maxim to every aspect of their lives. Maybe I'll do that myself from now on. For example, if a woman is fascinated by a poet whose words can charm an audience of enraptured girls every evening, she doesn't need to have him for a husband. She can listen to the poet and then go back and sleep with her boyfriend, who might be interested only in ledgers and black magic. If she's enthralled by a certain violinist, it isn't mandatory that she take him to bed, make him the father of her children, and put him in the kitchen to cook *marmitakos*, those great tuna and potato stews. If, for example, she's mesmerized by the genius of a certain chef, she doesn't also need to have meaningful conversations with him about the troubled cultural situation; she doesn't need to turn the maestro she admires into lover, father, friend, refuge, critic, and companion.

Fortunately for the survival of our social fabric, reasonable people don't need to be spellbound, enthralled, fed, amused, coddled, lectured, and accompanied by one sole, multitalented person. They have chefs to cook, violinists to listen to, poets to give readings, comedians to make them laugh, lovers with whom to have sex, therapists to listen to their neuroses, and husbands to live with and keep them company. They are packaged separately. If people really kept all their eggs in one basket, society as we know it today would function very poorly. Restaurants would close, orchestras would fold, poets would be silenced, because, with a basket of this sort, everyone would have what they needed at home. And then what? Eh?

And then what?

This is why Absolute Love has always been and always will be subversive. And dangerous. If you diversify—that is, if you have the *proper* allocation of eggs—the lover might fail you, the companion or father or chef might die, you might be left without the possibility of developing a particularly passionate vocation, but in the normal course of events, you would still have some other niche where you could find support. If, on the other hand, you have concentrated everything . . . By choosing to concentrate, I knew my eggs were a high-risk investment. I knew it was hazardous. But the risk of great suffering didn't keep me from fulfilling my ambition to have all my eggs—forgive the repetition—in the one basket.

It was worth it.

And now (a few days ago), the explosion. It's hard to know what will happen from this point on. Naturally enough, the first thing that occurs to a lowly wordsmith whose nest has exploded in her face is to recover that nest through words. For us, it is the most reliable means of keeping the void at bay. Writing has always proved an excellent way of discovering what will come next. You write and you learn. You write and things progress. You begin a story without knowing where it will lead; you write it precisely in order to know where it will end. Or, to be more modest, you write to discover what the next step will be. I know what my next step will be: to talk about him, about life with him, about life without him. I'm not the only person doing this. The mark he left is deep and fertile. His friend D. spoke to me yesterday about a play inspired by him. His friend Z., a former student of uncommon talent, sends me poems he dedicates to him. His friend R. is going to write about their common childhood in his next book. I'll offer one of many versions, one more version. Mine.

Cometa was muse material. He didn't need to die for this to become obvious. Everyone always told him he had a writerly disposition; so, to put a different wrinkle on the oft-repeated comment, I often told him that, over and above his writerly disposition, he had the stuff of which muses were made. It exasperated him, and he would laugh. He laughed and wrote. Laughed and lived. Laughed and existed. Laughed and drank. Laughed and raged. Laughed and made *bacallà a la llauna,* his cod and paprika specialty. Laughed and sang the *St. John Passion.* Amen.

And in this way, his transformations inspired us. It's true that certain people are like personages, as if somehow, involuntarily, they compel you to tell a story that is their own, but that they don't feel like telling or don't have the time to, because they're busy doing other things, for instance. Such as reciting poetry to a woman one doesn't know, listening to a friend with a problem, or cleaning anchovies with such dedication that they are left without the energy to describe it. And someone else must do the telling. This is my job now. This alone should occupy my days now. I write the pain, the raw, atrocious pain; I write, therefore, what is destined to be erased. In reality, what you are reading is written over what I am writing now, which has already been erased. What you are reading now rests on what has already been erased. Raw pain contributes nothing; it is shrill and impoverishing. Any minimally sensitive reader can readily imagine the pain caused by the death of a loved one;

perhaps she has even experienced it herself. The thing to do with shrillness, if you've given vent to it, is to rid yourself of it to the degree that you can. And keep erasing, until a different force, beyond pain, takes its place. Bewilderment, for example.

The fact that love can actually last will always strike me as strange. The fact that it can survive routine, repetition, living together, boredom, gestures long familiar seems remarkable. That was my case, and never before had I experienced this. And therein lies my bewilderment. As a driving force, bewilderment is cheerful, the strangeness of it is productive; it creates enigmas that you must puzzle out. Tapping into this source of energy, I write and erase, drawing smiles out of dark shadows, something I do for a while each day, a short time only. Because this book is being written in short spurts, as though the keyboard had a tendency to freeze. A modest stretch of time, no more than an hour. It hurts.

To write, I'll have to organize things. I'll name my chapters A and B; otherwise I'll get lost. I like fighting my natural tendency to disorderliness by classifying and arranging. That's why I always respond with statistics and percentages; for example, when I reply to letters, I always move from point A to point B to point C. If I don't, I know I'll use the slightest excuse to digress and time will cease to be of importance. The same thing happens when I'm in the car and not in a hurry. I just let myself go. I love reaching a goal by pure chance, by instinct. That must be why I find pleasure in searching for a parking space. It's one of the best moments of my day, particularly if the goal happens to be a complicated neighborhood in Barcelona. Now that he's no longer here and I have even more time— now, when I feel that all the time in the world has been drained away—it strikes me that the pursuit of a parking space will become even more attractive. It's an activity that doesn't leave the mind free, open to boredom. The search keeps you focused on the pedestrian who's walking in a certain manner (the way one walks with the intention of going to one's car, searching for it, glimpsing it from a distance, stepping down from the sidewalk), focused on the person taking off a jacket or jingling car keys. This activity has a relatively immediate usefulness as well as a final reward. Sooner or later you do find a parking space, and you feel you've accomplished something truly useful and at the same time quite difficult. You have managed to kill time in a very simple way, which is my great obsession: how to kill time from now on. Even more than before, I'm sure I'll enjoy getting lost now, whether in the city or out on the highway. It makes no difference to me; the important thing is to lose your way, on foot or by car, as if maps or navigation systems hadn't been invented. That's the joy of it. Glancing at the sun, noting if it's setting on this or that side, and moving "in the right direction," but without clear points of reference. This exasperates my friends when I drive them. "Do you think we'll get there?" they ask when they realize that to go from Carrer d'Enric Granados to Plaça de Francesc Macià I decide to take a spin through the neighborhood of Sant Gervasi. "Till now I've always managed to find my way," I reply with the intention of causing them to reflect on this irrefutable fact. But I'm afraid they don't really understand me.

However that may be, I'm sure now I'll derive even more pleasure from killing time in the car; I'll spend hours at it, but I haven't reached this point yet. It's only been a few days since he's been (what do they call it . . . "dead?"), and I'm not planning to get lost, in the city or in the country. On the contrary, I'm trying not to budge; I spend the day at my computer. If I must go out, I follow the same route. I don't stray one millimeter. Because, if I do, who knows? Once you're lost, who knows what might happen?

Along these intersecting avenues of words, I'll need to keep things in order and not get off track, because then, who knows? A simple classification, then. A chapters, B chapters. The A chapters will be about how we met, us, life with him. The B chapters will be about how I lost him, life without him. This will also serve as a mnemonic device (I've been a bit confused lately): A for affection, amusement, acceptance; B for barbarous, brutal, bare, burgeoning. Easy enough to remember.

Moreover, this classification could prove useful to potential readers, because it affords the possibility of reading only alternate chapters. In this way, the apprehensive reader can be spared the barbarity of death, pain, the end of pain, and the first moments of joy—altogether quite barbarous if you think about it. On the other hand, the reader who is bored by stories of triumphant love (stories that are triumphant always reflect a certain simpleminded complacency) can skip the A chapters. This brings me to the problem of names. In the A chapters, narrated in third person, characters will have to be given names, because in third-person narration, it helps to identify the characters. This can get tricky. Because neither of us had a name for the other.

We dispensed with ours when we met. The first thing we did was to rid ourselves of them. For my part, I'd never quite known what to do with mine. The idea of hearing myself called by the same name throughout the day—regardless of my own disposition, attitude, or mood or that of the person speaking or—has always seemed strange to me. I even find it hard to understand the meekness with which many accept their names. Or the enthusiasm, for the truth is some people use and abuse a name, drawing on it even when the context renders it unnecessary, like those who refer to themselves by their names or even scold themselves ("And I said to myself, 'Jordi, you shouldn't do that.' "). Or those who, though alone with their interlocutor, insist on using a name, as if there were some possibility of confusion ("Where did you leave the cigarettes, Maria Rosa?"). And if the person doesn't hear them, they repeat the question. Including the name.

Cometa and I were alike in our aversion to giving each other names. It's as though I were allergic to the idea of being trapped in a fixed identity, under the mantle of a particular title. He, too, seemed reticent to call me by my name; I don't remember a single time that he used a specific name for me when he phoned or left me a note, and he certainly never used my legal name. In any event, no name ever lasted long enough to fulfill the labeling function it supposedly had. The names changed, lasting sometimes but an instant, sometimes days, and occasionally they reappeared, deformed, shortened, cleft; we spoke to each other in strange languages, with strange names. But this was never a problem for us; the problem arose when we needed to give them a fixed form.

I suppose that's why it took us so long to decide on a name for our daughter, not so much which one, but whether we really needed to settle on a particular one in perpetuity. Our friends would say, "Children need to be given a name. A fixed name. If not, it's unsettling for them." And I would respond, "They'll have plenty of other reasons to be uneasy, important reasons." Cometa, however, was very sober-minded in matters concerning children. He was indisputably a strong advocate of giving children names. The problem was that he wasn't inspired by all the hogwash surrounding the choice of a name, not in the least. As a result, between him (who refused to make lists and vote for the prettiest names and then count the votes for each) and me (who didn't believe it was necessary to give a name at all, because it would be ineffective and would never be used), it took us a long time to settle on one.

We found one the day we were returning from a trip to the Grison Alps, a trip that, for reasons not relevant here, had become an emblematic peregrination since the beginning of our relationship and was a place filled with incomparable memories. "Sils, for Sils-Maria?" I said, at that time still thinking of life as an album of trading cards of Beautiful Great Moments. To which he, always the traditionalist, responded, "Let's leave it at Maria." And that's what we did. We had had lunch the previous day in Silvaplana, at that little place where one hears only the humming of bees, the rustling of the tree foliage in the garden, and the clinking of silverware being used by the few guests: an especially fortunate combination of sounds. That night a dramatic storm had hit the Piz Corvatsch, and we watched from the window of our room, through the blur of clouds. The following day, as the first rays of sun on a radiant morning cast a brilliant sheen on the dew-specked grassy margins of the road, on our way to the Austrian border, not knowing then as I do now that it would be the last time we made that trip together, on that day, in the car, we agreed on the name.

Everybody seemed to like the name for our daughter. Maria, name-of-names, a name so generic, a name so nominal it's almost not a name at all. We probably thought that in choosing it we could stick to our objective of forgetting the name and concentrating on the person. As it was, we could actually have settled the subject quite easily, because she arrived with her name of origin, given to her by the Chinese institution that had found her near the Yangtze River. It was a Chinese name that we liked, but it wasn't easy to keep, adapt, or pronounce. You had to get the tones right, so if we didn't hit the correct musical note, the child ignored us altogether. When we called her Maria, however, she turned around with amused surprise. She would stand, rooted to the floor in front of the mirror in the hotel room, repeating it for hours, as if she were discovering herself for the first time. At that moment I began to reconcile myself to names; maybe they did in fact serve to make us happier: It was obvious that she liked her name (she still didn't speak, so was unable to express that thought), or maybe what she really liked was something else, such as a new life "with food and kisses," as she puts it now, and the rest was fortuitous.

In any case, having a daughter brought me into contact with a real world that was completely unknown to me until then, and I understood that a name was of prime importance in the life of a child. And in the life of the parents. You never stop saying, "I'm the mother of So-and-So," and from then on, that is how you are known in the child's world, which becomes your own. And when you are with the family, there are so many occasions to call to the child; phrases like "put on your shoes" are uttered countless times a day, and the impact on the child is clearly much greater if it's preceded by a name, as this prevents the child from choosing to believe she's not the one being summoned. But in the intimacy of our lives as a couple—a trio now—we continued to call her by different names, and to speak to her in strange languages that were new every day. She was eager to join in this game; she seemed to relish it.

And now, after the tragedy, I continue to change her name (the newly chosen one could be influenced by any number of things), and she does the same with me. Often the name arises after a trip. When I returned from Mexico I called her Díjole for several days. When we journeyed there together, she was Churubusco (a neighborhood in Mexico City); a few days later she was Pozole, in homage to the delicious soup some Querétaro friends had us try. My daughter has a curious relationship with names that clearly gives her pleasure. Some she likes, and she comes to me just to hear me pronounce them; others she seems somehow to need: "Today I'm having a 'Ga' day. Call me only names that begin with 'Ga' . . . hmmm, Gaguin?" she says for instance. And we understand each other immediately. Always. I know it means she's having a day when she requires cuddling, that she needs special affection. A few days ago I stumbled across a little notebook in which she'd jotted down the names her father used for her. Many of them end in "ix." Perhaps her fondness for the world of Asterix inspired her father to come up with Gallic names. Píulix is the last one on the list, and that is how I will refer to her in this story. Phew, now I have one.

As I read her list, I was reminded of the names he had for me, and I was hoping to find one I can use here. Having been a symbiotic creature for sixteen years, it's only natural that now I must choose among the names that he-with-whom-I-was-fused used for me. But which one? Some weren't meant to go beyond the intimacy of the couple. He assigned them to me according to his mood, the day, the weather. They were his best gifts. Some were names from the Jurassic period, such as Velociraptor, or for designating a fish on the brink of extinction, such as Coelacanth. Some were names of particles, such as Photon, or chemical elements, such as Strontium. Or purely sonorous ones: Trumph, Flips, Kotor. In general they were names with a lot of "o's", but they weren't necessarily round; sometimes they were square and had sharp edges or spikes. Some names sounded like diseases, or like cats or dogs, but were they really? Take Nostos, for instance. Every now and then he called me Nostos. It struck me as the name of a dog, more precisely, the name of a bull terrier or a bulldog. But no, as it turns out, it's a Greek word for "homecoming." I didn't know that, I have such tremendous cultural lacunae. Or, if I'd ever known, I didn't remember. Did he remember?

I've devoted these last days to consulting a dictionary to see if the names he'd given me have any particular meaning. I always took them as they came, without considering if they did or not. He called me Kobold for a relatively long time. I liked it; it was comfortable and warm. But, as the name lasted, I asked him what it meant. "It's a gnome," he informed me. I complained that gnomes were tremendously ugly creatures. But he replied that, on the contrary, gnomides were very beautiful. I didn't even know that gnomes had a female version, but in the end I found the name appropriate, for I'm partial to kingdoms of the dark, and, like the kobolds, I would have enjoyed living with him underground, protected, being a naughty little elf, a gust of air that whirls up the dust, a comical torment. But I've only recently discovered, to my surprise, that the kobolds are relatives of the Greek *komboloi*, those cheerful dwarf humanoids who made fun of everything and were part of the court of Dionysius, one of Cometa's favorite gods.

I've found other names he gave me and whose meaning I didn't know. Muon, Eon, Onsra . . . Muon (a particle similar to an electron but which only remains stable for two millionth of a second) and Eon (an indefinitely long period of time) could have been intentional, or perhaps they were a fabrication of his unconscious (words you know but have forgotten). But, Onsra? In my opinion it's almost impossible for him to have known that "onsra" means "to love for the last time" in some South Asian language. Ah, chance, now that is a true komboloi.

But in the end I'll stick with the last name he gave me. I'll go with Lot. It's not derived from the Germanic Lotta that was popular in Catalunya many years ago, or from Lotis, the nymph forever occupied in escaping from Priapus, or from the delicate lotus flower. Nor is it from the biblical Lot (whose wife turned into a pillar of salt when she looked back), which it could have been. Or from *carallot*—such an endearing word, one he often used affectionately for both of us—which is derived from the Spanish *papalote* and means dimwit in English. A few days ago he exclaimed, "Papalote!" and I immediately responded, "What is it?" Of course I knew he was calling to me (you always know when you're being addressed by the person who loves you symbiotically; that's why people like us don't need names for each other).

Here again, I don't believe he chose the name for any particular reason or because he remembered the exact meaning; though perhaps he did, I'll never know. But once again, I found myself confronted by the surprise that in Mexican Spanish *papalote* is a kite—the kite that Mexican children fly in the sky. As would usually happen, Papalote was almost immediately shortened to the two-syllable Lote, then to Lot. The shorter versions usually lasted longer, bobbing around for a few days until they expired. This time we disappeared first. So then, we'll go with Lot. For, much like *papalotes*, Lot showed a true devotion to being handled by skillful hands. Nothing pleased her more than to be handled with talent, even though she always ended up doing as she pleased. One of her faults.

As for his, it's already been chosen. I'll call him Cometa, which is Catalan for "comet." That's the nickname he had when I met him. It suited him. Why they called him that, I don't know. But I can imagine a hundred reasons. Comets always escape. They give off heat. They leave a luminous trail. They seem ethereal in the distance, much like his leptosomatic body, like his shape when you saw him approaching from afar, slender and elongated. Because, like orbital comets, he always returned, but, like orbital comets, there was always a hovering suspicion, a remote possibility, that he might not return.

Cometa, comet . . . Coherent trajectory. Irregular form. Burning ice and frozen fire, like the poem by Quevedo he recited so well. I'd chosen the name for a character in a novel I was writing. The novel has of course been interrupted. No need to imagine fictional lakes in which to bathe when the ocean has suddenly swamped you. Be that as it may, the name suited him. Even more so now. Because, when comets disintegrate, they spawn around them a shower of stars. And we await them, here and now, on these nights of utter darkness. And they always arrive.

I get up. I check on my daughter, who's sleeping. "Píulix, Píulix," I whisper to her. As usual I have to extricate her head from one of the Asterix volumes her father gave her. I look at her and murmur some of the names I remember. Perhaps as many as twenty. Then I go back to bed. To bed. I spend my day immobile; there, I've said it, just in case. In the morning, I write. To myself, to others, to my entire e-mail list. All morning glued to the computer screen. You don't have to move much to write. Your fingers, a little, on the keyboard, as though playing a never-ending symphony with the mute button on. I'm afraid to move. If I move my body, who knows what might happen: It's as if I were a castle made of toothpicks. So, I spend most of the day in front of the computer. Until my daughter gets home. A little later, Cometa's sister arrives, delicate as an elf, warm and radiant as a flame. And the house is filled with joy, because they are cheerful and transmit joy. Then comes what for weeks will be the most longed-for moment: the Campari hour. Or the Gin Fizz hour. The sweet apathy that precedes nighttime sets in, and it is the end of the day. The end.

Tender is the night after Campari. I only used to have these drinks at hotels, in very specific places. I needed them to whet my appetite, as people tend to say. At home we drank mostly small-town stuff: our beer, our water, our wine. None of this modernity, everything old. I liked the idea of keeping specific drinks for specific places. Americano for hotels by the sea, Campari for hotels near monasteries, Gin Fizz for nights on the town in Madrid, strong liquors from local crops for stays in rural houses. Each drink in its own place. In short, those who know me know I'm extremely meticulous with my obsessions. Or should I say *was*? Because all my habits will have to change now. There's one problem, though: Where is the encyclopedia of cocktails? I gave it to Cometa as a gift some time ago, but we never used it. At home, he wasn't a sophisticated drinker. In any case, he always preferred a good brandy to a cocktail.

I'll buy a cocktail shaker tomorrow if I can find the encyclopedia. If not, I'll buy the shaker and the encyclopedia. I have a mission now. Or rather, two. (A mission, a mission!) It's fundamental to have a mission. I flip channels with the remote. I always thought that if one day I took over the remote, I'd devote myself to watching the most despicable shows to bring myself up to speed on the inconsequential gossip on the tabloid talk shows that Cometa was incapable of watching without falling into a state of abject depression. So of course we never saw them. And yet, now that I am free to watch them, I don't. I only want to channel surf, and every now and then I trip and get stuck. I get hooked on a sentence or an image that inevitably leads me to the same place. Right now, I've paused on *The Purple Rose of Cairo*.

The movie's at that scene where the sweet, doughy-faced explorer emerges from the screen and approaches Cecilia, a waitress from New Jersey who's in the audience, and tells her, "You must really love this picture." Disconcerted, she looks around and asks, "Me?" He keeps at it, "You've been here all day. This is the fifth time you're seeing this." Again she asks, "Are you talking to me?"

Poor Cecilia, her eggs in her lap, trying to find somewhere to keep them, some of them already poorly placed. Like a young student, an adolescent girl who, when asked a question, always says, "You mean me?" "Me?" Yes, girl: you. He's talking to you. Not exactly the type of woman who takes the initiative, this Cecilia. A category of women I find strange. Not that I think I'm a particularly enterprising person, no. As a matter of fact, most of the time I never see my initiatives through.

But have them, I do.

A1

You Must Really Love This Picture

It was an October afternoon, 1987. She was having a terribly sad day. And she had nothing particular to do that afternoon. A perilous combination. She decided she would head to the bar where she thought she might find Cometa. Actually, she was sure he'd be there: He was a creature of habit, regular habits that nonetheless weren't obsessive and could be breached if a more appealing option presented itself. Her clockwork regularity, however, could not be disrupted. Precisely because she had no plans that day, something quite rare for her, she chose a most unusual course of action: observing Cometa. This could prove a risky undertaking, the kind that could change your life. Approaching him was not easy for her. They hardly knew each other. Their few prior encounters were probably of no consequence to him. But for her, nothing was ever routine. No word, no glance: Everything was up for interpretation. It was one of her favorite pastimes. She'd been thinking about him for quite a while, but they never spoke. A chance meeting the previous spring ("Would the *Senyora* like a cup of tea?") had revealed to her the degree of his refinement. They'd seen each other since then at work, had greeted each other. Nothing more.

Now she wanted to gauge something else: the power of seduction that Cometa and his environment could wield over her devastated spirit. And so, that afternoon she'd resolutely made up her mind to enter the bar and leave it transformed. She would leave transformed or not leave at all. She'd never entered any place (not even the university) with such an ambitious project. In the end, it was only a bar, though actually it was much more. She'd often heard it mentioned and approached with mounting curiosity. It was a special place, magical; and everything seemed to suggest that it was destined to enter into the gallery of local myths. Whether you paid for your drink or not was irrelevant, for the two remarkable men who ran the bar (and bankrupted it, but made it a legend) never devoted much attention to money matters. They could quite easily book a musician from New Orleans or Philadelphia, pay his flight and accommodation in a luxury hotel, and have the place empty that day for lack of advertisement and marketing know-how, which simply did not flow through their veins to the same degree as their sensitivity and tenderness. Hardly anyone paid for their drinks, except Cometa, who, owing to his strange relationship with money, was always eager to pay at the slightest opportunity, using any pretext to rid himself of the cash he had on him, as if it were a soiled handkerchief, a dangerous substance that should be jettisoned, the farther away the better. Located in the historic quarter, near the monastery of an ancient village, the bar had stone walls that gave off a warm, diffused light, a convent-like atmosphere that enhanced sensuality, and that old farmhouse air that renders love more earthy and wild. For a long time (no doubt too long in business terms) only insiders knew of its existence, so the place was never full, which only heightened its appeal.

It must have been closed when Lot arrived that afternoon, but knowing nothing about opening hours for bars (eight o'clock in the evening), she pushed on the huge wooden door that stood ajar and slipped inside. The room was occupied by three people. Philippe, in the role of bartender, was drying glasses with agile aristocratic hands, his beautiful feline eyes lost in space. Miquel, in the role of boss, was grumbling in his tender, childlike manner, spitting out insults as he attempted to light the wood stove. Cometa, in the role of customer, was seated at the bar, his back to her. He signaled to the bartender, who stopped drying the glasses and put on, for the umpteenth time no doubt, the searing sound of a sax that seemed to be wrenching each note from the bowels of the earth. Though she was not yet aware of it, this was the version of "Lover Man" that Charlie Parker had been on the verge of not recording because he couldn't make it to the studio, and when he finally did arrive (or rather, when he *was made* to arrive), he was so high no one thought he could possibly do the job. But in fits and starts he managed, as we know, to finish the song. The rendering was so strange that, during the recording, there was a general sense that the take would be scrapped. More than strange, it was disturbing. But this version didn't simply hit the market, it became a reference point in the history of bebop.

But Lot knew nothing about the versions of "Lover Man." The only thing she knew was that someone was playing inside those stone walls as if he were suffocating. She too found herself short of breath when she wanted to open her mouth to address the man seated at the bar; that's why she said nothing, but merely observed him, something she had no difficulty doing as he was absorbed in the music, concentrating on the notes, abruptly sending them kisses before returning with a melancholy air to his drink and cigarette. When the music stopped, he requested the song again. And the bartender repeated the operation.

He hadn't even turned around when she entered. Nonetheless, the man working behind the bar informed him that a lady had arrived. At that point, Cometa greeted her courteously (a courtesy so extreme that it always made Lot assume it was a means of controlling the savage insolence she'd sometimes observed in him), and once again he was lost in the notes. She approached and sat at the bar, at a respectable distance so as not to disturb the solitude he was perhaps seeking. They hadn't arranged a meeting. They knew each other from work, where he was also known as a character, at least some of the time; so she could have fallen in love with him there as well. Seated at the bar, with "Lover Man" playing in the background, and immersed in the film references that Lot's generation had grown up with, Cometa seemed even more character-like. No doubt about it. Which is to say, he was much more novel-worthy, more real to her—or, better put, more vivid—because of the intensity with which fictional characters affect us, compared to their flesh-and-blood counterparts.

Cometa often buried himself in the depths of that convent-like tavern. When he wasn't at the bar he sat on a stone step in a dark corner, from which his solitary, smoking presence silently contemplated . . . who knows what? When he tired of "Lover Man," *A Love Supreme* played once, and then the music stopped for a moment. At that point, he addressed the man acting as bartender: "Play a song for this woman." He wouldn't have used the word "woman," though, no way; in a sentence like this, he would never have said that. He would have said "lady" or "*Senyora*." That's what he must have said that day. And his bartender-friend put on "Sophisticated Lady." No doubt the bartender thought the song couldn't possibly disappoint—whatever it was that shouldn't disappoint and whatever the relationship was between his customer-friend and the newcomer. It was a well-known song, infallible in Billie Holiday's voice, one of those songs that never loses its brutal intensity no matter how many times you've listened to it, a song that only someone with the musical sensitivity of a centipede could ignore.

After Cometa's laconic request, he reverted to staring straight ahead. She looked at him from the side. From then on, whenever she thought of him, she visualized his profile, perhaps because he was more the kind of man who sat at the bar rather than at a table. Lot observed the side of his face as she listened to a line from that song she was hearing for the first time, or maybe not, but in any case, it was the first time one of its phrases stuck in her mind: "smoking, drinking, never thinking . . ." The idea of renouncing thought caused a profound impression on Lot. At first, the line stayed with her like any musical phrase that plays over and over in your head, nagging and persistent. But the truth is, it perfectly illustrated Cometa's relationship with time, existence, the despair of thinking, the pain of thinking. For a man like him, the escape from obligations, however brief, could only be associated with sitting at a bar, the one pretext that afforded him the happiness of the gods and allowed him to momentarily forget the large and small crimes of humanity that repulsed him and were so difficult for him to dispel from his everyday existence.

Lot later realized that Billie Holiday's line advocating that we *not* think referred to the future ("never thinking / of

31

tomorrow"). Which was even more appropriate, as this would be one of the most interesting lessons Lot would learn from Cometa: his manner of ignoring the future with Olympian energy in order to concentrate on an ever-richer present, thus paradoxically managing to be at peace with the future, because he never scrutinized it with speculations, projects, or riddles about what lay ahead. To live with him was to live in a constant apology of the present.

This scene at the bar is a perfect example. Hours pass but the situation doesn't progress toward any kind of future. "Play a song for the *Senyora*," he'd said. That was all. For hours. Well, at least he'd given her a song. Did it mean anything beyond the courtesy required of the moment? Probably not. She had no choice but to try to read him. Being a novelist, Lot knew how to read people's thoughts. This is one thing novelists have in common with the paranoid. What distinguishes one from the other is that paranoids are absolutely certain they can read other people's thoughts correctly, whereas novelists know they might be mistaken and are simply placing a bet. Lot attempted to read. The truth is, it wasn't easy to read him, even less so from that angle. Generally speaking, he was difficult. Difficult when he was absorbed in thought, as he was contemplative by nature and his thoughts were too rigorous and complex for her, who had never studied metaphysics. Difficult, too, when he didn't appear to be thinking at all, as in those prized moments when he was enjoying his "glass work" (the term by which he and his friends referred to the drinker and his glass), those moments when all the demons of the day dissolve into the music, and all the horrors of humanity soften in the welcoming shelter of night. Concentrating on reading him gave Lot a headache, and she opted to abandon the pursuit and focus only on his attitude, which, like a disheartening neon sign, said: "Leave me in peace."

What should she do? Maybe that neon sign was also a reflection of his thoughts. Maybe his thoughts would remain beyond her grasp. It was clear that she'd have to come up with a strategy: Immersed in his musical daze, imperturbable to any other stimulus, he was obviously not going to step down from the screen to come looking for her, as Baxter the explorer had done for the waitress. It's true that Lot didn't mind watching the same movie over and over, but (since she'd always been held hostage by the future) she began to wish for the next scene. In the meantime, she tried to gauge the desire she might be able to awaken in him. To do so, she relied on a few signs she had discerned on those occasions when they had coincided. There were three, although in reality they offered but little.

The First Sign: a look. The year before, they'd run into each other at a lunch meeting. At the time, she still didn't know many people at work, only three or four colleagues, women who would later become close friends. The section of the table where she was seated began a conversation about song lyrics. It occurred to her to make an offhand comment about the sexist and occasionally whiny tone of Mexican songs, something about which she really knew very little. With roguish smiles, several voices warned her that she had formulated a risky opinion and should try to keep it from reaching Cometa if she didn't want to become the target of his sharp wit. And yet, the same people who professed to wish to shield her from public derision slyly conveyed her opinion to the other end of the table, where Cometa was sitting. When it reached him, he rose, ready to contest the affront that someone had dared to offer, clearly a person lacking in sensitivity, ignorant of the profound poetry residing in the *corridos* and the *huapangos*, in the lyrics by Esparza Oteo and Chava Flores, Chucho Monge, or Manuel Othón. But it turned out that the ignorant person was a woman. Cometa had raised his slender and noble lance, ready to defend the honor of the poets of the people, when he realized this. "Ah, it's a woman," he said in that extremely respectful tone of his, disappointed to be unable to enter into combat, disarmed by the misunderstanding. Immediately recovering from the disconcerting moment, he looked Lot directly in the eye with his dark, unwavering gaze, raised his glass, and, with a splendid baritone voice, started to sing.

To prove to her that Mexican men did not set store by trivialities, even less by playing the victim, he sang a stanza from "La chancla." He followed it with a few others to illustrate the humor in the lyrics. And finally, to reveal their infinite tenderness—rather than a sexist attitude—he sang "La casita":

La casita
tiene en el frente unas parras
donde cantan las cigarras
y se hace polvito el sol...

[The little house
covered with vine
where crickets sing
and the sun at dusk declines . . .]

He didn't stop at the end, but rather with the stanza that goes:

Pues con todo y que es bonita
que es muy chula mi casita,
siento al verla un no sé qué.
Me he metido en la cabeza
que hay allí mucha tristeza.
Creo que porque falta usted.

[Though my little house is pretty
just as lovely as it can be,
I get this feeling when I see it.
Inside my head a thought abides
that too much sadness there resides.
For what it lacks is you.]

Once he had demonstrated everything he wished to demonstrate, he unpinned his eyes from her and sat down. Lot's mouth was still hanging open long after he'd again struck up a lively conversation with the people sitting next to him at the table and had no doubt completely forgotten about her. She was so sure of this last detail that, come to think of it, this first sign couldn't be considered a sign of anything.

The Second Sign: courtesy. He treated her with great courtesy at work. But he did the same with everyone else. And it's true that she offered him few opportunities for interaction. She avoided him. He intimidated her. She was convinced she could talk to him only about metaphysics, Bach cantatas, fractal theory, or things of that nature. Or cuisine, or soccer, but she knew nothing about them. Of all of these, she deemed the first topic the most accessible, and secretly began poring over the *Critique of Pure Reason* with the hope of someday being

35

able to address him. But one morning at work, she witnessed a scene that astounded her. A colleague was sitting beside Cometa, plying him with boring details about her lost earring. The whole thing began with the loss of the earring, which she described in painstaking detail. She explained where she'd lost it (at home), how she'd asked her boyfriend to help her look for it. He was spared none of the direct discourse women often use in describing events: "'Pere, would you help me find my earring?' I told him. 'Of course, honey. Be glad to,' he replied." She explained to Cometa that she had then said: "It's bound to be somewhere here in the house." She told him how she had described the earring to her boyfriend (yet another description of the earring). She listed the places they had searched for the earring. She explained how they had finally found the earring. After this account—delivered in a soporific tone—she pulled out the earring for Cometa to admire. Lot, who struggled to imagine that anything could possibly interest Cometa less than an earring, could scarcely believe it. And as if that did not suffice, the girl concluded her account with a thoroughly banal reflection on chance occurrences—she dared to philosophize with him about chance! But there was a point to it, as the role played by chance was so important that a week later she managed to lose the other earring. She then launched into the same account, identical from start to finish, as parsimonious in its delivery as the previous one. And yet he observed her intently, with a calm, friendly, nonthreatening look, totally concealing the desire to strangle her; perhaps he didn't even experience such a desire. The patience he showed vastly exceeded what Lot had expected of a man as temperamental as he was. That is how she discovered that she didn't need to read Kant in order to talk to him; she could discuss the most boring trivialities without driving him away. Lot considered this fact auspicious, a positive sign. At the very least, he would be polite to her (in all probability, that is).

The Third Sign: the cup of tea. This incident took place long after the other two. A lunch meeting in the spring had just ended; she wasn't feeling well and wanted to have a coffee with him before heading home. The first café was closed, the second too full, so finally they went to his place, and he made her tea. He only had tea. Lot didn't like tea, but she would have liked to like it. She liked people who drank tea; they were more pensive, more serene than coffee lovers. She even enjoyed the tea that day, as would happen with many other things she'd never appreciated but would come to enjoy through him. She was tired and decided to tell him why her heart had recently been in such a state of ruin. "It's because of the wedding," she blurted out. (By now she knew you could talk to him about earrings, and surely "earrings" and "weddings" could be lumped under the same heading.) At first he didn't understand. He must have heard at work that she was about to get married, but he probably didn't remember. Weddings and earrings would have certainly figured among the topics that for him went in one ear and out the other. So she confessed she was riddled by terrible, insidious doubts. She wasn't sure of anything. Every day she told her boyfriend, "I'm sure we are making a mistake." She repeated the exchanges between them, explained that she was in a real funk as she went about the preparations. And nothing could turn out well like that (as a matter of fact, the only preparations that went well were those meant to discourage her future husband, who was finally convinced that she was right and gave up the whole nuptial business).

"I don't know what I'm doing, telling him these things, making it all seem so negative," she told Cometa, who had remained silent until he asked her with disarming simplicity:

"But do you love him or not?"

"It's not that simple," she replied. "At first I liked him a lot, so I made him fall in love with me, and I intended to then fall in love with him (the sooner the better with these things, as far as I'm concerned). And in fact he did fall in love, but when it was my turn, something was missing . . . I couldn't manage to fall in love as I'd planned, couldn't manage to love him as I'd expected, though I kept trying. And besides, he has all the qualities of someone who can be loved, but the more determined I was, the worse it went. I want to love him; I want it more than anything, but I can't. He says if I can't, I should call it off. But I can't do that either."

Cometa refilled her cup and said, "Women are strange creatures." (In this kind of sentence he would never have said "*Senyora.*")

She continued, "But I say, it isn't Absolute Love if it's riddled with doubt from the very beginning, is it? Relative Love, ordinary, garden-variety love, maybe, but not Absolute Love." She paused, hoping the concepts of "relative" and "absolute" would spark his philosophical interest and perhaps encourage him to offer some guidance. Not a chance. Faithful to his custom of asking what the interlocutor always assumes is obvious, he inquired:

"And what is absolute love?"

Never at a loss for words on the subject, she could have articulated many ideas, but remembering *The Big Sleep*, she said:

"It's the big fixer. The one that drives away all your demons. Not because you don't have them anymore, but because you

38

stop seeing them. The one that quells your anguish, not because it makes it disappear, but because it just ceases to cause you anguish. Absolute Love makes everything right. Remember the last lines between Marlowe and Vivian in *The Big Sleep*?"

Too bad—he didn't remember. Even though, after John Wayne, Bogart was the actor he was most keen on, and Bacall his favorite woman among all women. Even though he'd seen the movie a hundred times, Cometa never remembered things on demand or when requested, only when it suited him.

"Well, when Marlowe concludes his investigation and is about to leave, she tells him, 'You've forgotten one thing— me.' And he says, 'What's wrong with you?' And she replies, 'Nothing you can't fix.' You understand, don't you?"

He smiled, perhaps at Lot's naïveté.

"The idea of love symbiosis," she continued, "inspires me. If you're with this person, you don't need anything else. I hate principles such as 'You have to fend for yourself,' or 'Contentment is through inner harmony,' and so forth. Ridiculous! No! It's marvelous to find a man, a woman— whoever it is—who fixes you, entertains you, and changes you. Isn't it wonderful to be able to live through someone else, instead of through yourself (since you are acquainted with yourself to the point of boredom)? A man with whom to live in perfect symbiotic intimacy, like a remora and a shark."

She was reflecting on the fact that symbiosis represented an advantage for these two bonded creatures, but then she began to doubt whether a shark could get anything out of a relationship with a remora. She wanted to find another example, but couldn't think of one, and so she concluded:

"In any case, the notion of absolute love is exhilarating. But I could only give myself completely to a man who constantly feeds my soul, who possesses infinite resources. Why would you want a man, unless it's to mine his resources? That's what I'll always look for. If he doesn't exist, so much the better: I'll keep searching; I enjoy searching. But what if he does exist? Wow! It's in all the songs, every kind of art, writ large and small. Is it just a bunch of lies?"

After this inspired speech, she waited. But he said nothing. Not that the man she sought existed or did not exist. Not a word. And yet that very afternoon her spirit began to mend. How? Not a clue. What did he say that had managed to rescue at least her afternoon, if not more? He must have said something after her surprising confessions (surprising to him, since they hardly knew each other). But the only thing she remembered him saying was:

"More tea?"

They drank tea. And she felt suffused with an infinite humanity, even though they hardly touched, and he hardly spoke. But Lot kissed him on the lips and was surprised by their softness; they embraced and said good-bye. She felt that he'd comforted her or given her valuable advice. But he had said nothing, done nothing! She would soon learn that this was one of Cometa's strange virtues. His friends often spoke of his "helping them in critical moments," "giving them extremely good advice." But what form did it take? It was hard to say. How was it that simple phrases sounded wise coming from him? Was it perhaps his calm, deep bass-baritone voice? Was it because his thinking, speaking, and acting were one and the same? Was it because he didn't actually give advice or opinions, though he would occasionally deliver a comment that would knock you off your feet? Was it because Cometa seemed never to want anything from the other person, thus making the other feel respected and at the same time special, free? Why was it? She didn't know yet.

That evening, after reviewing the three signs, Lot made a curious discovery. She was twenty-seven years old that autumn of 1987, but she'd lived through long and intense love affairs and felt old and experienced. For the first time she understood why the easy, loving men of her life had awakened in her a kind of cruelty, sometimes an uncommon verbal violence, a destructive force that frightened her, a confrontational energy that made her miserable, and them too. She began to understand that she wasn't prepared to offer love in exchange for (only) love and a handful of standard virtues. She hadn't known what to do with the men who had arrived with their hands full of love. It made her feel guilty. What she wanted from them wasn't to receive love, but for love to drive *her* mad. Her. She remembered the cover of a book she'd read when she was sixteen, *L'Amour fou*, by André Breton. There was a luminous sky on the cover and a sentence that had always produced an equivocal sentiment in her: "*Je vous souhaite d'être follement aimée*," May you be madly loved. When she was sixteen she hadn't grasped what it was she disliked about the sentence. Now she knew: it was the passive voice. She was the one who wanted to give, not receive. The idea of feeling herself appealed to, needed, an object of adoration petrified her. On the other hand, to adore madly, to feel an infinite thirst and delay the moment of satiety (odious satiety): That is what she wanted. But to have that, she needed a man who was never on the lookout for women. A man with enough finesse and skill to make her feel that he didn't need her. A man who was never waiting for her, because the present would always be enough for him. A man who, even without having anything, had more than enough. A man ready to guard his freedom above all else, even her. In a word, what she had always been seeking without knowing it was this: someone to whom she would be superfluous.

And there you are, that man was him.

It was him.

It's not easy to find a man to whom one could be superfluous, she thought. *Or rather, it isn't easy to find a man, who, not needing her, wouldn't prefer to be without her.*

The platitudes of the time had confused her. The platitudes of the time dictated that the *new woman* wanted a man who was considerate and attentive, a man who shared decisions, responsibilities, errands, and tasks. And, as she wasn't an *old* woman, she thought she was one of these *new women*. She believed it. But no, she really wasn't one of them. Why would she want a man with whom to share decisions? She found nothing quite as odious as having to reach a consensus about the most banal, everyday matters. Nor did she want to share tasks, quite the opposite: divide them, distribute them according to the merits of each. And she certainly didn't want one of those solicitous men, a man who remembered her birthday, who brought her little gifts. In fact, all of those thoughtful gestures made her nervous. Maybe it was hereditary. She remembered standing with her parents in front of a jewelry store when she was very little. Her mother had exclaimed in admiration over a diamond ring in the showcase. Her father had said, "Maybe one day I'll be able to buy it for you." "Absolutely not," her mother had replied. "I'm not a capricious person; if you must give me something, I prefer it to be land." Lot's mother hadn't liked thoughtful gestures of that sort.

42

As for Lot, she wanted neither land nor diamonds. She belonged to a generation that hadn't been hungry and had little appreciation for material things (it was a brief generational parenthesis, almost as if their nonmaterialistic attitude had been a mistake, one that was promptly rectified). But Lot held fast to her penchant for prioritizing goods of the spirit and soul over practical matters. What she was looking for in a man was much more complex. She wanted one who enjoyed a privileged inner life. A unique personal atmosphere that he might transmit to her and, perhaps, share. That is what she sought.

We are still at the bar. It's two o'clock in the morning, and it doesn't look like the place is going to receive any more visitors. Maybe from the street it looks closed. It's not improbable that the owners have forgotten to open the outer wooden portal through which she had slipped when it was still too early to be open. She's racking her brain for a way to get Cometa out of there, so she can continue near him, without asking his permission. It's complicated. She's always been discreet when it comes to falling in love. She has a mother—yes, the same one who didn't want diamonds, the same one who wanted to keep her eggs in separate baskets—who has inculcated the precept that one should never run after a man. And she's not planning to. But, unfortunately, Lot can't stand a man running after her either. In this situation, who's to run after whom, if she can't and he never does? How are they to come together? The night doesn't look very promising. There's only one solution: let him do his thing. Let him finish whatever he has to finish. And then, when he's ready to leave—which doesn't appear to be any time soon—they'll leave together, and she'll walk beside him. Not behind him, not in front.

Yes. They'll leave together, in a natural way, without saying a word. It's an autumn night. Their footsteps will resound on the silent pavement along the street leading down to his place. Lot will have the impression that she hasn't breathed fresh air for a long time. They'll walk side by side, Cometa taking her in with that bewildered look he has for things after a few drinks, as if they had suddenly magically materialized in front of him, as if they might disappear from one moment to the next. She'll wish to stay in this town forever. Cometa won't say a word, he'll be whistling *A Love Supreme*, and at every instant it will appear that he's forgotten about the woman walking beside him. He'll probably declare his undying love for her at some point, but in the next moment he'll have forgotten and will continue walking by her side. He'll seem distracted, but not from aloofness, contempt, or indifference, but from a great delicacy, a special tenderness. Unencumbered. She will think: *I could disappear now and it wouldn't matter; I could leave and he wouldn't phone me; I could disappear into thin air and he'd say, "Hmm, how curious!" and he'd keep on whistling.* Over and again, Lot will ponder the discovery she's made this evening: *What a lovely way to be superfluous!* she'll exclaim silently. And, perhaps precisely for this very reason, she'll wish to stay and accompany him wherever he goes, even to hell if need be. And she'll continue walking by his side, with the certainty that, together, they are going somewhere.

B1

You Mean Me?

A rainy Friday in the autumn of 2003. All through the week a phrase has been gnawing at my brain (*I have this presentiment*), like one of those catchy tunes that stick insidiously in your mind, which you can't rid yourself of and you have to make an effort not to end up singing. I too have made an effort not to articulate the phrase. Every day this week I would have said, "I have this presentiment." But I didn't. It's better this way; it does no good. I've avoided it partly out of superstition, partly out of tactfulness: You can't articulate something like that in front of the person who is the object of such baleful foreboding. It's ominous and impolite. So, no one has voiced the phrase at home, not Monday, not Tuesday, not Wednesday, not Thursday. The week ends today, Friday. Today the phrase will chart unsuspected, vertiginous paths.

A rainy Friday in the autumn of 2003. Sixteen autumns have elapsed since we first met in a bar. A bar that's gone through many transformations over the years. The two owners closed it and left town to work elsewhere. Some time later, they died. Ph. wasn't much older than thirty when he had an accident, two months before his first child was born. That night, he was on his way back from talking, listening to, and no doubt spending a long time with M., his friend and former associate, who at fifty had just been diagnosed with incurable cancer. The charm of the bar's first period ended with them. Recently, another friend of ours has salvaged it and restored it to its original version. It's not a place he and I often frequent. We never go out at night. Only during the day.

It's been a strange, exhausting week. For some time he's had an unusual pain, a burning sensation not related to any physical effort. He describes it as a kind of fire in his shoulder; it burns and then suddenly disappears. We've gone to the doctor, of course, even if not persistently, because he's reluctant to go, always has been. "It's the cervical vertebrae," we were told the first time, when we went to the emergency room in the town where we were vacationing. Despite the treatment, the pain continued with unusual characteristics, and a few days ago he went to his trusted doctor, one of those intuitive doctors who has a well-deserved reputation for getting it right, and besides, he's a friend. But medicine is ambiguous, and myriad minor details can contribute to perpetuating an error, especially when the patient isn't one to spend his life examining his health. And, besides, at no point has he had any of the conventional symptoms of that thing that two hours from now will stab him with a deadly dagger. He's always been a peculiar guy, in body and soul. He has trouble identifying pain. He says it's because nothing has ever bothered him. It was a different story when he was little. But he doesn't remember it now. When he was little, he suffered from ancient and literary diseases, such as a typhus, which nearly killed him, or an alcohol-induced coma, caused by a nanny who gave him a baby bottle filled with rubbing alcohol, which she had poured from a container supposedly filled with water. He also enjoyed a few collapsed lungs when he was young and has marvelous memories of that period. Forced to rest, he received a never-ending stream of visits from his friends, enjoyed the most rewarding conversations, and read with insatiable voracity while his parents—who rivaled each other in culinary genius—cooked the most delectable dishes for him.

The memory of that period was so heartwarming (though it wasn't without its difficult moments, as attested to by his letters, some of which his friends still have) that, asked today what he would have liked to be in life, he often replies that his vocation was always that of a convalescent. I think he came up with this when he was quite young, perhaps after reading *The Magic Mountain*. That's when he discovered what a wonderful vocation convalescence was, for in no other state is it possible to read and think with so much time on your hands and with the clear conscience that you're not shirking any of your responsibilities. No other state offers reflective people the magnificent lucidity that comes with the proximity of illness and death. In any case, his periods of convalescence were extraordinarily enriching. But they weren't repeated. After the age of twenty, he spent thirty more years without being sick for a single day, never visiting a doctor, never having suffered, according to him, the slightest discomfort. To me, *never experiencing the slightest pain* is such a strange phenomenon that it always made me doubt whether he identified pain properly; perhaps his pain threshold was so high that he didn't devote the necessary attention to it, or maybe he didn't want to bother anyone with his minor aches and pains.

All of which is to say that he's not accustomed to speaking of physical pain, much less his own, and it's hard for him to describe it. So, when I attempt to force a description or the doctor does, he's always evasive, minimizing the pain. Nevertheless, this week he's made an effort to find the words. "I only know," he repeats, "that it's the strangest thing I've ever felt."

"Could you be a little more precise" I ask him. "Could you use an adjective?"

"Incandescent," he says.

And then, immediately, he says it's only lasted a few seconds; already he wants to talk about something else; already he's putting together a little dinner, chopping onions, whistling; already he has sped away from his body at supersonic speed. Enough. He doesn't want to talk about it any longer, he feels—in his words—magnificently well.

Two years ago, after thirty without setting foot in a doctor's office, cancer struck him. Struck us, I should say. Since he seems intent on dispensing with the body and occupying himself solely with the spirit, I'm the one who keeps track of the detailed blood tests, with the number of lymphocytes and leucocytes, and of all his pains, which he seems to forget with the ease with which he forgets—so he says—anything that might encumber his spirit. This critical situation did not, however, cause us to be unhappy, not at all. I'd say it was rather the opposite: With his capacity to forget and my capacity to extract anything intense and worthy of observation from any given situation, we've had two wonderful years.

Besides, his cancer wasn't the type that usually recurs. And, furthermore, it wasn't lung cancer, so often deadly, and the one we most feared because it had carried off many members of his family. It had been such a deep-seated fear of mine that only now that time has elapsed can I look back and see him, circumspect and perplexed, serene when confronted by the news, above all worried about me and our daughter, true to his usual style, saying, "Shit, this is serious." And I see myself enthusiastically reminding him at every turn, as if congratulating him, "But it's not lung cancer! You realize? It's not in your lungs!" And, true enough, it wasn't in his lungs, it was a *nothing* cancer, one of those that—once you've been sliced open from top to bottom in a seven-hour operation, and they have changed your metabolism forever—only recurs in a small percentage of cases. He didn't find the fact that it wasn't lung cancer of particular interest. But I did. And my euphoria contributed to the cheerful climate we continued to experience. If he had lost part of his joy, that part I now contributed: The dreaded cancer had finally struck, and I felt (because it wasn't in his lung) as though we'd just won the lottery. Meaning, immortality.

Ever since I met him, his immortality (and by this I am referring exclusively to an expanding future, nothing more) was the only lottery ticket I was interested in. The cancer that had to strike, struck; the threat was no longer an unfamiliar perspective. We lived through it, and it didn't resemble anything I had imagined. Lung cancer could also strike, of course, but I decided that it wouldn't. Full Stop. Fears and anguishes behave thus, in an irrational manner. If fears have many irrational components, dispensing with them does too. It's simply that, during this kind of vicissitude, you often arrive at a point

49

where you feel invincible because you have already had your quota of suffering, and therefore nothing more can befall you. Absurd. But the important thing is that it works. And for me it worked beautifully.

His illness taught me to live the present more intensely. Having him at my side had shown me, from the very beginning, how important this lesson was, but I lacked the final, definitive touch that comes only with practice: His illness gave me the impulse I needed to learn how to live the moment fully. During the first weeks, the days passed with a sharpened sense of terror and were followed by an immense and intensely celebrated joy every time we learned that things weren't *so bad*. In a short story, I once wrote about the collateral beauty of an illness. Beauty manifested itself often in our illness. It appeared in the most remarkable places. It sprouted from friends—mine and his. From copies of *Capitán Trueno*, the classic comic book that one of his friends brought him, the same guy who was the meticulous custodian of the treasures of their shared childhood and had never discarded anything associated with the two of them, the friend whose personal transformation started during this illness as he grew into a man. It sprouted quite suddenly during a phantasmagorical nocturnal trip to the airport mailing facilities while attempting to send an urgent biopsy to Boston, an additional benefit offered us by our health plan: It could easily have been a nightmare, but instead of that, beauty sprouted and we ended up laughing over a dinner by the sea. It also sprouted, quite unexpectedly, from a young nurse we didn't know who had just finished performing a scintigraphy (the definitive test for determining the prognosis of a tumor; it detects bone metastases, which are usually irreversible and thereby rule out any further operation). What was certain to be a miserable night until we learned the results the following day became a cause for celebration: Through an open door I caught sight of him hugging the nurse, both of them with tears in their eyes. Apparently, breaching his ritual of extreme courtesy, he'd asked her if she could offer any advance news, and she— breaching her ritual of not providing any information—told him she didn't see any sign of The Beast, and they were both moved.

I too was moved when he came out of the room; I hugged him and fell in love with him again. I fall in love with him regularly, for one reason or another. The following day, it was because of the skeleton. We went to get the results, now anguish-free thanks to the nurse's kindness, and when I pulled the scintigraphy out of the envelope, I was impressed by the elegance of his bones. "They're gorgeous!" I exclaimed. I tried to show them to him, "Don't you want to see how lovely your skeleton is?" But no, he didn't. Not the slightest interest in anything of the sort. But he was happy. "I can assure you that I understand a bit about skeletons, and this one is so elegant!" I added. And it was true. My fondness for medicine turns to extreme hypochondria when something is bothering him, an anxiety I only manage to keep in check by pumping myself with medical information. This means that I have perused the Internet, searching for reports and tests, and I have studied countless scintigraphies, X-rays, tests, biopsies . . . A friend kindly offered to help me by letting me use her physician identification number to subscribe to two highly specialized magazines and a database of radiological images. I can, therefore, give a qualified opinion, perhaps not necessarily medical, but certainly aesthetic: I am now able, for example, to offer an informed opinion about the elegance of a skeleton.

Those flash points we lived through two years ago were exceptionally fulfilling. Any close-knit couple is familiar with these moments. Ever since we met, we have had to face the death of people we loved dearly, and at the rate of about one death every other year. These are difficult trials for a couple, ones that tend to either unite or separate. They brought us closer together, as this illness does now. And yet, even when fused by this bond, the sick person stands alone. Utterly alone. I can't know how he hurts or what hurts him, or if he has fears that his exquisite discretion prevents him from revealing. The relationship with the sick is unfair, asynchronous: I recall having dinner together—the four women who most loved him—to celebrate that both the operation and the tests performed during it had turned out well. We were immensely happy. Friends kept phoning and receiving the news with exclamations of relief. A sense of calm and euphoria spread like gunpowder among those who loved him. And, in the meantime, what was he doing? He was in the ICU spending one of the worse Lovecraftian nights of his life. Our elation over the news didn't allow us, who loved him dearly, to sympathize with his pain that night. We were filled with such joy that we didn't show the slightest commiseration for what he was enduring, those hours that, according to him, were the worst of his life.

The joy at continuing to have him. That was the only thing that counted.

After serious complications over the following days, he was finally discharged from the hospital on an icy twenty-third of December; I went to pick him up with our daughter, whom he hadn't seen for twenty days. It had snowed a lot and the sun had finally come out that morning. He was weak when he left the hospital, but happy and free. He didn't have to undergo any further treatment; everything had ended in the best possible way.

It's been two years since then, and he always remembers with immense gratitude those mornings on sick leave, the strolls through the market in search of the ingredients for whatever meal he was in the mood for, the excursions with his friend A. to hunt for wild mushrooms, the winter afternoons with our daughter listening to *Peter and the Wolf*, the intellectual fertility that he saw gradually increasing in him, the trip to the snow that February . . .

It's been two magnificent years, punctuated by tests that allowed us to say, on each occasion, "Everything's OK." Nothing other than that, until this little pain. During the last few days, the doctor has set things in motion again, using as a starting point the pinched cervical diagnosis. A week of tests and more tests, searching for the one word that terrifies me and that he seems to ignore, that terrible word we never mention (metastasis), while I have secretly reviewed everything I have found on the subject. This is also the doctor's fear. If the tests today come back fine, not only will this fear be ruled out, but the tests scheduled for the end of the year in order for the cancer to be declared in full remission will no longer be necessary. The six-month checkups will be over.

The sentence that has stuck in my head like an irritating earworm will be dismissed or confirmed this afternoon. I have only to open an envelope. It's pouring rain on Avinguda Tibidabo. From the car I contemplate the gardens of the aristocratic mansions, pelted by the rain and the sound of heavy traffic. One of them houses a hospital where today people go to receive their death sentences. He gets out of the car to pick up the envelope. A few days ago, I accompanied him to get tested. I noticed then the drawings and paintings that famous people had given the radiology hospital. All of them expressed gratitude. Some of the people are still alive, others aren't, but all of them expressed enormous gratitude toward the place where they had gone in search of their sentences. I found it curious. I mean, it's logical to be grateful to your surgeon, your doctor, your nurse, but I didn't know that radiologists also conjured so much gratitude. Or maybe it's this particular radiologist. Maybe this radiologist is such a good radiologist that he never finds anything wrong. Nothing abnormal. Yes. It must be that.

From the car I see people leaving the majestic mansion. One after the other, they leave with their envelopes and open their umbrellas to protect themselves from the rain. A strange place to come looking for one's death sentence. What a refined manner, precise to the point of nausea, we now have of receiving our death sentence or our always provisional pardon. Notice, one day, the number of people wandering around Barcelona with a large envelope, one of those that you never know where to put because it's too large to fold and, to make matters worse, it doesn't fit anywhere. If you stop to take note, you'll glimpse many such people. Let's assume some of them have had routine tests, some are recalcitrant hypochondriacs, the kind who rush to the doctor for no reason at all. But there will also be some—not an insignificant number—who are collecting either their death sentence or their temporary reprieve.

My train of thought is suddenly cut short when I see him coming out. He gets in the car and tosses me the envelope, as though to say "disagreeable mission accomplished." If it were up to him, he'd leave the envelope in the car unopened, perhaps indefinitely, or at least until he takes it to the doctor on Monday. But he knows I could never last the weekend like that. He knows I'll open it immediately. Before he starts the car, I've already read it. Not detected. So, no. No anomaly has been observed. "No." The most beautiful word in the world.

No!

No!

My joy knows no bounds. The baleful omens disappear before the evidence I hold in the envelope. From behind the wheel he says, "So then, I won't die tomorrow, huh?" That's what he says (a bit of pessimism to counter my enthusiasm). As we head up the Arrabassada toward the Tibidabo Mountain above Barcelona, I read the report more carefully. There might be nothing else, and that little pain of his would remain unexplained for now. But the afternoon is so perfect that yes, yes, there is something: There's a pinched cervical vertebrae (inconsequential, of course, compared to metastasis) and it affects precisely the spot on the spine that always troubles him, the C5. "It corresponds exactly to the C5," I exclaim with enthusiasm. And once again I'm unable to engage him. It doesn't matter. In the torrential rain the forest is again green and protective. My body relaxes. We have to stop by the house to pick up our daughter before leaving for the weekend. When we get there, he asks me to leave the envelope on the bed. I'd really like to take it with me and spend the weekend studying pinched vertebrae, a field that hadn't piqued my curiosity until now. But I do as he asks, as I almost always do. Or almost never. I put it on the bed. And we leave.

We've hardly spoken on the highway during our trip. And now we've arrived. There's no fog. Sometimes our beloved fog fails us, as it has this week when it's rained so relentlessly. The house is cold, a pleasant feeling. He's in the basement, turning on the heat. He always stays down there a while, to speak to the departed, as he puts it. And, as always, the pizza gets cold, but I abandon any notion of calling to him out of respect for his peculiar excursion into the terrain of profundities, childhood, paradise lost. As always, our physical separation brings a slight unease that spreads through my body. But I'm accustomed to this now, and it doesn't lessen the well-being of our relationship. He didn't mention it, but while we were on the road I had the impression that he was again accosted by this strange pain that comes and goes in waves. I suspected as much because he didn't ask me to talk to him as he usually does when we travel ("Tell me something, anything . . ."), but fatigue explained the silence, I suppose. At one point I think I said: "Are you OK? Do you want me to drive?" It's a routine question, with an invariably negative answer, because according to him, nothing rattles his nerves quite as much as watching me drive. He insists that he's fine, but tired. We have arrived, and he's in the basement. I'm getting the violin ready for my daughter so she can take it to her grandmother's tomorrow. She's had her first violin classes a couple of weeks ago. And tomorrow will be her first day wearing her new coat. I'm preparing the violin and the coat. Despite the pain that I suspected during the trip, I'm immensely happy because, as a general rule, pinched vertebrae don't kill you. Life resumes its normal rhythm.

Life is momentarily suspended when you await test results. Life will resume tomorrow. Tomorrow morning, new coat, new violin. Tomorrow morning, another look at the plans for our future house in Buzy. Another look at gardening magazines. An old childhood dream of mine. A year ago we discovered a magnificent spot in the Pyrenees, at the foot of the Col de Marie-Blanque. A road with a white picket fence led there. It was a very Norman countryside with intense green fields. The village, too, is charming. The hens cluck freely in the square with the stone washing trough; there are a few fourteenth-century houses and a Neolithic dolmen at the entrance to the village. Even he, who wasn't remotely interested in the possibility of buying anything and had never had any petit-bourgeois dreams, exclaimed as soon as he saw it, "What a magnificent place!" It turned out that the strip of land we spotted had belonged to the community since time immemorial and was for sale at a very good price. We bought it. I found it hard to believe that my old dream was about to come true.

That was when I began writing a novel, about a year ago. It bore the title *La casa dels seus somnis—The House of Her Dreams*. I think the title was ironic, but I'm not completely certain. In the novel, the young girl protagonist is fascinated by a man named Cometa who is living in the house next door to her; he has a lover, but the adolescent girl wants to make a father figure of him. Later, the protagonist, now an adult, looks for a house like the one where her charismatic neighbor had lived, but she can't find one. As I wrote the novel, I began to realize that the house of her dreams didn't exist, that there are no houses without the people who live in them, or had lived in them, and new houses without spirits don't become dream houses until they have been sufficiently lived in. Who knows if the little house in Buzy that will be ready next summer will be the house of my dreams? Probably not, because novels have a wisdom of their own, and you can divine things in them that are not apparent in one's conscious life.

In my conscious life there will be a house of my dreams—it's been decided. Planning a house: one of the most common diversions to temporarily forget about death. But I've never been much like Ivan Ilych, whose first death knell finds him hanging curtains, and he suddenly realizes the emptiness of a life in which curtains have been more of a priority than the inner self. No, it would have been impossible to live with a person like that. However, contrary to my partner, I do have a certain facility for enthusing to the point of obsession over plans for wild gardens or pamphlets about wooden terraces where we'll read and converse as we have an aperitif facing the splendid countryside. In your conscious life, you have to apply for a mortgage and sign off on the house plans (for which we have appointments three weeks from now). In our conscious life, this afternoon we had to collect the test results that—starting tomorrow—will allow us to continue cheerfully with our plans. Tomorrow will be the end of this nerve-racking week; tomorrow (not today, because I'm too exhausted) I will again consider whether we want a straight or spiral staircase. Contrary to him, a man of the present as I've never known another, I can't remember a period in my life when I wasn't absorbed and obsessed with some project or another. In my case, obsession means obsession. Looking for the man most suitable for me. Looking for the hotel most suitable for a vacation. Looking for the dog most suitable for my daughter. Looking for the land most suitable for the little house of my dreams. Looking for the most accurate diagnosis for him. All of this involved a perpetual, sleepless dedication that bordered on addiction. Until now, it's always yielded good results. Tonight, I don't want to be absorbed by anything; tonight is relief and joy, and a fatigue so intense that I think I might fall asleep awake, while having dinner.

But after dinner the pain returns. (The pain isn't important, science has declared that nothing has been detected, nothing can be seen, no metastasis, a pinched vertebra, yes.) "It may be a pinched nerve or whatever, but today it's unbearable," he says. And the alert mechanism, deactivated when I opened the envelope and read the report, is reactivated. I'm wide-awake: "Let's go across the street," I say to him (there's a hospital). "No, let's wait, you know it goes away immediately." I don't want to insist for fear of overwhelming him. He asks for an aspirin and I'm starting down to the kitchen to look for one when he says, "No, wait a second, give me your hand. I want your hand." A strange request coming from him, who never asks for anyone's hand. He stares straight ahead, at the wall, a fierce look, as he experiences what must be a sharp pain; I see his profile. His profile. After a moment, he says: "Yes, I'll take an aspirin." I bring him one. He takes it. He walks around the house. He says he feels better. He tells me to go to sleep. "Monday, Monday," he says. "We'll see about this on Monday. Right now I want to wait."

We try to sleep, him watching a film with *his* John Wayne. I remember because he says, "It's not John Ford, but (at least) it's John Wayne." That's what I remember, through the cloud. Half asleep, I wonder how I will be able to hold out till Monday; besides, there's a match tomorrow. Two hours at the stadium can't be good for a pinched vertebra. And yet, even with my alarm mechanism activated, I drop off, exhausted after our sleep-deprived week. And then, I don't know how, I don't know when, I don't know if he's still watching the movie or if it ended some time ago, he leans toward me in a strange way.

A strange way.

That's what it was.

That's what it is.

This is it.

But no, I don't recognize it. Not even now.

"What's the matter, *amor*, what is it?"

(Does it have to be this way?)

He says nothing.

His gaze serene.

Clear.

Some sort of automaton emerges from me. Someone who phones, someone who, inexplicably, makes arrangements, someone who calls and speaks and calls again because the ambulance doesn't arrive and she can't stand automated messages and is looking for the keys to the garden gate. The future suddenly becomes very brief: She sees herself confined in a hospital room waiting for news. The automaton asks herself if she will be able to bear the wait, possibly a wait of several hours. She phones again. It's raining hard.

She looks for the keys. To the front door, the door to the porch, the gate to the garden. The three keys. She wakes up the daughter, phones the grandmother to come and get her. Even though the grandmother walks, and is coming from farther away, she arrives before the ambulance. Just before it. I put her coat on, the new coat. But we forget the violin. As Grandmother is taking the girl away, down the rain-sodden street, the ambulance arrives, slow and silent, and the girl suddenly turns back just before she disappears around the corner. "The violin, I want my violin," I hear a little voice call. Her eyes fix on the orange light that floods the street, as Grandmother tugs on her and they disappear around the corner.

A few minutes later, the doctor comes up the stairs. The light in the bedroom goes out during the attempt to revive him, the doctor asks for a lamp. As I am unplugging the one in his sister's room, the doctor asks. "What illnesses did your husband have?" I catch his use of the past tense (had?), but I decide to ignore it and consider it an unconscious slip. With absolute conviction, I give him a detailed account of the cervical vertebrae problem, as though discussing a non-life-threatening illness might put him off track, and by putting the messenger off track, the message might be altered. But the messenger is implacable. As I'm leaving the room, the lamp in my hand, he tells me: "These things are difficult to say, but . . ."

I don't let him finish. I interrupt and serenely discuss his clinical history (the lamp falls and shatters; strange, I'm not aware of having relaxed my grip). I ask, "What about the pinched nerve?" The man makes a gesture as if to catch me, strange because I'm not aware of having leaned over, of having fainted, just the opposite, I hear myself (I hear the automaton) speaking firmly about the peculiar occurrence of the pinched vertebra. I want him to explain it to me, not to hug me. "Let me see," I say. "Couldn't this be a case of a sudden spinal cord compression brought on by the pinched nerve?" It doesn't matter that what I'm saying might be completely ridiculous, what I want somehow to convey to *Senyor Ambulance Man* is the following: *There were two options here: metastasis or pinched nerve. Metastasis has been ruled out. Therefore, you, Senyor, are left with only the second option. So, explain to me how a pinched nerve could do this.*

The man doesn't take it personally. He says, "It's a typical cardiovascular accident. Cerebral damage can only be avoided by acting in a matter of seconds, after that first moment, nothing can be done, or there are aftereffects." (Typical? Typical in what way? Typical for whom?) He says, "We often encounter this." The lost letter, the purloined letter is there in front of my eyes, filling everything, and the automaton doesn't see it. I hear "cardiovascular accident" but my brain will take a long time, weeks even, to process these words. I continue asking questions. It's amazing how blind we can be when influenced by an assessment different from the "right" one. A pain in the left arm: Even an idiot would associate that with a heart attack. But we knew far more than any idiot. We knew that many syndromes that appear to be symptoms of a heart condition are in fact manifestations of the dreaded metastasis. And we knew that his electrocardiograms had always been perfect, that the last CPK analyses were fine, that stress tests showed nothing abnormal, and that his circulatory parameters were normal. I tell this to *Senyor Ambulance Man*: "How could it possibly be a heart attack, if he had none of the symptoms?" (other than the main one). But no, he (who gets it right because he's not influenced by any previous tests or additional signs) stubbornly insists: heart attack. So, the automaton gives up. I give up. The man is clearly not qualified to explain such a rare case, perhaps the only one of its kind in the world: the case of a pinched vertebra that suddenly caused a fatal spinal cord compression. So I decide to ask him a simpler question:

"And if you had come earlier?" the automaton asks, with the intention of investigating further (*Inbestigating*, as Cometa would jokingly say!). She poses the question without even a hint of reproach.

The man responds, "Perhaps we could have saved his life, but his brain would have been irreversibly damaged."

Correct response. That's more or less what she wants to hear, so that she may return to a few minutes earlier. She wants to talk, talk so that time will stand still. She isn't expecting a response such as, "Well, look lady, if we'd come ten minutes earlier maybe we could have saved him; but of course, we're used to our job and we take things easy, and, even though there wasn't a single car on the street, even though we had only to cross the street to get to your house, we took twenty minutes to get here; you understand, don't you?" And, naturally, the automaton would have responded, "Of course, it happens to the best of us. No one's perfect." And the man might also have said, "You could have gone to the hospital hours ago, you fools!" But he doesn't, and that's to be appreciated, and besides, the automaton would have replied the same, "Ah, yes, of course, it happens to the best of us; no one's perfect."

The automaton says things, asks questions, and makes phone calls; it's as if the automaton is a kind of ectoplasm that has emanated from me and accompanies me; it doesn't join me and I don't think it ever will again. Ever again. Perhaps in this separation there is a division between body and soul that's equivalent to death. Perhaps the separation of body and soul occurs not in the one who dies, but in the one who remains.

"Do you need anything else?" they say. "No, nothing else. Thank you." What could I need? If one day I am able to do without him, it's that I am able to do without the air I breathe, just that. But automatons don't think about these things. They don't think, they don't know, but fortunately, they act. Nothing permeates automatons to any degree; she has heard that he is dead and she accepts it instantly, but she accepts it automatically. "I don't need a thing," she repeats to the strangers. "Nothing, thank you." An arrogant sentence, even though she speaks it out of consideration, or so she believes.

That Friday was several days ago. I don't know how many. Not many. From time to time I feel dizzy when I picture my daughter's face as she suddenly turns around, asking for the violin, the light of the ambulance on the wet street, my mother pulling on her arm, the two of them disappearing as the ambulance brakes. These instants of bewildering dizziness don't usually occur at night. As soon as darkness falls, the insufferable pain of day begins to abate. And I give myself over to the remote control. I'm channel surfing pointlessly. It's been a while since I left *The Purple Rose of Cairo* behind, and now I've stopped to watch the end of a very apropos program about Dizzy Gillespie and his friends. I resume surfing and return to *The Purple Rose of Cairo*; the explorer, Tom Baxter, has emerged from the screen pursuing his love for the waitress.

He says to her, "I can learn to be real."

She's shocked and responds, "You can't learn to be real. Some of us are real, some are not."

No, no, Cecilia! Things are not that simple. You can be real yet not corporeal. You can be real and be dead. You can be real without being actual. The permutations are complex, the combinations countless. But I understand what you mean, Cecilia. "To learn to be real" is, for example, to leave the nocturnal world, the world of poetry, and allow yourself to be transformed into an apartment man. "To learn to be real" is to allow yourself to be torn from the Transylvanian mists where you move about like fish in water and be put in a house with parquet floors and a mailbox where you get insurance policies and bank statements . . . And everything that goes with it.

A2

If Parker Were Playing

In the weeks following their first encounter, Lot began to visit Cometa's home. Or the places he frequented. She did it when she felt so inclined, but in small doses, so as not to unsettle the lycanthrope. She didn't want to climb into the screen and share the set with him, and even less to snatch him away from it. Not abruptly. Not yet. She wanted to enjoy her peculiar amatory freedom to the fullest. However, nowhere is it written that such a state of affairs should last forever. One day or another, Lot, given her enterprising nature, was going to want to have a hand in shaping his destiny. One day or another, she would want, perhaps, to spend all the minutes of the day with him. But that day hadn't arrived, nor was she in a hurry for it to arrive. She was very slow when it came to surrendering her heart; she had learned to cultivate her affections with parsimony, so as not to misuse them. For the moment, she continued to reside in the orchestra stalls, which is what she most liked: a spectator of Cometa's mime, listening to his perpetually new discourse.

Nothing she observed in him was banal. There were days when she had the impression of having entered a chapter of the Quixote, a tale by Poe, a story by Beckett. She was never quite sure in their encounters what kind of climate he would offer. After a while she learned to identify some of the signs, primarily musical ones. Cometa paraded his musical head wherever he went. He did nothing without music. He wrote with music, thought with music, cooked with music, breathed with music. At home, he either had music permanently playing, or he whistled it or sang it. It wasn't simply an accompaniment for him, it was part of his very essence, and to be attentive to what he whistled or sang or listened to was the best way to know what to expect of him.

If Wagner was playing, you had to prepare for the worse. It was a dangerous day that heralded a storm. A raging Cometa might appear, his voice booming like thunder over some minor detail, such as the aioli sauce not taking with its usual thickness. A day like that (if finally the aioli was not thick enough) would probably end with him reciting Rubén Darío or Quevedo, tears in his eyes; or, on the contrary, hours later, after he had achieved the most perfect of aiolis by sacrificing quite a few of eggs, he would be enjoying a sumptuous meal and, if that was the case, the music would have changed. If Schubert was playing, he was probably waiting for you, preparing a delicious, surprising dish, immersed in serene thoughts. If Schwarzkopf was singing the *lieder* by Strauss, he would probably be seated, wistfully jotting down observations in one of his characteristic pocket notebooks, reading Spinoza, and glancing up at the window in hopes of discerning a dense fog. If, however, he was singing the *lieder,* he was probably shaving, happy because he was on the point of going out to do something pleasant, such as meeting friends, having herring for breakfast, teaching a class he was looking forward to. If the *Goldberg Variations* were playing, he was probably engrossed in one of those mathematical problems that tormented him from time to time. If Jorge Negrete was playing, or some Nicaraguan or Mexican revolutionary song, many emotions probably awaited you, in addition to a variety of *frijolitos* and tacos, which would be followed by a long siesta. If Schoenberg or Cage were playing, you should expect the chill of an entomologist. And if Charlie Parker was playing, well then, you should expect nothing (he would not be aware of your presence at all).

Sometimes there was no music (for example, when Barça was playing) while he watched a soccer match, a sacred moment that he often shared with his friends. But occasionally, just the two of them would watch a game together, and then she would entertain the hope that one day (for the moment, there was no need for it to be any time soon) he would agree to learn to be real, as real as any man reclining on the sofa, drinking beer, and watching a soccer match. As real as any public school teacher who keeps to his schedule and enters his grades. For he was also that. But when Lot noted the passion he dedicated to his classes, to watching a soccer match, to observing the beauty of the players' moves, she realized that this would not be the path to normality either.

With him she lived from surprise to surprise, in a perpetual state of excess. Cometa was extravagant, excessive. But that would not have been startling to Lot: She too was like that. Cometa's excesses were, however, of a different nature. He was excessive even in his judiciousness. In his courtesy, in his serenity, in his loyalty. In his passion, in his vehemence, in his eloquence, in his pain for the world lived in the first person, as though every dead Palestinian, for example, took from him a piece of his innermost being. From the time he was little—five or six years old—when no one had yet been able to inculcate in him a sense of social conscience, he had taken it upon himself to spoil the family dinners by making them aware of the scope of the tragedies broadcast on television. It didn't matter that the tragedy was remote; he lived it in the first person if it was a human catastrophe (natural ones didn't move him, they were natural, after all! But the evil intrinsic to the human condition affected him deeply). He was also exaggerated in his lack of resentment or envy (almost as if he were unfamiliar with any malicious sentiments, as if he were incapable of comprehending them and they caught him by surprise every time). Excessive but never quite sufficient were his inimitable phrases, the boisterous laughter he wrenched from some of his acolytes, the tenderness he showed, the life he offered, the expletives with which he sometimes left you paralyzed. Excessive was, at times, the concern he sparked when he retreated from himself. It was an exciting world with which she had an ambiguous relationship. It was an intense life, the intense life Lot had always wanted, the kind that snatches you away from everydayness and from yourself, the one Lot had felt sprouting inside her but had not known how to live. The intense life that had always beckoned to her but from which she had always felt excluded. Riding on the tail of Comet Cometa. That was the way. Now she knew. But she also wanted more. Especially as the weeks went by and he—despite professing his love for her—gave no sign of wanting anything more than what he had. Lot, however, began to want more. She wanted to be permanently at his side.

In the beginning, she thought it was possible to be with him but within a world of fiction. I'll wait for you in the early mornings; I'll come with you without disturbing your nights; I'll wait for you at home, sleepless, while you listen to *A Love Supreme* over and over. While you act the vampire. While, enveloped in plumes of cigarette smoke wafting among the stone walls of your favorite haunt, you stare straight in front of you. While . . . But he kept saying no, being together doesn't work that way. If they lived together it had to be with the condition that they abandon the reign of Dionysus that she had also grown enamored of . . . It was he who set conditions for himself. But setting them didn't mean that he intended to subject himself to them. Not yet. She wasn't in a hurry either; she was enjoying their movie too much. It was a time of wine and roses that Lot wanted to live fully. So they let the weeks pass, then the months that soon turned into years. Unhurried years of private recitals of Spanish Golden Age poetry and jazz, dinners with friends, irregular hours, intense scenes. From time to time, however, Lot grew impatient and wanted a more long-term, orderly life to begin.

On one occasion, Lot asked him to clarify the future for her. "Future?" he said, as if he'd never heard the word. "What future?" And she replied, "You know what I mean: for you to clarify once and for all whether you have any intentions of becoming real or not." For the first time he seemed interested in pleasing her in one of her projects (he was in love after all), and he said, "This thing of ours is forever." But if you stop to think about it, he hadn't even used the future tense, only the present, which doesn't mean a commitment to anything.

The "forever" gave the phrase a certain whiff of future, it's true, but the temporality of "forever" is ambiguous; it can move backward or forward. Lot began to lose patience. She demanded a more concrete response.

"Only that? Forever? How? How forever? In what way forever? Could we share the house, have projects, children? It's as if you had just arrived from another planet . . . You seem to know neither past nor future, neither nostalgia nor ambition. You don't submit to anything, you act as if everything was new at every moment, as if everything had to be rethought at each instant and no conventions were of any value to you, and *that*, in order to lead a normal life, is an obstacle."

"Until now my life has been absolutely normal," he insisted, demonstrating a lack of knowledge about his own life that verged on boldness, or complete unawareness; or perhaps, as usual, he only intended for her to explain what normality meant to her, to her and the bulk of humanity. But that day she didn't feel like rethinking normality (and thanks to this obstinacy they were actually able to move forward). She acted offended:

"How can you say that your life has always been normal! It is anything but normal!"

He said, "Come on, love, don't exaggerate!"

He said it with that tone he sometimes used, typical of the town of Almacelles, unlike his usual ceremonious and chivalrous old Spanish ways, which made him seem even more unreal.

"To be concise," she replied, "do you have any background, any kind of history in the real world?"

That's when he answered that yes, he did, and offered proof.

He explained, for example, that apart from being a civil servant—a public school teacher—like any other student, he'd also given private classes to earn a living. He'd been married. And for a long time he'd also tended a vegetable garden and had swum every morning. Indeed, is there anything more real than marriage or private classes? Not to mention the excruciating exams to become a teacher in the public school system, real to the point of nausea. Growing carrots and swimming every morning sounded pretty real too, even though it was a bit poetic, and therefore more suspicious. But, in general, Lot was rather more convinced.

For a short while. It didn't take her long to realize that the evidence he'd presented was, if not altogether false, certainly incomplete. Some friend or other always turned up, keen to fill in the gaps; nothing pleased them more than reviewing episodes from Cometa's past. In this fashion, Lot learned that he'd done his university degree while sporting plaid slippers and an unkempt beard, and despite his rather plain appearance, he had managed to make the blonde with the Scandinavian profile—the most beautiful girl in the college—fall in love with him. She was so beautiful that his friends called her precisely that, *La Bella*, which gives you an idea of how beautiful she was. As for marriage, it is true that he married (La Bella), but it is also true that after dating for five years, the marriage only lasted a few months because of his tendency to consider home a port of call, a place through which to pass. And they separated, each leaving the other with the best of memories, as well as an enduring friendship. Yes, he had been a student, as real as any fifteen-year-old student who leaves home to study in the big city. But with certain peculiarities. Such as wallpapering his room in the pension with the Sistine Chapel or spending his food allowance on orchids that he took to the Liceu Opera House to a *lieder* singer who fascinated him. He lost a lot of weight on account of the orchids and came close to starving to death (for it would have been an unpardonable heresy to die of thirst). It's also true that he had given private classes. But these were equally strange: He was a tutor for a curious Barcelona family who paid him an astronomical amount to give their daughter math classes. They came to collect him in a chauffeur-driven car and returned him as if he were a valuable but fragile treasure that the family had to protect. As for the time he was actually "married," though not in a formal sense, he *did* do certain homely things such as tending a vegetable garden, but his moonlight conversations with the tomato plants were of uncommon duration and abstraction for communion with vegetables. As for the matter of swimming, in no way did it resemble the swimming activity of the majority of mortals; he only swam alone, which, in the immense, old mansion belonging to his wife, was easy to do. And then there's the question of his swimming style, gliding weightlessly over the water, perhaps because of his rather slight, aerodynamic constitution. Between one woman and another, there had been a large number of others whom his chivalry (or his bad memory for that sort of thing) prevented him from mentioning or hardly even remembering; but there was always someone nearby, eager to remind you in a friendly, graceful way.

He had now turned his back on many of those youthful, romantic proclivities, including his penchant for strolling the streets in plaid slippers; he had evolved toward a more serious way of dressing in which quality, classic shoes were a primary element. In most areas of his life he now adhered to the traditional, but at any moment he could be crazy enough to join a revolution.

Was it really possible to hold out hope that he would willingly abandon this seductive world through which he moved with the freedom of a clochard, the generosity of a gentleman, the complicity of those who loved him, the frankness of a terrorist Diogenes?

That is what Lot asked herself every time she dreamed that he would come down to live in the orchestra stalls. And then one day, he finally said "yes." Yes, he would learn to be real for her, a strange woman herself, but a woman after all; and it is a well-known fact that women are obsessed with changing things, shaping them into something real. He said "yes" while on a train to Galicia. They were alone in a wagon-lit compartment having a drink when he made the promise, or something similar to it. She recognized it as a solemn promise, because she knew how much he disliked playing with people's feelings. Because she knew him well. If she had not, perhaps she would have doubted the veracity of his words, for a few minutes after his promise Cometa stuck his head out the window and sang to the starry night: "*Que me ha pillao, que me ha pillao (¡que me ha pillao!) el carrito del helao . . .*" [I was caught, I was caught red-handed, my hand in the ice cream!] A couple of girls walking along the platform stopped to contemplate the baritone at the lit window, singing with a refined, powerful timbre, brandishing his glass to the night like the oriflamme raised in a lost battle of cavaliers, in that hushed train station in a small town in Castile.

"¡Que me ha pillao!" he concluded. The girls were young and pretty, and as he never lied, he manifested his admiration for them and declared his instant infatuation. One of the girls approached him, and as the train slowly started up again, he kissed her so passionately that Lot thought she was an old friend. "You know her?" she asked when he finally pulled his head back inside and raised the window. "No," he said, surprised that you had to know someone to declare such ardent, transient infatuation.

Lot began to understand that the two of them would never do things like kiss at the right moment, or toast each other because they had decided to share a life together. And she, who thought she wanted these things, realized that she liked the idea that nothing happened as she had expected or as the movies had taught her to expect.

Lot enjoyed scenes like the one on the train. She liked the fact that the scene in which he had finally said "yes" had ended with his enthusiastic homage to the beauty of two unknown girls. She loved how he made literature of each instant in the most natural of ways, and she began to wonder if it really was a good idea to attempt to set her life on a conventional path. Once again, Lot postponed her project: She didn't mind waiting, and she was afraid that any change might put an end to her state of inebriation.

She was inebriated by a love that didn't diminish, inebriated by an unfamiliar joy. He had repaired her life in marvelous ways, he had cleansed the sickly thoughts, he had plucked her from chaos, confusion, shadows, madness. He had introduced her into a world where madness signified health and energy for new and fantastic undertakings (as Don Quixote said,

"¡Todo el mundo se tenga!"—Let all the world stand!), where confusion was enlightened by rays of keen discernment, and shadows became an essential part without which the light could not shine. Cometa had extricated her from that place and had taught her a profusion of things.

And how did he do it?
He did nothing.
Cometa never did anything!

Or rather: He never seemed to do anything to influence anything. He had the charm of the nonaction man. The reflective man who, among other things, reflected the truth and your actions and returned them to you; and that was enough to learn important lessons. The man who, with Socratic irony, would tear apart rationalist naïveté's without the slightest smugness . . .

That—that is how he extricated her. But, from where? What had he extricated her from, if she could no longer remember what she was like before she met him?

B2

Deep as a Root

The automaton is waiting for it to be eight o'clock to call her friends. She's not alone, there's family. People coming and going. Bureaucrats, doctors, doctor friends who are drawing up certificates, because apparently you need to die wherever you're a registered voter, if not, things get really complicated. That's fine, I, for one, like things to be complicated in moments like this; it's good to have things to do, things that dilate the moment but are related to the moment, such as trying to think what doctor friend you can phone at five o'clock in the morning to sign the certificate if you don't want things to get even more complicated. And, with a bit of luck, you might be distracted and miss the moment when they take *him* away (through the triple doors of happiness that we opened for him every evening when he arrived—the inside, the porch, the garden). That curious moment when *some strangers* remove him *from his house.*

And the body's not the important thing. At no point was I inclined to throw myself on my beloved and weep, my cheek against his, screaming his name amid exclamations of pain, not even when "they shot him" or when *Senyor Ambulance Man* gave me the news. I'm an effusive person, Mediterranean in my disposition, and I'd always imagined that in a similar situation that is how I would react. But I don't, and I surprise myself. The fact that he's not here, in his body, presumably inspires in me a profound sense of strangeness. And also a deep respect, as if the slightest caress could be a violation: He can't ward off my kisses and show his annoyance (as he often did when one of my passionate, clumsy caresses would cause an anchovy to drop from his fork just as it approached his mouth), nor can he exclaim in amusing irritation, "You really have the worst timing!" and add in exalted tones, "*Kairos, kairos!*" (Apparently that's Greek for having "the gift of good timing," which I clearly lacked.)

I suppose I also want to avoid the memory of cold skin (I don't know how long it takes for a body to turn cold). That's what I want to avoid, above all, for I once touched the face of a woman I loved several hours after she died, and I've never forgotten that coldness: The memory of her marble cheek appropriated forever the memory of the live cheek I had kissed a thousand times. And now I don't want anything to cloud the very precise memory I have of the texture and temperature of his warm skin, of his touch. I don't want to perceive anything different, anything that might expunge the true memory. I want to always remember his exact temperature. That's why, when at some point I go up to the bedroom to kiss him, I do so ever so carefully. This, despite the fact that I am not even allowed to do that, because the law states (and automatons respect the law) that when someone dies who isn't registered in the place of death, the judge has to come, and nothing should be touched until the judge arrives and rules out, for instance, the possibility that it was murder.

We are, therefore, downstairs in the kitchen. It's still dark. Dawn is only beginning to allow us to discern the roses through the window above the sink. But not yet the ivy; it still blends into the darkness. People come and go all morning, until I begin to perceive the roses and the ivy more clearly. The kitchen window, the roses, and the ivy will define this night, and they are the only indication of the passing of time. Periodically, certain thoughts gurgle up spontaneously: "She'll forget him, she'll forget him, she'll forget him," I say. (I'm referring to my daughter—who else?) "Have you forgotten your father?" asks P., who lost hers when she was five. "Have you forgotten your father?" I don't respond. "She'll forget him. She'll forget him. She'll forget him," continues the automaton. A rash, passionate clamor exclaims, "No, no, no, she won't forget him."

"No" to what was yes. "Yes" to what was no.

My father died in a similar fashion, on an autumn day, with no warning. I was eight years old. I arrived at my parents' shop on Rambla de Ferran and found it closed. Mamà always told me, "Don't be late leaving school, because we close at half past one." I stared at the shut door. I remember my incredulity perfectly. I studied my watch: Was I late? No, it was fifteen minutes before the half hour. Was it possible that my watch wasn't working right? And while I was studying it intently, trying to discover what anomaly had occurred for my watch to mark a certain hour and the shop door another, a neighbor appeared, charged with taking me to some friends' house. I remember few images of that moment. I have a bad memory for visual details. That must be why, when I do manage to retain an image, it sticks with me for life. And that must be why, when I pass the Rambla and my eyes happen to spot the clock on the station, I always visualize half past one. That's why I make an effort not to look at it. And if for some reason I need to know the time, I ask a passerby.

I wonder if our daughter will forget the image of the rainy street where for years she used to wait for him when he was returning from seeing friends. She loved watching him slowly approach, his spindly shape at the end of the tree-lined street; he'd raise his arm with the newspaper in his hand to greet us and she'd run to hug him and climb into his arms. I don't know if she'll forget this same tree-lined street where her father and his friends spent such a happy childhood, fraught with adventures and legends, the street where so many times her father had helped her learn to ride a bicycle, all the way down to the soccer field at the end. I don't know if she'll forget that strange October night when she left the house at four o'clock in the morning. If it hadn't been for the violin, I feel certain that her visual memory would not have stored any particularly remarkable image. But she'd suddenly turned around and seen the street, glistening in the orange light of a useless ambulance. All because of the violin.

When the ivy is clearly discernible, the automaton phones her friends to give them the news. Curiously, she keeps saying, "*Si, si,*" because they keep saying "No". There are some who don't contradict the news: They accept the blow silently. Then they say, for example, "I'll be right over," or they ask a confused, "What?" But others keep repeating "No" many times over, in different tones of voice. Or they respond with a forceful comment ("You can't be serious, what kind of joke is this?"); with a denial of the fait accompli ("I refuse to believe it"); with spontaneous, impulsive reactions. In a word, the whole spectrum of "no's," to which the automaton answers with the whole spectrum of mimetically opposed "*si*'s." And if they utter three hopeful "no's", I reply with three desperate "*si*'s." That's what happens with sudden deaths. When they aren't sudden, interlocutors don't usually say "No." They say: "Ah." Or, perhaps, "Wow." But when interlocutors have just woken up on a Saturday morning with their plans for the day radically altered, it's only natural that they say "No." We never lose our belief in the power (no doubt immense, but not unlimited) of words. One of them said "No" eight times. I counted them. Perhaps other things they don't do, but count, automatons do.

Funeral parlor life commences midmorning. The event reminds me of a reception, a literary cocktail party, except for the fact that there are no canapés and no cava, for in this country it's frowned upon to eat on these occasions. Like at receptions and cocktail parties, little groups form and you can join a group or stand apart. Some wander around alone all day. To wander about alone in a funeral parlor isn't as pathetic as being by yourself at a cocktail party. Some people run into each other after a long time. A friend of mine asks me about one of Cometa's friends:

"Which one is G.?"

"The one over there with the black hair," I respond, pointing vaguely at him.

"I don't see anyone with black hair, do you mean the guy with the white hair?" And, yes, I realize that his hair is completely white, and all these years I'd never noticed it.

At some point, my women friends suggest I call my daughter, because if she suspects that something has happened to her father, she'll need, they say, to hear my voice. *My reassuring voice.* A friend has listened in, to confirm that my voice sounds sufficiently reassuring, and, yes, "You were great," she tells me later. Yes, I've managed. I tell her, "Papà's in the hospital, darling, he's very sick. I'll come and get you tomorrow, OK? Above all, don't worry about anything." "Yeah, *right*, Mamà, how do you expect me not to worry if my *estimadíssim* [most beloved] Papà is in the hospital?" "*Estimadíssim*," she says, she's very fond of superlatives. And I suppose she'll go back to playing princess with E., and she'll still have that crystalline laugh her father fell in love with at the hotel in Hefei when he provoked her first peals of laughter.

Later, someone will tell me that my daughter told her friend, "I think my father died. Because when I went to give him a kiss, he was really still." She'll tell me about this herself. I'm astounded. When could she have kissed him? (She never left the house without giving him a kiss.) When could she have? How many things happened that I didn't see, hear, control—like my grip on the lamp?

It's raining. It's rained nonstop these past few days, like the time of Noah's ark, but, in this case, seven days and seven nights. It's evening now, closing time.

I don't want this day to end. The terror of tomorrow, of waking with that feeling that it's all been a bad dream and then realizing that the dream is real. It's a feeling I'm familiar with, something I've experienced during every painful episode in my life. But curiously, this time it's different. For the first

84

time after a personal tragedy, I don't wake up the following day with the feeling that it was all a nightmare. Even in my sleep I'm never detached from reality. In my deepest sleep, I've never stopped knowing that the nightmare is real. This gives an idea of how deeply misfortune has thrust its dagger into you: when it plunges so deep into your heart, as deep as a root, that not even the soundest sleep can dispel your awareness of what has occurred. I wake and there is no contrast between the two states. There's only never-ending despair.

Words, words, words. His friends improvise funeral speeches. I'm mesmerized by the beauty of words. I could die of gratitude. I don't want the day to end. Today is the day to fight desperation with words. He was really annoyed lately at funerals and weddings. He hated the way the ministers of the church spouted such nonsense, at times even heretical. The interpretation they often made of the Gospels horrified him. I couldn't understand why he listened to them. "Why do you listen? At Mass no one ever listens. Who listens?" He thought that was a lack of respect, and refused to behave in that fashion, no matter how much of an atheist he was. It was one of his traits. He always listened. And, of course, nonsense is not unique to religious funerals: The drivel you hear at civil funerals is considerable! And, since it isn't bound by any ritual, the rubbish is doubly odious, to such a degree that at times the most emotional moments wither in a sea of cloying, hackneyed expressions.

This is not the case today. The words are lucid, profound, deeply felt. They are spoken by friends who represent the three different worlds he inhabited. The speeches are different, pronounced in three distinct tones, and I savor them like an exquisite dish I don't want to finish. In a dense, brutal, excessive way, the words recreate him, even more so than if he were present. There's an excess of him, the last excess, a day when absence is stronger than presence. And this will never happen again, not with this intensity.

And that's why I want to stay here.

But it's not possible.

Outside it's still raining cats and dogs.

I don't recognize the cemetery nor do I know how we got here. (Maybe because it's raining cats and dogs.) I know somewhere there's a fallen angel, sculpted in white marble. I've often seen a similar or identical figure in other places, but this angel is a beautifully sculpted relief that gives the impression of having been chiseled with tremendous delicacy by the brute force of an ax. The angel is sleeping with the soundness of eternal sleep, and the rose in its hand is always on the verge of falling, conveying the conviction that the next time you come it will have fallen. But no, when you return, it's always there. My mother commissioned it for my father. "Commissioned" isn't exactly the word; my mother never commissions or orders anything, because she's never delegated anything; so no doubt she stood over the monumental mason until she had the angel of her dreams. She maintains that the sculptor's work was particularly inspired because he was moved by the youth of the severed couple, and that's why the angel is so beautiful (being the eternal contrarian, I thought Mamà was exaggerating, until I realized the uniqueness of the sculpture). I come with her every year. That's how I know this cemetery. But it's not the same place today. Have I ever been here? I don't recognize anything. A curtain of water until I get out of the car. The rest is fire.

The program after the funeral is going to be very animated. I say program because now more than ever I need to program every second of my life (no unoccupied second, not a single unoccupied second); I need to know what should be done with every minute of the day. And what I need to do is:

1. Have lunch with my women friends.
2. Talk with his family.
3. Pick up my daughter this afternoon, who's at a friend's house, and tell her that she won't be seeing her father again. Ever again.

Point one. Everything goes according to plan, no incidents. My friends give me tremendous support. They don't want to leave after lunch; they want to accompany me to the restaurant where his family are eating. "No, it's only a matter of walking down the street, to the end. I have to start practicing," I say. "You'll have plenty of time to practice, there's no reason to start today," Ml. tells me. But I insist—true to my motto of *the sooner the better*—and I tell them to go back to Barcelona.

Point two. The restaurant where his family are having lunch is at the end of the street. It's hard to walk this street. But I'm still numb and arrive without incident. (I thought it would be much harder, but I need only take one step after the other.) As soon as I enter I feel the warm atmosphere that they create wherever they go and that comforts us all. Some people who know us come up to me. Suddenly a friend greets me and—as he doesn't know what to say—he blurts out, "I saw you on TV." (Huh?) Well, that's just great. So the nitwit saw me on TV? I feel nauseous, not for any particular reason, the poor guy didn't know what to say. In the end, it'll be just one of many comments I'll hear from people who can't find the words to confront death; but I feel nauseous, not for any one particular reason, for everything, and I leave to go collect my daughter.

Point three. My daughter is playing princess with E. and M., my friend's children. My friend, the mother of the twins, is a childhood friend. We met at school when we were about seven. When my father died, I stopped talking. I was shy before, but after that I adopted a type of behavior that, while not exactly autistic, looked a lot like it. I couldn't talk, it frightened me to hear someone addressing me, and if I didn't talk to anyone, the chances increased that no one would talk to me. My friend helped me through that period. She was shy, but not to the extent that I was. One day she said something to me, I don't remember exactly what it was, but it was intended to bring me out of my darkness, and it did. That's when our friendship began; it's lasted until now (forty years), and I can assure you that I did begin to speak again. And now my daughter is talking nonstop with my friend's daughter, playing, entertained, happy, unaware. I let her play longer. And longer. And longer.

In the car, as we're driving home, silence. She doesn't ask anything. "Are you OK, Píulix?" She says she is. But she doesn't ask anything.

The three of us drove this same route exactly a month ago. After dinner at my friend's house with the children, we were caught in a tremendous downpour. In just a few minutes all the cars around us were at a standstill in the middle of Carrer

Acadèmia, and people had to get out to push them because the water had reached bumper level. We were ecstatic about the adventure. The two of us were—he wasn't. We headed up the ring road to avoid the flooding street. "What a great adventure!" Píulix exclaimed when we got home, and I agreed. He was irritated by our excitement and told us we'd been on the verge of getting stuck, or even worse, being swept down to the river, and from there probably to the sea, or who knows, even to the ocean.

"You're so theatrical, darling!" I said.

"What ocean would we have reached?" our daughter asked with great interest.

"The two of you don't have any notion of danger, you're oblivious."

"That's true, but we had a great time!" I exclaimed as we chased him with a towel to dry him off and smother him in kisses that he pretended to rebuff, because he didn't like to be kissed by a couple of crazy, reckless girls.

Today the adventure is of another kind. Never again will there be that glorious feeling of "we are all safe and together, which is all that matters," that feeling that often arises when you're indoors with your close-knit family during inclement weather. The inclemency is inside me now; it has settled there, for good I suppose. I have to try to keep the inclemency from devastating my daughter's heart. *Importantíssim*. The first step: the announcement. I've waited for her to ask, but she doesn't. Actually, it's better. I don't think it's a good idea to tell her here in the car, with my back to her, as I drive. I'll wait till we get home, in our bedroom. When I was a few months older than she is now, after verifying that my watch said half past one, I was taken to the house of some friends of my parents.

I stayed a couple of days. It seemed very long. They told me my parents were away on a trip. I thought it strange. On a November afternoon, a Sunday, the friends who were keeping me (during that time we never left the house, I suppose to protect me from hearing any news that someone might divulge by accident) took me home. I'd been uneasy that last day with them, troubled by a dark foreboding. But I was happy and eager to be going home; there was only one dispiriting detail and it was that my wool dress was scratchy. When we arrived, my premonitions vanished: I saw all the lights through the windows, and through the door I could hear people talking. I remember asking the friends who accompanied me, "Is there a party?" I don't know if, at the time, I had any notion of the modern concept of a surprise party, nor do I know if that's why today I find surprise parties so beastly. But they didn't have to respond, for the door swung open and my mother told me that bit about Papà's-gone-to-heaven-and-we-will-never-see-him-again. Premonitions, jubilation, reprieve, and the announcement of the worst. Even in that, it resembled the Fridays with their X-rays: premonitions, jubilation, reprieve, and the announcement of the worst.

"Papà's-gone-to-heaven-and-we-will-never-see-him-again."

That was the sentence. I've never forgotten it. As I've never forgotten the scratchy wool dress, the hour my watch showed, or my father's brothers taking me, after I was given the news, to buy me the board game I'd always wanted—but the stores were closed because it was Sunday.

As for the phrase, I always thought my mother must have rehearsed it many times; she had spoken it like an automaton. I remember thinking that the "never again" part was over the top; "never again" just wasn't possible. I think I remember she said it very fast. I suppose someone told her that the clearer the better. I've been rehearsing in the car. Just in case, like me, she'll remember it all her life. We don't have a heaven, which is such a useless construct. We do, however, have a basement filled with childhood memories where family ashes end up, next to the bottles of aging wine, the fermenting vinegar, and the tools and fishing rods that hold such endearing anecdotes. But this won't be of any use to her at the moment. I'll need to invent some place similar to heaven. I'll tell her he died, so it'll be clear, so that right from the beginning there won't be any confusion. After that, we'll think about heaven. As I'm parking the car, she finally asks in a whining voice:

"Is Papà in the hospital? Because, if he's in the hospital, when we leave on Monday he won't be able to come with us!"

I tell her the exact words I'd planned to say. Not one more. Not one less. When she hears the word "died," she gives me a half-smile of disbelief or one that says "a great adventure." I'm sure she thinks I'm exaggerating. She listens as if the news was something unreal, grandiose, so colossal that she is unable to cry, something taken perhaps from one of the stories she loves. A few seconds later, she starts to weep. You'd give anything if that heart-wrenching weeping had never had to be.

It's better to remember, for instance, that a few minutes after her heart-wrenching weeping, as she's wiping away her tears, she says, "What are we going to eat now? Because, what if he's taken his pots and pans?" Pots and pans are very important to her (she loved watching him cook), she's always hungry ("When I'm grown, Papà and I will cook for you,"

91

she used to say). And it's good for me ("And you'll only have to wash the dishes, like a queen"), good to have someone thinking about survival, now that my own wish to survive is faltering. I only know how to cook vegetables, soups, and chops. And wash dishes. I've always believed in specialization, and we were a scrupulously specialized couple who never needlessly duplicated tasks. He drove on the motorway. I drove in the city. He cooked. I washed pans. And we did everything else like that.

"You'll have to learn to cook," she says with that adorable practical instinct that children display in opportune moments.

She forgets. She becomes distracted. She weeps again. She's distracted again. But we aren't done yet. The news hovers above her head but it hasn't really settled. After a moment, she asks:

"Why did you tell me that, about Papà being dead?"

I have to start over. She wants to change the message and I can't allow it. She wants to change the message just as I wanted *Senyor Ambulance Man* to change it (You have two options, metastasis or pinched nerve, though actually only one: a pinched nerve). In the same way, she's saying: You have two options, messenger woman: Either he's in the hospital or you're joking. I know he's not in the hospital, so why are you telling me this horrid joke.

"Why did you tell me that about Papà, that he died?"

There can't be any truce.

"Because that's what happened."

She seems to accept it, but a few minutes later she asks the same question and I respond:

"Because it's the truth."

She asks only one more time. And no more.

Several days have passed and here I am, protected by the night, as I always am at the end of day. I've made progress. Instead of surrendering to channel surfing, now I'm watching Amenábar's film *The Others*. But I get bogged down by that sentence where the servant appears from out of the shadows and says to the young mother, who's alone, "Shall I make us a nice cup of tea, ma'am?" Like a wagon stuck in the mud, like a bone stuck in your throat, *shallimakeusanicecupofteama'am* is lodged in my head, a slow but sharp stab, then I no longer feel pain. I only feel that the film has come to a stop, the long night has come to a stop. Everything has stopped.

That's better. The problem is somehow to avoid the arrival of hellish, accursed morning.

A3

The Land of Boredom

Cometa had extricated her from the quagmire of the land of boredom, where her two previous (protracted) love stories had shipwrecked, one after the other. All of us have an animal totem, some sort of taboo monster that haunts us. Cometa's was the Shark. An imaginary shark that only attacked in nightmares. Lot's was Boredom. And the worst part was that she could never find interlocutors who fully understood her plight.

She eventually realized that victims of boredom don't usually inspire compassion. If they live alone, the metaphysical depression that boredom provokes makes them more or less worthy of compassion. But if the boredom monster attacks and they have a partner, then prepare to grin and bear it. "So, what's the matter with her? Is she bored? Is she afraid of being bored? Something's boring her? Bored with her partner? Bored by her partner?" No one seems to fully understand the misery of those who are terrorized by a monster (an invisible but omnipresent danger) that rules over their world.

Lot taught in a lycée, surrounded by adolescents who fell head over heels in and out of love; and she often noticed a discrepancy in the way they were treated. One teacher, for example, mentioned a very diligent student, a girl, who had suddenly stopped studying, "I heard that her boyfriend broke up with her and she's in a lot of pain." The other teachers sympathized with the girl; they understood her situation. Everyone looked serious, or to be more precise, grim. There was, however, another occasion when a brilliant student suffered a serious crisis for the opposite reason: For the first time, the girl had discovered the finiteness of love, the finiteness of passion; she was experiencing it firsthand and the disappointment was agonizing. She'd been convinced that her love was forever. Or at least for a few years. But after a year, her heart no longer fluttered when her guy walked in the room. She wasn't anxious to see him anymore; the world no longer revolved around him; he wasn't enough to offset the glumness of Sunday afternoons. What had happened? Had she tired of the relationship? If she had, then she'd probably have to break up with her boyfriend. But no one said, "Poor thing, she has to break up with her boyfriend and she's in a lot of pain." Strange. Why didn't she elicit the same degree of sympathy, or more, than the girls who were abandoned and who, after all, walked away free and full of energy, heading toward another relationship, unburdened and with no sense of guilt?

To be incapable of loving when you are determined to continue loving is a terrible thing, one of the saddest things that can happen to you. Infinitely sadder than being abandoned. That's what Lot thought, accustomed as she was to not being able to love those with whom she fell in love. She'd reached the stage where she couldn't conceive of anything worse than the weariness and the indifference that attacked her soon after starting a new relationship. No hunger, no thirst? There's nothing's worse than the absence of desire, nothing darker than not wanting what you have. *This* is boredom. An endless tunnel through which you don't advance, because there is no objective, no exit, not even the wish to leave. An oppressive tunnel that leads only to desperation and, of course, suicide. Monster of monsters, no one described it as well as Baudelaire. When Lot was fifteen she discovered his poetry, and she felt that finally someone truly understood her. Yes, the poet was completely right, the poet who said:

And yet, among the beasts and creatures all—
Panther, snake, scorpion, jackal, ape, hound, hawk—
Monsters that crawl, and shriek, and grunt, and squawk,
In our vice-filled menagerie's caterwaul,
One worse is there, fit to heap scorn upon—
More ugly, rank! Though noiseless, calm and still,
yet would he turn the earth to scraps and swill,
swallow it whole in one great, gaping yawn:
Ennui!

Boredom. These last verses had driven her mad with alleged lucidity when she was fifteen. At the end of the poem, the poet calls the reader a hypocrite. What an appropriate adjective! The reader who so often fails to recognize the greyness of her life, denies it, rejects it, even to the point of choosing endless tedium over any kind of change, anything unexpected.

Other than Baudelaire, Lot never found anyone who agreed with her on this point, not when she was fifteen, not at a later age. Nor did the men she'd known understand her horror of being bored with the other. Nor did Cometa. And so, for years Lot had plodded along, accompanied but alone, through the quicksand of this monstrous land. She was forced to perform a real juggling act when she felt herself being sucked down, the monster wanting to drag her into the depths. This had happened each time she had fallen in love. A brief period and then—swoosh!—that sinking sensation.

Twice she'd fallen in love. Her first love, a lovely guy. For two years she eyed him from a distance, platonically. At fifteen she started going out with him. At fifteen and a half she was already reciting Baudelaire while playing sinister chords on an electric organ by candlelight, in the darkness. Not a good sign. Nevertheless, that love was beautiful and tender. But, yes, that is where she first encountered the monster. After a while, what she had so desired began to waste away. She was thirsty for fruits she hadn't known. She felt herself an exile from an uncertain future. She felt doomed. She recited Baudelaire and suffered tremendously, as only adolescents are capable of suffering for love, for affection—or for disaffection in her case. She did love him; she wanted to grow old at his side. But old age seemed so far away. She saw clearly that it would not work out, that her love life would be more than that, but she persisted. Her heart, however, no longer skipped a beat when she awaited him. But she was adamant. They were together for six years, until she met another man. Her second man.

This second relationship never knew a moment's peace. She felt terribly guilty that boredom had taken from her the love she had felt for her young, adolescent friend. She never managed to love the second man whom, nevertheless, she liked in a very special way. She felt trapped between the past and the future. And as she'd never been very diplomatic, she often told him, "I have the impression that you're positioned between the before and the after, between the past and the future, yesterday and tomorrow."

It's true that he turned out to be the perfect bridgeman. Depending on how you look at it, all lovers are a path to another lover. But there are some who are more than that, some are perfect bridges. It's not that she, whom we know was seeking Absolute Love, had begun the relationship with the intention of turning him into a bridge, not at all. But her intuition immediately told her that this was not a land where she would stay, but a bridge to a land from which she would never return. It's a fact that we often know things that we don't realize we know. During that strange relationship, Lot felt almost permanently bad: On the one hand, she couldn't manage to get beyond the longing for a past that, paradoxically, she didn't want to recapture. On the other hand, she knew she was doomed to a future that she herself was constructing with this man. She felt she was that strange bird who, convinced that she was making a nest, was really building a cage.

At the time, Lot was probably close to becoming a borderline alcoholic, though she wasn't aware of it. This is how it went: Though it may seem peculiar, in the same way that generations of Spanish children had associated the old-fashioned snack of bread dipped in wine and sugar with something healthy, Lot had always viewed an aperitif as a harmless drink for accompanying clams, which were the important thing. And if the clams made her thirsty, well, she drank more vermouth. She made the same kind of association between cava and ham. And ham makes you thirsty too. As for the bridgeman, perhaps because of his lack of drinking culture or his sense of attentiveness, not only did he fail to see any problem in this, but he awaited her at lunchtime with a plate of clams and a bottle of Martini vermouth, and he awaited her at dinnertime with ham and cava. And so, a dual pattern of states of mind began to take shape: a sick fluctuation between euphoria and sadness. The sadness arrived with the midday aperitif, when she suffered terrible pangs of guilt about her first love, an infinite sadness that the bridgeman didn't understand. "You can't spend your life like Colometa in Rodoreda's novel *The Time of the Doves*, always thinking about your first love without getting over it; besides, you're the one who left him," he would say.

Sad and misunderstood, Lot awaited the evening ham, which had the curious virtue of dispelling all guilt; and then she was able to enjoy herself, engaging in the pleasures that emanated from the night, until the hour of the clams returned. Guilt set in with the vermouth and clams and disappeared with the cava and ham; the following day, it returned with the clams. And Lot never once associated it with drinking, only with eating.

Probably the only thing that saved her from addiction was her peculiar immunity to licentiousness. The same tedium that caused so many problems in her affections and love life kept her from becoming addicted to anything for long. Sooner or later her interest waned; she had only to wait. And so, after a while, without any particular effort or regret, she gave up cava and vermouth and moved on to wine and Campari. This facility for abandoning acquired habits had saved her from becoming truly addicted (and not for lack of trying) to cigarettes, to chocolate, to Pac-Man. She might get hooked for a while, but in the end she never had to make an effort to break away. Sooner or later, usually sooner, she tired. Sooner or later she lost her appetite, her thirst, her desire, and a different appetite, thirst, desire would appear, perhaps resembling the previous, perhaps radically different.

It's true, however, that during those years with the bridgeman, she had come very close to transforming that brainless alcohol intake into an addiction. How ludicrous that she had to meet Cometa, a passionate, expert drinker, in order to learn that when you're thirsty, you drink water.

She was terribly thirsty one afternoon when she arrived at the bar where they were to meet. He was always very punctual and had been sitting in front of his untouched gin and tonic for some time. Feeling parched, Lot said: "May I?" And, to his amazement, she drank it down in one gulp. "I'm just really thirsty," she said when she finished.

"She's thirsty," Cometa said to the bartender. And he asked for two tonic waters, which she downed with the same enjoyment and the same pleasure. It truly irritated Cometa that she showed such lack of respect for his gin and tonic, that she could drag a sacred drink down to the level of a liquid fit for frogs, and that she was capable of imbibing it with the same disposition, the same indifference with which he drank a glass of water. He explained it to her. And she understood. It was only the beginning of her beginning to understand things.

Reaching the land of Cometa—the land that lay on the other side of the bridge—was like arriving in a country where everything made sense. Was it possible that she might free herself forever of the quagmire of boredom? At his side, there was nothing unimportant, nothing that was taken for granted. Everything was done correctly, conscientiously. And it could be explained, with reasons. As the relationship with Cometa progressed, neither tedium nor guilt put in an appearance. She felt freer than she had for a long time. She grieved at the same time for the loss of her first love and her second: For the price of one mourning, she got two. She'd always carried her guilt around with her (initially, for having abandoned her first love, and later, for having caused her second relationship to deteriorate to an untenable degree), and then, suddenly, she was freed of it. Nothing better than Cometa to tame guilt: He was an expert at it. It was almost enough to observe how he conducted himself for her to be able to unburden herself. By doing always what he believed, he probably never had anything to feel guilty about. It's also possible his peculiar sense of oblivion helped him to circumvent useless guilt. In any case, Lot had never known anyone—other than a psychopath— who was so totally devoid of any sense of guilt. Or perhaps he simply had a truly thorough education, and, as Epictetus's maxim states, "One who is well educated, neither blames another, nor himself." And so, finally, Lot's guilt began to melt away like ice in the sun, while she simultaneously came to realize how arrogant we are when we feel the same guilt she had, for there is no one for whom we are truly irreplaceable.

Even though the threat of boredom did not materialize, the terror that the monster inspired in Lot was so great that she was always alert, expecting to discover its lurking presence at any given moment. She found it hard to believe that it might not suddenly reappear. When would that perverse alarm be triggered, the one that had brought her previous love stories to their end? She knew it well, the diabolical alarm that whispered in her ear in a perverse voice, "Admit that you're growing bored with the way he speaks, you're growing bored with the way he is silent, you're growing bored with the way he makes love, you're growing bored with the way he looks at things . . . Do something, do something!" The voice would not let her give up, would not let her leave the other in peace. Quite the opposite, it stubbornly demanded, "Don't run away, don't escape, do something, cause an accident, make a scene, don't be bored, act!"

This time she wasn't willing to allow perversity to win the game. The day she heard the diabolical voice, she wouldn't stick around to make the other person's life impossible, hammering away at him, revealing how his every gesture bored her. No. She would leave; she'd have to leave before it was too late. It was settled: She would never be cruel to Cometa, she would never let perversity impose itself.

Until then, perversity had been the antidote to boredom. Perversity has nothing to do with wickedness, only with a certain failing. When she felt that a kind of sickening peace was approaching, bringing with it warnings of the quagmire of boredom, she always knew exactly what to do to avoid it: a hurtful expression, the appropriate word to make herself hated, the right gesture to show her disgust. Anything that would make that gentle routine explode, anything that would compromise that loathsome predictability, anything to keep the dreaded monster at bay . . .

Certain signs were the harbingers of perversity. The signs lay in the little details. It all started in the same way. It started with something insignificant, a triviality. She referred to it as "the little detail." We already know that she doesn't like thoughtful little gifts or gestures, but this is a different concept. The little detail was a venial sin—*venialíssim*, trifling, insignificant, minute . . . A triviality capable of ruining the best reputation, a mere trifle, but capable of destroying the best first impression. This brings Lot's mother back on the scene. She was the one who provided the example *and* the training for spotting those "little details." Lot's mother would sometimes let drop a comment about a certain person whom she had found adorable for some time: "Today I noticed a little detail . . ." This meant that the person in question had committed some irreparable faux pas, and nothing she did from that moment on was of any consequence.

The "little detail" is not a great defect, but it kills everything: It's that unfortunate sentence the other person utters and you can never forget; the one word that clearly indicates that your boyfriend is a cheapskate; the slightly larger piece of fish he puts on his plate that reveals how rude he really is; the word that exposes him as selfish; that slight touch of baseness that puts into question his moral character.

Was it that Lot did not have any selfish, offensive traits of her own? Was she perhaps faultless? Of course not! But what do her flaws have to do with all of this? Nothing at all. The dog that hunts for rabbits, the pig that forages for truffles, doesn't have to be perfect: It has only to smell the rabbits; it has only to look for truffles. That's their destiny. And so, Lot was destined to "spot the little details," and this practice—at times useful, at others detestable—became second nature to her. When you've been trained to see the details, you look for them, you can't help it.

With Cometa, nothing seemed destined to be any different. As was her wont, Lot braced herself for the arrival of the cloud that would create the tedious climate she knew so well. But it didn't appear. As there was no boredom, there was no need to search for little details to entertain herself. However, being well trained in the discipline, it was nearly impossible for her to avoid rummaging for the "minutiae" that would make her fall out of love . . . But she didn't find any, and she hadn't counted on that. Where were the little defects? Where were the little deceptions that concealed some hidden flaw?

There were no hidden flaws: The ones he had he never tried to conceal, and he ended up making the most of them. There were no little deceptions; Cometa always showed all his cards. Always. And that disarms even the keenest hound dog. Time passed and she remarked with surprise that the intense passion periodically resumed, and it was interspersed with periods of the peace and calm of married life, with a man who had finally become someone real—or something similar to that—and with whom family routines seemed to glide smoothly. Lot had always believed that because of her sticky problem with tedium such a life would forever be off limits; and being the stubborn person she was, she found it difficult to admit that it could be that easy. At every instant, she was surprised to have found someone who could emerge triumphant from her unforgiving scrutiny. One day she told Cometa:

"You know what? You've, you've, you've . . ."

"You've what?" he interrupted impatiently.

"It's that . . . Wow, I've just realized . . . you've . . . no word exists for the opposite of 'to disappoint.' You can't say you've 'undisappointed' me, or you've been 'undisappointing' me every day!" she observed. "Why don't we have a word for the opposite of disappoint? It should exist, don't you think?"

"Bah," he said with a tone of skepticism.

"Well, just that: You've . . . the opposite of disappointed me. There should be a verb for it, don't you think?"

Years passed and she continued to be perplexed by her ability to keep the Tedium Monster at bay in the company of this man. Commentaries and exclamations of surprise recurred, a surprise he didn't seem to share:

"Can you believe it?" she'd say. "We've been together for ten years and I'm *still* interested in everything you say, I'm *still* interested in everything you do . . ."

Or maybe:

"Can you believe it? We've been together for twelve years and I *still* wait for you every afternoon with the same eagerness."

Or maybe:

"It seems incredible that I could feel this way, after such a long time together!"

In the end, he found the "still" and the "incredible" rather irritating.

"Would you kindly stop watching over this love as if it were an *escudella* stew, waiting for it to boil," he said one day.

"*Escudella* . . . Yes, that's it, an *escudella* stew. I'm researching . . . trying to determine the ingredients. I'll identify them one day."

"I don't know why you marvel at being happy. Stop marveling at being happy and devote yourself to being happy, for heaven's sake!"

"I can do both things at the same time, in case you didn't know. We women can do two things at the same time. More than two . . ."

But the perplexity provoked by swimming in that joyful *escudella* kept her investigative proclivities in a state of constant engagement. And, slowly, her fear of seeing the Tedium Monster reappear gave way to the terror of losing the company of the man who had battled it and won.

B3

What We Talk about
When We Talk about Killing Ourselves

Time has been returned to me without my asking for it. Absolute Love is hard work; it absorbs a lot of time, a lot of energy. I had mirrored my time to his. My schedules to his. My age to his. And I was all too happy to do so. Ever since I was little I've been afraid of having too much time on my hands, but this has never happened in the last sixteen years. Because I added his activities to mine: Even if I wasn't the protagonist of his, even though he was living them and not me, I was there; I was always there. If someone were to ask me what I was doing, where I was, for instance, on the day the World Trade Center collapsed, I couldn't tell you for sure. But ask me where he was, and I know exactly where and with whom. When we were apart for a few hours, my mind always accompanied him. And when we were together, his inner climate—his every smile, his every sign of irritation, his every new dish, his every emotion—regulated my mood. In a word, to be left suddenly without an occupation of this import clearly transforms the time that lies ahead into an interminable desert.

So much for time. As for space: on arriving in town after being gone since Friday, I experience an unsettling feeling. Have you ever had the impression that everything around you is a set, a fake landscape, a stage identical to the familiar one, yet absolutely strange and never seen before? I'd been afraid of seeing the town without him. But I don't see it, because it's not the same place: Someone has transformed it into a stage set. As a result, I'm scared: I find it deceptive, and therefore hostile. It deceives me in the worse possible way: disguising itself as the town it was. There are, therefore, no painful memories, but nor are there memories that I can associate with him. And this lack of familiarity is so strong that it sometimes provokes an unbearable physical malaise, especially when I leave the inside of a building and find myself on the street again. At times I have to go back inside until I can regain my vital signs, my breathing. Then I head home with the intention of not going out again. Home, home, to our haven, to the house, fast. Fast! To home.

I suppose it's the indifference that makes the town so inhospitable, meaning precisely that nothing has changed: No river of tears has flooded it, no black sky has collapsed onto the streets. People stroll nonchalantly. Everything flows with the indifference that characterizes towns and cities, whose movements are never contingent on death, that is, not when the person dies an individual death.

At home, however, everything is different. His presence is powerful; it accompanies you. You can touch his clothes, his annotated books, his ideas spread about the table in many little slips of paper. At home, the objects are not indifferent. They speak. The oversized envelope left on the bed—on top of the duvet cover with the large yellow peaches—speaks; it is the envelope that contains his provisional pardon, the one he didn't want me to take with us. Our daughter's things speak, as she reencounters them and associates them with her father. "Look, this is the book Papà gave me on Thursday."

One of the things that impresses me the most these days is being able to say "Thursday." It's still not necessary to say "that Thursday": Last Thursday is right here, so close, yet so inaccessible. "He gave you one of his books?" I ask my daughter. He never gave away his books; he was generous with everything except the books that had become his: He knew them, was intimate with them, and he didn't like the idea of lending them. When he wanted to recommend one, he preferred to buy it rather than lend his.

But he couldn't refuse his daughter. She'd fallen in love with one of those little old books from the Crisol collection, a book by Juan Luis Vives published by Aguilar in 1944. I suppose it was because it was tiny and bound in red leather. It couldn't have been because of the title, *La mujer cristiana. De los deberes del marido. Pedagogía pueril* [The Christian Woman. Duties of a Husband. Child Pedagogy]. Last Thursday we heard her reading the beginning of it out loud: "The feminism of Luis Vives in the Valencia of the Edetan people, and later of El Cid, and then of Don Jaime the Conqueror, who purged it of the impunity of the Hagrites . . ." Later, we heard her howling like a ravenous little dog, as she often does, until he went to get her some cookies. Then we caught a crunching sound as she nibbled, followed immediately by silence. She must have fallen asleep. That is how she fell asleep on Thursday. Thursday.

The objects belonging to the one who is no longer present suddenly assume a disproportionate importance.

They hold the person's smell and touch. My daughter takes great care of his things. She likes to feel their proximity: jacket, wallet, books, notebooks, the presents he gave her, the figurines he bought for her at the stationery store, the wolf of the three little pigs (it was the latest one), the violin strings that were changed last Wednesday. Wednesday. The need to embrace and caress the imprint he made on them is enormous. This is a moment of rapine: his objects spring to mind and you need to appropriate them. Where are the photos? Where are his fountain pens? His binoculars? The notes he left me?

Overcome by a sudden frenzy, I search for the notes. I kept them in a drawer. We never wrote letters to each other, just brief messages. Two lines at most. They were our letters, but everything's mixed up in the drawer and I can only find one of his last notes. It's a sketch, an elongated worm made of spheres drawn with a quick pen, two words—eternal love— written in German (it probably didn't sound as corny to him in German) and a message: "I'll be home at ten." That's all the correspondence we ever sent each other. There was no occasion for anything else; we were never separated long enough to have to write.

After a few days, you stop looking with such single-minded eagerness. You just happen upon them. You open your appointment book and you find a little drawing. It's an amusing illustration, a rather wide, ungainly skeleton he'd drawn for our daughter in a restaurant in Tuscany when she'd asked what we were like inside. They'd just shown us the fish they were going to cook for us. Waiting for fish to be prepared after seeing it, fresh out of the water, always put Cometa in a good mood. The skeleton was cute and I kept it in my planner. We walked back along the stone footpath by the sea, waves splashing us in the night.

You open the closet and see his jacket, and him in it, and you feel the touch of his fog-cold skin when he arrived for dinner during our vacation in the house of the three doors. You open the other closet and you see the dress you wore last summer and you wonder what you'll feel next summer when you have to decide if you'll wear it again.

You open the kitchen cupboard and you see the kidney beans he bought in the town of El Barco de Ávila, where he had the mystical revelation that he should stay and live forever in a place like that.

You take the cap off the toothpaste and you know it's almost finished, and the next tube of toothpaste won't be the one he used.

You open the mailbox and find the hand-addressed envelope that he regularly received from Librairie Vrin, the old philosophy bookstore in Place de la Sorbonne that we occasionally visited ("the only ones who ever write me," he often said).

You open the freezer and see the *escudella* and the *fabada,* his bean stew. (Now that should be nice, to wolf down a *fabada* two months from now and be able to say: *He made it.*) At least that's interesting. I don't make any changes: I want his objects to accompany me forever. For the time being, they'll pound away at me until every wave wears down the pain, transforming it into fine, soft sand. I don't plan to remove things from the closet. Much like the smoker who gives up smoking (and every time he does something he'd previously done while smoking he feels a powerful, intense, unbearable absence), it is only through repeated actions that we can learn to incorporate his things into our lives, until finally they are under our skin. At that point, his things will no longer cause us pain, and it won't matter where we go, they'll go with us. Píulix participates in this with her characteristic cheerfulness. It's almost as if his things, scattered around the house, intensify her father's presence rather than saddening her by his absence.

But a shadow has been cast over certain areas. The living room/dining room is one such case. The place where we ate the dishes he cooked. The place where he read while Píulix climbed on top of him or counted his ribs, the place where the two of them listened to *Peter and the Wolf* on winter nights. The place where on Wednesday our daughter scratched out her first notes on the violin and he was moved—recently he was easily moved by things related to her or to me. The same place where two weeks ago I, who never put on my music, dared to play Charles Trenet while he was in the kitchen cooking *kokotxas* (hake cheeks) and he suddenly appeared when he heard "*Que reste-t-il de nos amours*," wanting to dance the last part with me as he whistled the tune. It was unusual for him, and yet, at the same time, it was one of those amorous outbursts that could only have come from him, for just imagine—if I'd been the one to request the dance, one burned *kokotxa* would have sufficed for all hell to break loose! No, no ... you couldn't play around with these things, especially if he was in the kitchen or if there was music involved.

In any case, the living room was very much his space. And now the objects in it are challenging us: "Place me in the present, make me useful, give me a purpose!" We lost the living room in my home when my father died. It was almost as if it had been closed off. After that it was always lifeless. Of course, I belong to that generation where parents didn't let children set foot in the room. The living room was sacrosanct and immaculate, a place for entertaining that resembled a model room in a show house or a furniture store, one that children weren't allowed to contaminate with their grime. Our living room wasn't a particularly venerated place, but it was very much his space, and now it's difficult for us to make it our own. We need to do something, urgently; we can't allow our living room to disappear from the house. (In my planner for killing time: Give new life to the living room.)

When the moment for killing time arrives, I'll have a lot of things in my planner. But I haven't even started it yet. I spend my days answering letters and responding to phone calls: from students, acquaintances, friends who have reappeared from the past. Everyone has something to say, and if someone doesn't say something, I do. If need be, I'll take the initiative. I search my memory in case there's someone left who doesn't know; I check to see if there's an acquaintance who hasn't shown any signs of life, and if that's the case, I'll give her a nudge, help her get her act together. And when I'm done with acquaintances, I'll start with strangers.

Any available stranger will do: the plumber, the carpenter, the mailman, the telemarketer who phones asking for him . . . Yes, they too will learn. "No, he's not in." And if they insist: "He died the other day." They stop insisting.

The problem is how to delay the moment when there is no longer anything to communicate, nothing related to his death (and therefore to his life). When that moment arrives, when the time comes when there is no one left in whom I can provoke a certain degree of shock, no one with whom to share this blow, then that arduous moment will have arrived when you must rebuild a life you have no wish to rebuild, confront the absence, and return to the landscape of boredom that you never wanted to revisit.

Because . . . No, no . . . I never want to feel the threat of boredom hovering over me again . . . I'll choose death before that.

You have believed this ever since you met him.

Ever since you merged with him, you have thought: If he isn't here, I don't want to be either.

And so?

What are you waiting for?

The two of you talked about it for years. Until your daughter arrived (because when you have children together, you can no longer tell the other *I-can't-live-without-you* and not scare the hell out of them). For years you did, in a manner of speaking, promise each other just that. If not, what exactly does "I can't live without you" mean? Is it a lie? Is it a metaphor? What is it exactly? Maybe it's that you interpret everything in a literal sense, something you've always been guilty of.

The time has come to reflect on this point: What exactly is the literal meaning of a sentence like this? It's not an infrequent one. When couples have been together for a while, to prove their devotion, they get in the habit of saying things like: "I couldn't conceive of life without you." I just opened a book by Saul Bellow and found a dedication to his wife: "To Janis, the star without whom I could not navigate." And I thought: This needs to be substantiated. If Janis dies, will he navigate? Will he continue navigating? What are we expressing when we say this? The intensity that cannot be expressed in any other way? And, to what degree is this just a figure of speech?

I had no doubt that in our case the sentence expressed a deep-felt desire. Even more so for me: We writers are often fragile, often dependent on someone who is by our side and who is *everything*: admired character, constant source of inspiration, unlimited support, teacher, love, lover. Not only did I take these sentences very seriously, but I have always been surprised to discover that there are couples who are prepared to survive the other without the slightest compunction. After he died I remember a friend telling me, "Fortunately, he had the heart attack after he got home, and not a few hours before while driving." Since I'd always thought that the prospect of the family dying together was like a gift from heaven, I had to ask her to repeat the sentence because I didn't understand what she was saying.

The problem occurs when what you most feared happens and you don't die. This proves really surprising. You're not yet thinking of killing yourself, because, naturally, you imagine that dying of love is a slow, slow thing, and you're waiting for the death throes to kick in. The shock is so great that at times you have to look at yourself in the mirror to believe it: You're amazed that your body has emerged unscathed from such inner devastation. I catch a glimpse of myself pushing a cart in a shopping center with mirrored walls, and the contrast between what I see and what I feel is striking. Apparently, I am a living a person who walks around and pushes a cart. My face too is quite normal: a distraught grimace, true, but it's a whole face, not falling to pieces, not decomposing. The body is here too, solid, still standing. And even though I steady myself on the cart, I appear to be the one who is pushing it. Mirrors are deceptive, they silence pain. The body silences pain. The body is preserved. How can such a divorce exist? How can a stupid little blood clot kill you and yet grief like this does not?

You wait and wait; you begin to suspect that you might not be the Isolde you thought you were destined to become, but the only thing you achieve is a mild case of anemia and an enviable figure because you're not hungry and don't eat. You start to tire of waiting and you think maybe you should help the situation a bit. It's not enough to eat little; on the contrary, in a time when everything edible is toxic to a lesser or greater degree, nothing improves health more than not eating. You need to do more to move things along. But how? A colleague sends me an e-mail: "What helped me was to go to Iraq when things were so messed up there." Something to consider. I make a mental note in my planner for killing time: Become a war correspondent.

Then, of course, there's my daughter. She's both a deterrent against my wish to disappear and a force driving me toward it: I'm haunted by the fear of offering her a sad life. Because, this I know for sure: better a dead mom than a sad, toxic mom. (But, maybe you won't be the sad mother you think you'll be?)

The truth is, the greater part of your day is taken up with graphic, visual, plastic, full-color fantasies of killing yourself. You are not convinced by the model that comes to mind, the suicide prototype from your adolescence: the image of Sylvia Plath with her head in the oven, her two lovely children in the next room snacking on the bread and butter their mother has left them. I used to think it a heroic gesture, freeing them

116

of a mother who (despite possessing one of the literary gazes that has best captured the euphoria of being alive) could not rid herself of the desperation of a bleak, miserable winter and a love betrayal. This model presides over my thoughts about suicide these days, repetitive, obsessive, serious thoughts.

How serious? We'll never know. There's always something a little ridiculous about suicidal ideas that aren't carried out. You know you must make use of the moments when you're inebriated by pain in order to see it through, but the idea becomes slightly more ridiculous with every day that passes without acting on it. And in the meantime, you talk about it. In an abstract way, of course.

"It's fucking anti-aesthetic," my friend O. says when I tell her about Plath. "Head in the oven, that's out of the question."

My friend is an expert in people who want to kill themselves and in people who do kill themselves. She's a psychiatrist. We met when we were fifteen and were enthralled by our readings of Virginia Woolf, Katherine Mansfield, Sylvia Plath, and similar writers.

"And besides, your oven is electric," she says with a shudder.

"The bit about the oven was just a manner of speaking."

"It's always been clear to me," she says. "If one day I were to decide, it'd be in a nice warm bathtub."

"Too slow for me; you know I'm impatient, the faster the better." I sigh at the difficulty of choosing. "But it's incredible that removing yourself from the equation is so complicated!"

"Complicated?" she says. "Not at all!"

"Ah, no?"

"Potassium injection."

"What?"

"Potassium chloride straight into the vein. Pills, don't even think about it. I have a patient who took fifty tranquilizers the other day and he's alive and kicking."

"No kidding."

"Yeah . . . He never stopped talking about killing himself and when he takes a shot at it, he screws it up!"

The rest of the time we discuss the relationship between suicide and suicidal thinking. It's not true that people who talk about suicide never kill themselves. Actually, the majority of those who do carry it through have threatened to do so, and they've talked about it over and over. There are also, however, those who have never talked about it.

"I think I can recognize a suicide when they walk through the door to my office," she says, adding: "And you're not one of them."

I sigh, I don't know if from disappointment or relief. But then I realize one minor detail:

"But I've never been to your office," I tell her.

She remains silent, the reference to her work darkens her expression, shrouding it in doubt. For days she's been telling me that she lacks perspective when it comes to me. The strong bond between us doesn't allow her the detachment she needs to assess how I'm doing: She can't treat me as a patient because I'm a friend, and she can't treat me as a friend because she sees a potential patient in me.

Yet, perhaps she's right when she says she doesn't think I'm suicide material. Though it's not something I ever plan, I do have constant recourse to a powerful weapon for keeping my death wish in check: words. Words can sculpt an idea and shape it until it becomes a manageable paste, a soft, manageable suicide paste, increasingly less serious, increasingly more comical. Words strip the death wish of its solemnity; words divest you of the energy needed to move from thought to action. In the end, the same happens with my suicide plans as with my travel plans. I talk so much about a trip, I consider it from so many angles, that finally I no longer feel any need to visit the place, because I have the impression that I've already been there. The same applies here: By exhausting the subject of killing yourself, you contribute to the feeling that you've already killed yourself. And so, I continue to talk about it in an abstract way.

I talk about it and people talk to me about it.

We're having lunch at some friends' house where I often eat on Sundays; they have been present in every chapter of our lives, and now they are watching me for signs of depression. They are treating me to a weekend in a spa and a trip to Rome in the spring, all three of us with the girls. X. is looking into low-cost flights, and when I show interest, he says in a surprised tone:

"Ah, but you and Píulix will go by plane too?" He knows I used to move heaven and earth to avoid getting on a plane; I only flew if it was absolutely necessary. And now he's amazed that I react with such indifference.

"Of course we'll take the plane," I say.

"Since you never wanted to fly before . . ." he responds.

Then we hear his wife's cheerful voice explaining to him as she drains the pasta, "Yes, but that was different; now she doesn't care if she dies!" So we book the first deal we can find and immediately change subjects and start talking about the spa.

My friend brings out the list of available treatments and reads them, "Hydrotherapy Immersion Bath. It's like a bubble bath with essential oils, but under water."

"And do they drown you?" I ask.

"Yes, but there's an extra charge for that," she replies and continues. "Eucalyptus bath, petal bath, salt bath; wow—blood bath, now you might find *that* one interesting."

And in this way, the miraculous power of words triumphs over action. Through the use and abuse of words you distance yourself from the idea of suicide, and it grows smaller and smaller. It's true that it lingers there for a while, in the background. Protective. But every time the oven makes an appearance and you haven't put your head in it, you have one more reason to laugh at yourself. What is it that separates the suicides that haven't been carried out (always a bit pathetic, even comical) from the ones that have been (which, in contrast to the first, leave you in a state of infinite dismay)? What exactly is the distance that separates them, so small yet so immense? What is that step? According to my friend the expert, it's that moment of confusion when your judgment is clouded, an instant of blind aggressiveness. In any case, a person with a wish to disappear will never know if she came close to acting on the idea or not.

In a town where I spent several of my summer vacations a few years ago, I met a woman who certainly had many reasons for detesting life: a husband who abused her, economic problems, depression, and a long list of misfortunes. More than once, as she wept in despair, she voiced this curious sentence, "I swear, if the train came through this town, I'd have already thrown myself under it!"

And yet, the train passed through the next town over. She had only to walk four kilometers.

I have lunch with my friend O. For days I've been asking her for books on the grieving process; I want to know what's in store. Today she remembered and when we're saying goodbye, she pulls something out of her bag.

"I brought you what you asked for the other day," she says.

"Ah, great!" I reply, thinking that today I'll have reading material to fill the sweet truce of night.

But it's only two sheets of paper, two sheets with the title: *The Mourning Process. Guidelines to Evaluate Pathological Grief.*

"Is this all?" I ask in disappointment.

"You'll have to fill in the rest yourself."

A4

Manual of the Good Charismatic

Nothing in the world had regaled Lot with as many enjoyable moments as the charismatic people she had known. Ever since she was little, those individuals who were touched by a special charm—she called them "the charismatics"—had fascinated her and sparked in her desires whose existence she would never even have suspected had it not been for them. She was deeply indebted to them. She would have learned little without them. As she was prone to boredom, she needed to be seduced in order to absorb any type of lesson, any kind of affection, but also any information. If she wasn't seduced, she found it difficult to even listen—yet another example of the unfortunate inconvenience caused by her susceptibility to boredom.

When she first took up writing, she felt all the more indebted to these charismatic people; she was sustained by her contact with people who were true "personages." Whatever might be said, literature has never been nourished by dull, harmless figures—which is not to say that it necessarily is by characters who immediately appear to be brilliant. No, often, essential characters are only discovered after a second glance, or a third; but they are rich, full of nuances and complexities.

Her encounters with charismatics had been the greatest attraction of her life, and they had marked her forever. First was her teacher in the City of Fog, a man whose personality reminded her of her recently deceased father. That probably set the pattern for the charismatics that would interest her in the future: those who would open tiny windows in the hard walls of her thinking. Some of her women friends had been charismatic. And then there was Cometa. Gifted with a charisma that was generally acknowledged by a sufficiently large number of people of different ages and conditions, he seemed to have entered Lot's life for the purpose of illustrating and refining the vague idea she had of the concept of charisma, a notion not easy to define. Much as a painter who devotes himself to painting thighs will search for interesting thighs and might one day discover *The Thigh* that will forever after serve as his model, when Lot found Cometa she realized that by taking his charisma as a model, she could unravel the mystery of that vague and obscure notion.

From the very beginning she studied him carefully, observing every aspect of his personality, asking herself where the key lay; it was obvious that charisma was not the sum of the elements that formed it, but rather an entirely new entity, and she was determined to discover the secret formula. Where did the enigma lie? What was it that had managed to make him irresistibly attractive to her, to whom everything eventually proved to be unbearably repulsive?

She had realized even before meeting Cometa—long before—that there were many misconceptions about charisma, some of them spread by those who were envious—people who are easily recognizable because they frown when someone is captivated by another person—and yet these very same people find it perfectly normal for someone to be enthralled by a painting by Brueghel, a canal in Venice, a certain building, or even an albino gorilla, such as the one in the Barcelona zoo. She found it impossible to understand this envy of charisma. She wouldn't have minded being charismatic herself; in fact she would have been thrilled. But she had so enjoyed the charisma of others that, given the choice, she would have chosen to enjoy it in others rather than have it herself.

After all, good charismatics tend to be very generous with their gift, since they have received it for free. As the etymology of the word (from the Greek *kharisma,* "gift offered freely by the gods") indicates, those in possession of this gift did not have to lift a finger to merit the distinction. The charismatic is born, so to speak, with a silver spoon in his mouth; things for which other people are reproached, he is permitted. Sentences that sound unfortunate in others sound masterly in him. Someone else makes the same joke and no one laughs. Another offers the same definition and no one stops to ponder the matter as if they had suddenly been presented with some great truth. They don't have to make a real effort: It is a gift they have been granted.

For all of these reasons, Lot was conscious that charisma could be irritating, not only for the envious, but also for lovers of meritocracy, for the chronically distrustful (they are suspicious of any sort of fascination), for the weak who are afraid of being crushed by a powerful personality, for the obtuse who, locked in the narrowness of their own interests, are impervious to charisma. And, finally, it is irritating for those who are self-assured and under no circumstances want to endanger their security in exchange for a more beautiful, freer, or simply more attractive truth, for they are determined not to lose their north, though it might lead to cold, desolate steppes, barren of ideas and emotions.

When Lot met Cometa, she was able to discern a few more aspects of this notion: Since charisma can be irritating, it's a good idea for the charismatic to appear fragile in order to be forgiven for being blessed with the gift. This was Cometa's case: He could easily be forgiven for being charismatic. Perhaps because of his almost weightless aspect, his elongated, spindly bones with their vulnerable semblance. Or perhaps because of a rare Franciscan quality of his that caused him to be loved even by the most disagreeable creatures (it was curious to see, for example, a friend's incredibly aggressive dog, that no one dared approach, allow itself to be calmly patted by Cometa as if it were a tame little rabbit). Or perhaps it was that gentleness of his that made him always attentive to those in need of it, or the total lack of pragmatism that made him prioritize the interests of others over his own. In any case, some of these traits, or all of them, were the price he paid in order to be forgiven for being charismatic. And he paid it happily, because he wasn't aware there was a price.

Later, as Lot made progress in her rather futile research task, she reached another conclusion: If you stop to consider it, to be forgiven for being charismatic is typical of any good charismatic, for people with good charisma make sure that their gift reverts to the lives of those around them; they transmit the pleasure of knowing and the curiosity of seeking; they help the other connect with himself; they bring out the best in the other rather than the worse.

By taking Cometa as the model against which to measure other examples of charisma, one by one Lot revised the ideas that had tainted her understanding of it.

As a young person, she had often associated charisma with erotic magnetism. Now, however, she realized that, though charisma appeals to an immediate erotic urge, it isn't necessarily of a sexual nature; it doesn't appeal directly to genitalia, as becomes obvious when you consider that people, without distinction of sex or age, are often receptive to charisma.

For a long time she believed that charisma was very close to ingenuity. But that's not the case: The witty, ingenious person is someone who is overly conscious of his own power of seduction and has built a repertoire of witticisms that tend to be repeated. He repeats what he knows to be amusing, and when he doesn't repeat it, it's because he knows that it wouldn't be amusing to repeat it. He uses tricks and knows how to release the appropriate spring mechanism to produce amusement or charm. But this charm is not innate. The charismatic person, on the other hand, never uses his wit with premeditation. And when he does use it, it's not to make himself shine, but rather to make the ideas he's trying to communicate shine.

Lot had often associated charisma with a certain kind of radiant friendliness. But no. In reality, she had only to review a few examples of charismatic people in order to realize that they weren't particularly friendly. Nor was Cometa. Kind, funny, histrionic, gentle, courteous, all of these things, but friendly, never. For days he would wander around with a sullen look on his face, or spend an entire dinner without opening his mouth; at work, he could be seen reading in a corner, unapproachable and circumspect, for weeks on end. He was capable of making himself so silent and invisible, so unnoticeable, that he seemed to disappear. Timid he was not, but nor was he an extrovert.

She thought once that she had finally found a synonym: It seemed to her that charisma and charm were twins. But in the end she reached the conclusion that they were merely cousins. A silent, absolutely angelic person can be charming. A child can be charming. There's something angelic in charm, whereas in charisma, the angelic is always accompanied by a slightly diabolical air, voluptuous and transgressive.

She had obviously heard countless times that charisma was associated with leadership. She was aware that the charisma of a leader, dictator, or politician was often combined with his ability to captivate others, hypnotizing them in order to convince them of something or another. Undoubtedly, the charismatic is able to attract followers through his speech, and therefore often holds a power that can be used for certain purposes. But if a person cunningly uses his charisma for a premeditated reason, he automatically corrupts its essence. What then, should be the relationship of the charismatic to power?

One day Lot discovered a text in Cometa's diary that shed some light on this point. For some time he had kept a diary, exiguous and extremely brief. A diary protected by a password that she'd attempted to discover in every possible way, except one: asking him openly for it. And when she did, after briefly playing around with her, he gave it to her. It proved to be a strange diary; only three times in the few short pages was there any mention of his inner life, not of himself or his feelings. And he'd begun it with the firm intention of setting down his most intimate secrets, but in the end it consisted mainly of reflections on his relationship with the world and its conflicts.

He was so little given to confession that he didn't even confess to himself: When he needed to confess something, he preferred public statements.

But Lot did discover one confessional entry that helped her understand the relationship between charisma and power. Knowing that Cometa had always declared his distaste for even the most insignificant expression of power, and that the slightest show of power (such as grading students) displeased him to a nearly pathological degree, Lot's first reaction while reading it was a smile. Written in Spanish, not Catalan, it read:

I will tell you of my tragic relationship with the political.

I know that I'm destined to command as others are to obey. It's not that I like this; in fact, I cannot see myself giving orders, and I tremble before the weaknesses and fears of others. I'm not a strong man; in order to be one, you need a fair amount of pigheadedness, which is always accompanied by a certain dose of stupidity, and there's no trace of either in me. Nor do I possess the kind of strength that is a consequence of messianic illumination; I'm nothing like a Messiah; I don't hold the solution to any human problems; I'm not the bearer of any message intended for my fellowmen.

And yet, I am confident in the dictate of my star: I am a man destined to command.

I know that many would like to command, and that the desire to have some degree of influence, however small, is the primary objective in many lives, if not all. But this is not my case; I have no wish to command, I am perfectly content simply to ponder these things or hoodwink my soul, surrounded by friends with a few bottles. (It doesn't trouble me; I know that no one is ever going to insist that I wield any power.) There is actually a considerable difference between wanting to command and knowing that you are destined to command; furthermore, to want power is a symptom of not being destined for command. I'm speaking of destiny, of an unwished for inclination of one's character, an involuntary need, something imprinted in one's innermost being that has nothing to do with desire.

Here, Cometa had shed light on the ambiguity of the relationship between charisma and power. Indeed, in order to command, you need to want to be in command. And, often, in order to know how to command, you need to *not* want to be in command, and herein lies the irresolvable paradox that explains—if not all, at least to a large degree—our political and social life. The passage also demonstrated that he was aware of the moral authority invested in him by others, though he refused to use it for anything that was particularly "useful" to him. Lot made a mental note: "Moral authority granted by others," and this opened up an entirely new line of research for her.

Ever since Cometa was little, his group of friends had tended to ask for his advice in critical moments, which were many. Because in that wild period of their childhood, the least objectionable thing the kids did was to lie on the train tracks and see who would be the last to jump up before the train arrived. They devised and carried out a long list of outrageous undertakings that would send shudders through us today. Within the family he was often called upon to resolve conflicts too, especially between his mother and his paternal aunt, who loved to argue; he constantly found himself in the role of arbitrator, which made him very uncomfortable.

"I always prepare meatballs in the Bilbao style, with chili, garlic and vinegar, and I add a chopped carrot," his Aunt Goldameier would say, for instance.

"Well, that's not how I do it," his mother would reply. "Onion, garlic, and parsley, yes, but never, ever carrots!"

And the eyes of the two women would turn to Cometa:

"Isn't it true that meatballs are better if you add a chopped carrot?" his aunt would say, staring him down with black, mischievous eyes.

"But I never make meatballs," he would counter boldly, trying his best not to take sides with either of the women. But his aunt, more inclined to argue than his mother, would insist:

"Ok, so you never make them. But if you ever *were* to make meatballs, isn't it true that they'd be much better if you added a chopped carrot?"

All his life he had been dogged by constant requests for his pronouncement on the most diverse subjects; they might address a mundane subject, such as cuisine or soccer, or they could be concerned with a world conflict or a social dilemma. But, just as he refused to reap any personal benefit from his charisma—other than the affection or support of loved ones—he couldn't stand for others to exploit his "messianic" gifts. Upon occasion, the insistence on securing his judgment or reaction was such that it would irk him considerably, and he would protest in a disgruntled voice: "I'm not the Oracle of Delphi! . . . How you love oracles!"

Another text, this time by von Kleist, offered Lot the last clue that rounded out her concept of charisma. It was a story about a boy who steps out of his bath and sees himself reflected in the mirror and is captivated by the beauty of his own image as he lifts his foot to a stool to dry himself. Yet, when he attempts to reproduce the gesture, he can't; and the more he tries, overcome by vanity and self-importance, the farther he is from that graceful image, until finally:

From that day, from that very moment, an extraordinary change came over this boy. He began to spend whole days before the mirror. His attractions slipped away from him, one after the other. An invisible and incomprehensible power seemed to settle like a steel net over the free play of his gestures. A year later nothing remained of the lovely grace that had given pleasure to all who looked at him.

And so, Lot learned that charisma needed a fundamental substratum of grace and charm (which brought her again to the etymology of the word). Good charisma is graceful. And charm only appears, paradoxically, by foregoing any interest in oneself, by forgetting oneself. It only appears when it is not sought. When it is, affectation—the mortal enemy of grace—sets in. Lot made a note: "Zero affectation." Therefore, if grace never appears on request or when it is planned, then it can only originate by accident. "Accident. Unpredictability," Lot jotted down. An important notion: Cometa's whole personality was inextricably connected with unpredictability. An unpredictability that was, to be sure, difficult to define.

Cometa was a man of his word and of British punctuality. One of those men whose word, once given, was tantamount to action. He detested improvisation, and his routines were precise. Paradoxically, these could change at the drop of a hat, and in striking ways because of his temperamental character, his frankness (which made him incapable of being one of those people who asserted that the emperor was dressed when he was in fact naked), his immersion in the present (which caused him to be wrapped up in whatever he was doing, without concern for schedules or barriers), and his instantaneous and exalted infatuations. To the heaviness of the academic intellectual, he brought a winged lightness. To a dragging melody, his spicy pizzicatos. To sentences a thousand times repeated, the least expected word, one that contained—like the final, black note in Mozart's musical phrases—that unexpected spark, impossible to program.

Intensely committed to the present (whether it was a *suquet de peix*—a fish stew—or his cod dish *al pil-pil,* a class or a sea outing, a discussion or the singing of a revolutionary song) he gave his all, to the point of exhaustion. How could an interlocutor be indifferent to how vulnerable he was to beauty, to passion, to compassion? How could one not understand that—if absorbed by a sublime musical note, a friend in need, or a cause he considered just—time ceased to exist for him? How could someone at his side not envy those instants of ecstasy in which, as the etymology indicates, he would abandon his position *(ex-stasis),* not as she would have—as a dreamer caught up in the future—but in the manner of the ex-static, for whom the past and the future are completely obliterated?

As is only natural, such a man never really belongs to his family or his wife, or to anyone. This was an extraordinary challenge for Lot. Because it transformed her daily wait for Cometa into an adventure. As the ecstatic/ex-static moment—the veritable substitute for inaccessible eternity—might suddenly draw him out of his routine, seeing him arrive always provoked in Lot a happiness disproportionate to the time he'd been away (a few hours at most). No matter where he was coming back from—work, lunch with a friend, buying fish, the bar—she was in the habit of receiving him as if he were returning from war or the jungle. There was an evanescent, diaphanous air about him, as though he were enveloped by the precariousness of things that are cherished and ephemeral. "You are without a doubt the man with the warmest welcome in the entire county," Lot would often say, for she only felt truly serene when she could embrace him.

They needed each other a great deal. Probably in a rather neurotic way. He phoned her if he was going to be late. She awaited him as though he was never going to return. And when he did arrive, he would laugh as soon as he glimpsed her through the window, racing down the stairs, anxious to hug him, jumping for joy like a madwoman. His arrivals, especially in the City of Fog, became a festive tradition that his daughter inherited. She too soon got in the habit of jumping. No one had ever seen *him* jump, but it always made him happy to glance through the door and catch sight of the two jumping girls who would throw themselves in his arms. Years passed and the jingle of the keys and the creaking of the garden gate as it opened continued to be the most longed-for sound of all, the most beautiful sound Lot had ever heard. *Let me never, never stop hearing this sound,* she implored at night, and she felt that she was asking for the impossible, much as when she had prayed to Baby Jesus as a little girl to recover things that were unrecoverable.

The fear of losing him grew day by day. It ran parallel to her eagerness to explore and document the ingredients in the secret formula of his existence, as though she believed that one day—if he should disappear, for she never contemplated the possibility that she might disappear before him—she could concoct a few laboratory Cometas that would make a few Lots happy. She believed in this kitchen-laboratory in a vague fashion, in the same way that she had believed in heaven when she was little. That's why she took note of the ingredients. But in the meantime (in case the kitchen, like heaven, turned out to be a fraud), she let herself be swept away by an intense joy whenever she heard the creaking of the garden gate at ten o'clock at night. And over time, her need to hear that sound grew. At one point Cometa wanted to oil the hinges, but she had begged him not to.

B4

Things People Say

In the weeks following his death, I've heard a string of picturesque sentences. I'm at a literary award gala. An acquaintance approaches me and tells me she's heard of his death and exclaims:

"You never expect this; we always think these things only happen to others, don't we?"

I would have said, "Listen, you nitwit, I on the other hand have always believed that this would happen precisely to me." I could also have said, "Has no one, during your long life, ever told you that death is the only sure thing that awaits you, infinitely more certain than your waxing appointment on Wednesday?" But I don't say anything. I simply string the sentence like a pearl, like another pendant on an imaginary necklace that I wear wherever I go.

Another example: The day after the literary award, a resolute neighbor sticks her head through the door and, with the same tone she might use to determine whether I'm in need of laundry detergent, asks me: "You got some books for coping with death?" And I think, in this house we have nothing else. But no, she's not referring to Shakespeare or Coetzee, or to Spinoza or Schopenhauer. She's not talking about poetry, or fiction, or philosophy. She's referring to a certain type of self-help book, the type of book from which has been extracted whatever is specific to thought (that is, thought itself), reducing it to formulas for "coping with death." Or whatever.

More somber still is the gardener's comment. The day after the funeral, when I ask him to continue coming from time to time to keep up the garden, he says, "If you want, I won't plant any more flowers. *¿Pa qué?*" What for?

Every day, all around me, I'm able to substantiate the degree to which we are disarmed by the tragedy of our interlocutors. I'm speaking, of course, of "people," not friends. Friends always know how to speak and how to be silent; in a way friends are in the same boat as you. I'm referring now to people you don't know well, neighbors, distant cousins. In general, people are very kind, even those who forget to be kind. They attempt to voice whatever words they can, knowing full well that they are useless, conscious that it's hopeless to try to use a Band-Aid when gouts of blood are gushing out. Yet, despite the disproportion, I love words. They help me. They distract me. Words are formidable. I prefer them to silence, although some silences can be very explicit . . . But I prefer words. It matters little whether they leave me pensive or perplexed, whether they make me smile or weep, whether they leave me dumbfounded or stunned: I appreciate them, I love them, I wear them on me constantly. Even in the occasions when most of us wield platitudes, I like to hear how each person uses them. Nothing that is said to me is dull. There are no useless words: They all interest me, they are all going somewhere or another. And, by golly, there are comments that deserve to be featured in an anthology of condolences.

Let's start with the platitudes. One of the most frequent ones for expressing commiseration has to do with the age of the deceased. If the deceased is elderly, more than seventy let's say, people believe that can be a measure of consolation: The deceased has lived a life that has ended at a reasonable point. Sometimes, the living who are older than the deceased don't see it that way. "He was young," they typically say if the deceased is seventy-eight and they are eighty-five. Because, of course, a life is never fully done. Nor is there a life left to be lived. In Cometa's case, he was too old to have died young and too young to die old. From which we can deduce that perhaps he died at the right age, since there is no ideal age for dying: They are all good, they are all bad.

Another platitudinous comment refers to the beauty of death. Many think this one was nice. "What a lovely death!" some say. Others, "Don't for a moment doubt that this is what he would have wished!" (But *he* never stated his opinion on the matter, at least not a concrete one, with his habit of resisting to choose what cannot be chosen.) It's true, however, that in general we like to consider—as though a long catalogue of possible deaths existed—whether we would like to die here or there, in this fashion or that. Someone, harping on the beauty of his death, offers: "You can't appreciate this now, but you will later!" Fine. But for the time being I do not appreciate it.

It is also quite usual, in these cases, for interlocutors to help you neutralize all the conditional perfect verb tenses. Every time you utter an "if only he'd," "if we had known," or "if we had thought," someone counters with a comforting phrase that tells you exactly what should be said. If you say that you can't get over the fact that you didn't react forcefully enough to make him go to the hospital, someone counters that it's never a good idea to get all worked up when someone is on the verge of having a heart attack (and you're relieved, because, just imagine if he'd had the heart attack after you had got worked up, instead of after holding his hand, going downstairs to get him an aspirin, and falling asleep beside him while he watched a John Wayne movie). If you say if only he'd had an electrocardiogram that same afternoon, someone informs you that her uncle collapsed right after a perfect ECG as he was going down the hospital stairs and died (and you are relieved, because it's always better to die in your own bed rather than rolling down a flight of stairs). If you say you wish you had anticipated this possibility—you who always anticipated everything for him—and that you'll never forgive yourself for not having a vial of nitroglycerin in the medicine cabinet, someone tells you that her father gave her grandfather a nitroglycerin injection directly into the heart at the first symptom of a heart attack and he died in his arms (and you're relieved about the grandfather's death forty-five years ago because you translate it into, "if you had given Cometa a shot in the heart, it wouldn't have made any difference"). If you say you wish the suspicions had been confirmed the first day he noticed the pain, several weeks ago, someone responds that some heart attacks are irreversible even before the person slips into a coma, as was the case of someone's brother who went to the hospital with a slight pain in his arm and was in a coma for a month, but died anyway, only later, when death was past due (and

140

you're relieved, because at least you've gone to Corsica and Avila and you've had a marvelous summer, which you might have spent in the hospital knowing nothing could be done anyway, like whoever's brother that was). And if you say if only he'd survived, there's always someone who comes back with the comment that he might have been left in a wheelchair. And, yes, you're momentarily relieved, but the truth is that it would have been the perfect excuse for him not to walk, which he hated—unless it was to hunt for wild mushrooms or meet up with a friend or do something pleasurable that wasn't sports related.

It's good to listen to people. The important thing is that, while you're listening, you distract The Beast that's ripping out your guts. And while you talk, The Beast grows weaker and time passes. You listen and you talk, you repeat the same thing over and over, they repeat the same things to you, and you wear down these gut-wrenching images. Until finally, through these homespun ploys of yours, you succeed in lessening the pain, simply by attrition.

In addition to wielding platitudes, it's also quite usual to draw comparisons. Generally speaking, the intention is to offer solidarity and consolation of *the-same-thing-happened-to-me* kind. A young woman says, "I lost my father not long ago," and hurriedly adds, tactfully: "It's not the same, of course." Another offers, "I have a friend who lost a child," and continues, "They say it's the greatest pain of all." Apparently there's a ranking, and the death of a child comes in at ten and a father's at six. But I know people who have experienced greater pain at the death of a father than at the death of a child. Would anyone dare proclaim there's anything abnormal about these people's suffering? I don't know what is comparable when it comes to pain. Each person's hell is an unfathomable enigma; who could make them the object of quantification?

Nevertheless, there seems to be a blueprint for mourning. And, in a certain way, you're forced to adjust to it. If you should laugh two days later, people think that you're doing so to make them feel good, or that you've adopted an artificial demeanor, or that you've gone mad. If, on the other hand, ten years later, you weep for your husband as you did four days ago, no one will even remember what happened to you. Actually, there's no need to wait ten years. Six months after he died, I'm talking to an acquaintance who was very attentive in the days following his death; when she asks me how I am and I say I'm better, she asks, "Have you been sick?" From the outside, other people's mourning moves at a very different pace. When you lose someone very close to you, strange, unpredictable, indescribable things happen. The comments that reach you offer an idea of the abyss that lies between other people's mourning and your own.

But, all in all, I prefer these fresh words to the colorless sentences of the so-called self-help books that I'm perusing for the first time. Some acquaintances (who don't know me well) send me a few with the best of intentions; and I've even bought a couple myself—a clear sign of my state of obfuscation—also with the best of intentions, as well as a degree of hopefulness; but above all with the goal of killing time. But I find myself getting annoyed by the message of overcoming and personal growth that they emphasize. *You can do this! You can do this!* they incessantly parrot. But I already fucking know that. What happens if I don't want to? That is the problem: wanting to. In any case, my mind is made up: I have no intention of overcoming anything. Not in the way they're suggesting. I want to absorb—incorporate—not overcome. No overcoming for me.

I turn the page, in case there's another more interesting idea. Ha, look here: *You'll want to die. You'll think about suicide. You'll want to disappear*, I read. That's pretty close to what I'm feeling. But then I read: *Don't worry: It's normal.* Excuse me? What are they saying? Is it possible that someone who just lost a loved one could give a shit about "being normal?" My friend and adviser on reading material reproaches me for my self-help lapse. "You'd be better off reading a Greek tragedy," she says. The following day she brings me a movie to help me kill time. It's not exactly a Greek tragedy. It's John Huston's *The Dead*.

Not all the messages I receive are platitudes, clichés, oddball sentences, conventional condolences, or self-help books. There are people who, for one reason or another, stay away from these hackneyed expressions. Poets, for instance. It's characteristic of poets to avoid cliché; it is also characteristic of them to manifest their sensibility on these occasions. Cometa counted several poets among his friends. And now, from their innermost selves words are spawned, unfolding like stars across the sky—verses that speak of Bacchanalian orgies and anarchic seas, of indomitable colts and springtimes that fertilize every hollow, of Beowulfs, of Quixotes and windmills . . .

H., a coworker, gives me a keepsake. It's a letter, one of many, and it touches me in a special way. A true gift. "It was in 1987," she writes, "and no one knew that the two of you

143

were dating. I saw you coming out of a building, talking to each other, and then, suddenly, with that typical gesture of his, he put his hand on your shoulder. And I understood that you were a couple."

The image moves me, the way you're moved when someone unexpectedly gives you a picture of yourself that was taken without your knowing. A curious parallelism comes to mind: When my teacher from the City of Fog died in 1999, I was especially distressed. I wrote to his wife, and, strangely enough, I offered her a similar gift, an image of them that I had never forgotten: One Christmas, many years ago, I spotted them strolling along Carrer Major loaded with packages and toys for their children. They were engaged in a lively conversation and suddenly he put his arm on her shoulder. I watched them walking away into the fog; I didn't try to speak to them, so as not to disturb the magic of the moment.

But not everyone who avoids clichés does so by means of poetry. There are, for example, his exalted, unconditional friends who avoid the commonplace out of pure devotion, and who, at times, get so carried away in my presence that they end up having the opposite effect than what they intended.

Some twenty of us are having lunch together, mostly friends of his, both male and female; it's the second large luncheon without him. A woman stands up and makes a toast. Then she solemnly pronounces: "We should acknowledge that none of us here at this table will ever leave the imprint that he did." Applause and clinking of glasses. I'm moved by the sentence and I clap too. I raise my glass and then start to sit back down. But she repeats the sentence, and, looking directly at me, addresses me: "It's true, isn't it?" I merely smile, anxious to sit down. She's at the other end of the table and continues to stand, while twenty pairs of eyes are waiting for me to agree. I recall the chapter of the unfinished book that bears the title: "Rubbing Out the Tracks," and I find an excuse to avoid the issue: "Actually, I don't know if he was really interested in leaving a mark . . ." But the uncompromising enthusiast isn't willing to drop the subject and replies: "Leaving a mark or not isn't something that was up to him. No matter what he said, the reality is that he has left his mark and . . . and none of us who are here . . ." (and she repeats the sentence, word for word).

The situation is becoming unbearable. He's my partner. Yet, he will increasingly belong to everyone; that's the thing about the deceased, they belong to whoever appropriates them . . . But he's still *very much* mine, and I'm guarded about it . . . Leaving less of a mark than him suits me fine. Not a problem. His male friends also seem willing to recognize, rather meekly, that they won't be leaving anything like the mark he did; aware that the situation is embarrassing me, they look away and start talking again among themselves. No one seems to want to compete for Cometa's imprint, and I'm dying to end the conversation, especially because one of the women—the one sitting beside me—seems to have a strange smirk on her face, as if she doesn't really agree with what the ineluctable enthusiast has just stated.

Ineluctable indeed: Now that we seem to have dropped the subject, she walks straight up to me, prepared to force me to admit in private what I didn't want to admit in public. She sits down beside me, between the woman with the smirk and me, and repeats the sentence. There is no way out of this, because two female friends who have joined us are also in agreement, and, aside from Smirk, I'm the only one who seems to question the mark left by the deceased. But suddenly, Smirk saves the day by speaking up:

"Look here—I'm still holding out hope that I might leave an important mark."

The other women counterattack, noting all the reasons why Cometa's mark *has* to be greater than other marks, and again I become so uncomfortable that I end up exploding:

"Come on! He also had his flaws! And huge ones!"

"Of course, of course . . ." the women hurriedly agree. "We weren't suggesting that he didn't." (And it's true, we've only spoken of his imprint, not of his shortcomings), but I'm encouraged:

"Flaws? Wow, did he ever have some!" And I start reeling them off, and if the shortcomings aren't significant enough, I exaggerate them (as he used to do, humorously, when he'd get worked up over his own faults and mine). The tension eases. The lady next to me relaxes her smirk. Everyone seems fine with the idea of not leaving much of a mark.

Others avoid clichés simply because sincerity suddenly bursts forth. Shortly after that wretched day, I attend a dinner as a member of a panel of literary judges. During the meal I feel myself dying, in an empty, foreign world, where the only thing that draws me back to Cometa's world is the account that O. is giving of the book she's writing about the years Ava Gardner spent in Madrid and of her interviews with the few people still around who took part in that world. We're suddenly joined by another member, who offers me his condolences. He mentions a woman friend of his, a writer whose partner died. And then he concludes with disarming frankness, "Poor thing, she never again did anything worthwhile." And I think: *Fucking brilliant!* Recently, when I'm approached by people who want to talk to me—and I'm tremendously grateful to them—I find that my thinking has become rather minimalistic. My only thought now is: *Fucking brilliant!* At the moment, I can't come up with anything else. I'll deliberate on this later.

And then finally, there are those who avoid clichés because they always have. This is the case of N., a friend of his family, ninety years filled with lucidity and a razor-sharp intelligence. She's just back from Mexico, where she lived in exile for forty years and where she now spends six months a year. When she learns of his death, she phones me; as soon as I pick up, with no greeting, she hurls an "I've got him in the file" at me. "Sorry?" I say. "Yes, child, I have a file with the heading *Those Who Won't Be Returning*; I keep my friends' obituaries in it." "I like the title," I say (it leaves no room for doubts). She has a couple of husbands, a few close male friends and some very dear female friends in it. Lately, the file has been growing bulkier. N. (who has always declared herself left-wing, a Red through and through) lets me know she's proud to have filed him away on the same day as two other friends of hers, Manolo Vázquez and Juana Doña. She interprets this as an unequivocal sign of destiny. "Three Reds, *so deeply humane*, dead on the same night, this has to mean something," she tells me. "No doubt about it," I say.

Was he a Red? I don't know. His role was more about denouncing the perils of ideology, about provoking his socialist friends with Nazi or Fascist songs, and his right-wing friends by singing "The Internationale." Even his goddaughter, the daughter of a good friend of his who was ultra-ecological and ultra-republican, used to show up at her ultra-ecological, ultra-republican kindergarten singing *Ich hatt' einen Kameraden* when she was four years old, something that could have produced an erroneous conclusion in narrow-minded people for whom the song was more relevant as a Fascist symbol than as a moving hymn for a fallen comrade composed a hundred and fifty years before the Second World War. The Spanish Fascist song "Camisa azul", blue shirt, was another favorite when he really wanted to piss someone off. After all, as an adolescent rebelling against his intensely left-wing father, he'd sung it when he enrolled for a month in a camp run by the Falange, the Spanish Fascist organization.

If N. is suggesting that being a Marxist Red was Cometa's true hidden destiny, perhaps she wasn't completely off track. A week before he died, he flung open the door to the room where I write, something he often did when he wanted to announce sudden decisions, amorous declarations, or special revelations: "Finally, at the end of my life, I know who I am," he said, "I'm a Problematic Red, the reddest and most problematic of problematic reds, and that's how I want to die!"

Before she hangs up, N. broaches the subject of the appropriate age: "When I look at myself," she says (because, despite her lucidity, she suffers the aches and pains typical of her age), "I envy those who die young."

But for heaven's sake, we all aspire to decrepitude! We all work, day in, day out, to be able to reach that point—just as free men often labor in order to reach a state of enslavement. We all toil away, hoping to be *like poor Aunt Julia! . . . That haggard look on her face when she was singing "Arrayed for the Bridal."*

I'm watching *The Dead*—tender is the night. The husband's magnificent final monologue as he's thinking (the realization many years overdue) about his wife and Michael Furey, the young man who gave his life for her:

"How poor a part I've played in your life . . . Why am I feeling this riot of emotion? What started it up? A ride in the cab? When not responding when I kissed her hand? My aunt's party? My own foolish speech? Wine, dancing, music? . . . Poor Aunt Julia . . . That haggard look on her face when she was singing 'Arrayed for the Bridal.' Soon, she'll be a shade too."

And he also says: "Yes, the newspapers are right: snow is general all over Ireland. Falling on every part of the dark central plain, on the treeless hills, softly upon the Bog of Allen, and, farther westward, softly falling into the dark mutinous Shannon waves . . . One by one we are all becoming shades."

The husband says: "Better pass boldly into that other world, in the full glory of some passion, than fade and wither dismally with age . . . How long you locked away in your heart, the image of your lover's eyes when he told you that he did not wish to live?"

The husband says: "I've never felt like that myself toward any woman, but I know that such a feeling must be love. Think of all those who ever were, back to the start of time. And me, transient as they, flickering out as well into their grey world. Like everything around me, this solid world itself, which they reared and lived in, is dwindling and dissolving."

The husband says: "Snow is falling. Falling in that lonely churchyard where Michael Furey lays buried. Falling faintly through the universe, and faintly falling, like the descent of their last end, upon all the living and the dead."

That's what he says.

A5

Muses and Countermuses

They delighted in words. Both of them, though in different ways. As is common within a couple, sometimes there were communication mistakes and misunderstandings. The precision of his speech, which others enjoyed so much, proved exhausting for Lot twenty-four hours a day. She, on the other hand, liked to toss out words without much logic and classify them later. Her manner of speaking often recalled the barbaric attitude attributed to Abbot Arnaud Almaric during the extermination of the Cathars, when soldiers were worried about killing Orthodox Catholics along with the heretics ("Kill them all, for the Lord knows those that are His own."). Far too often, Lot would say the first thing that came to mind, in hopes that Cometa would grasp what best suited him, or separate the wheat from the chaff. That's why she wrote. She sought, in her writing, to make the choices she was incapable of in speech.

For his part, instead of listening to her, he preferred reading her. And if he had to listen to her, he preferred monologues. He loved for her to tell stories. Any story. He even enjoyed her account of the bad movies he would never have seen, under any circumstance. Or stories a thousand times recounted. He often asked her to talk to him in order to calm or entertain him. Or to put him to sleep, an honor she shared with José María García—*Butanito*—whose program, which broadcast at midnight, Cometa used to listen to on the radio; he had only to hear the man's first words and he was sound asleep. When the program stopped being aired, he was never again able to fall asleep as easily.

She liked listening to him speak; his manner was tempestuous, forceful, unpredictable. Ultimately, one could say they communicated with a perfection that Lot had never known with any other man—provided they avoided dialogue.

Of course, his exacting standards regarding dialogue were out of the ordinary. He understood it in a Socratic sense, as a delicate maieutic far removed from the typical mechanical discussions that usually take place. And he managed to impose this rigor on friends and students alike . . .

But, Lot . . . Lot didn't respect anything when it came to bringing the conversation around to her own interests, and this irritated Cometa tremendously. He detested the feminine recourse to sophistry, stubbornness, and tricks that she had used at the beginning of their relationship. She disregarded the most elementary rules of logic through all sorts of ruses, which he skillfully took apart and she immediately put back together with no regard to rules, with no caution, until finally what had motivated the argument became irrelevant. The impossibility of engaging in dialogue is what really irritated him: "The *Logos*, the *Logos*, yet again you've destroyed the *Logos*! How easily you tell the *Logos* to go to hell, *Senyora!*" he would exclaim in exasperation. He often used the second person plural, even at times the majestic plural, to compensate for the vehemence of his attack; at other times the use of the plural took the form of a rather vague *vosaltres* in which Lot could feel herself comfortably included, in the company of all those people who toss soliloquies back and forth without rhyme or reason and with whom she could share the responsibility for having killed the *Logos* yet again.

"I've made up my mind!" he said one day in the car while he was driving, "We won't have any more conversations. No, no more dialoging. If you want to tell me something, do it in writing. And I'll answer you in writing."

Lot burst out laughing. Some time later, having forgotten the argument, she said:

"What time are we leaving on Friday?"

"On paper, I said—ask me in writing."

During their first years together, humor alone saved them many times over from dialogic catastrophe. But even if metaphysical rigor exhausted her, there was nothing she enjoyed more than the attempt to take it on! And nothing made Cometa more nervous than for her to do so. "You're a writer, forget about it! Isn't that enough? Is there any greater happiness, any more unfettered freedom than what you writers enjoy?" But she refused to forget about it. There was nothing in the world she would have wished for more than to possess a metaphysically privileged mind.

And yet, in that case, they might never have complemented each other so perfectly. Because it's true that, when it came to words, each of them contributed what the other wished for but lacked. And so, while Lot insisted that she was a passionate lover of rigorous thought, he in turn declared that nothing would have pleased him more than to experience the independence and sovereignty that a writer wields over the world she creates. In any case, he didn't possess a writer's obsessive nature: A story would have to present itself very forcefully for him to wish to tell it.

Both of them found their vocation in the character of the other, and they were stimulated by their respective aptitudes. His rigor was fundamental to her as a writer. She drank from the wellspring of his thinking, and she was convinced that she would never have written had she not known him, not because she lacked imagination, but because what she needed was to set limits to her imagination, to create boundaries, to have more structure. Cometa organized her licentious thinking. Things she had only surmised in a confused manner but had been unable to express, she now suddenly understood, with a clarification from him, or a joke, or a "damn it!" He was the one who had inculcated the conviction that she had to be accountable for each and every word she wrote, every comma, every period. So that she would never write an insincere sentence; which is to say, every sentence had to be endowed with meaning, even if that meaning was elusive (we know the writer shouldn't totally control her stories).

And so it was that, when they settled into their daytime life together, she began to write. And, curiously enough, he did too, even if his need to write was not as pronounced as hers. "I understand that you don't have the need to write," she told him. "If I could satisfy an audience as you do, if I were accompanied by your conviction of gesture, voice, expression, if I had your capacity to improvise, why would I need anything more?" But when she praised his talent, he would gainsay her,

"The spoken word is crude and messy. It's impregnated with the deceit of seduction. The written word, on the other hand, is unsullied."

Ah . . . but it was all the same to her: Unsullied or messy, she would have wished to possess the gift of eloquence and improvisation, wished that the sentences would flow, at once beautiful and full of meaning. She would have liked to weave words that the wind would waft away, to be able to seduce with the spoken word that envelops the gesture and the gaze and the hands and the voice—always the voice!

And yet, she found it easier to write. On the other hand, because of his meticulousness and his tendency to expunge, it was more of a challenge for him to commit his thoughts to paper. He'd always taken notes, wherever he went. Notebooks of all shapes and colors, half-filled with his lucubrations. No matter where he was, what kind of people he was with, what type of atmosphere he was in, whatever the moment, it was his thinking incarnated as words that allowed him to delight in and make others delight in the topics that drew his attention. A soccer match. A friend sitting next to him in the stadium. A ball misses the goal. His friend protests. "Quiet! I'm thinking!" Cometa cuts him off. The day after the match, he handed his friend a remarkable text on the geometry of the goal. The title: *The Three Posts*. A text that he never expanded on, like the majority of the things he wrote.

And then, one day, he began to write with a more concrete project in mind. It coincided with their moving in together. She was writing stories: first one, then another, then the next. He, on the other hand, commenced a pharmacy of words,

155

and forever after he wrote the same book. Like a condensed version of Penelope's cloth, seemingly without end, he wrote a lot and erased even more. The one unifying subject in those pages was oblivion and its virtues, the oblivion without which we could not live.

Year after year Cometa rose at five o'clock in the morning; he never needed to sleep more than four hours. And, submerged in tea, coffee, smoke, he would read for quite a while and then he would write. In those early hours when it was still dark, he would write and delete. The pharmacy that he filled with words became the never-ending book, the book he was always writing, the book that would never be finished. He deleted a lot. He trashed things that she considered valuable. Many of the things he mulled over served as inspiration for her. After all, he had always been a muse to her.

She also liked to think that she had inspired a few thought-provoking reflections in him. In fact, she frequently reasoned that if she wasn't his muse, at least she was his countermuse. Countermuses are often as effective as muses, if not more so. Countermuses are people whose attitude ignites a passion for thinking; and it's a well-known fact that a flame once ignited generates an immunological response that creates antibodies and other active biomolecules. For Cometa, observing Lot's way of facing the future was a source of inspiration *a contrario*. He found it strange, almost incomprehensible, to see her constantly projecting herself into the future. The excesses of her turbulent activity—always moving forward, always living in advance—were far removed from what he wished for himself: a present lived by distilling the greatest value from each detail, a contemplative life centered on the precise instant.

He spoke of this too in his never-ending book. No doubt she had something to do with it. Or so she hoped.

In September 2003, he told Lot, "It's done. I have only to fine-tune a few things. I'll give it to you for your birthday in November." The promise surprised Lot; it wasn't his style to plan so far in advance. He knew it would be the best present he could give her. Then the school year began, that little pain began, the autumn began—as always with its demands encroaching on them—and after a few days he said, "Maybe I'll give it to you for Christmas." She smiled. She'd become so fond of the interminable book that she didn't know if she wanted it to be finished. And the fact that he didn't finish it (because he was modest, or self-demanding, or because of his tendency to squander his talent) endowed it with added value in a world so full of things that are finished yet fake, of works quickly churned out, simple ideas sold at the price of gold.

At the beginning of October he said: "Now I'm sure it'll be finished by Christmas." Lot was almost sorry. The thought that he would finish it seemed so strange to her that she almost hoped he would find an excuse not to.

B5

Getting Through the Day

Six months have passed, seven, eight. It seems like years. Expanded, bloated minutes that slowly evolve into the next minute. Some things of course begin to change, some obsessions become attenuated or begin to bore you, because your tendency to boredom has its drawbacks—but also its advantages.

The most acute crises of desperation also become less frequent. The Beast allows me to breathe for long intervals. But you should never let your guard down. As a matter of fact, it's when you sense that a certain normality is setting in that you need to be the most alert: While you were distracted, trying to experience a modicum of happiness, The Beast has taken advantage of the truce to sharpen his knives. And then it comes down on you with an implacable ferocity and you find yourself unarmed. So, I keep The Beast in check. My trick is never to do anything to mask the suffering. Take Cometa's constant presence, for example: Is there any reason why I should remove his clothes from the closet? No. If I find I need more space—since he won't be complaining—maybe his space will shrink in an organic way. But is there any reason to remove his clothes *now*? Isn't it enough that his body has left? Why, on top of that, must I throw out his belongings? I find that incomprehensible. And so, I live with his things in a manner that renders them quotidian, so they don't cause me pain. And in this way, without realizing it, I create a sort of continuity in which his presence is assimilated into the house, like the air one breathes—to such an extent that I sometimes have the feeling that I've done things with him recently; and only when I check the dates do I realize that I did them alone and that he is no longer here.

The "if we had known" also begins to make less sense, as does my obsession with "the warning signs." In this story, actions and signs have created a recurrent pattern that is difficult to view without bewilderment. I'm referring to coincidences, the type of coincidences that Paul Auster is fond of and refers to as "patterns": the sketches of destiny whose regular forms seem to correspond to a mysterious design. Even if one doesn't want to see them as anything other than the fruit of pure chance, they are still striking.

It's striking that my daughter lost her father at the same age as I did. It's striking that we spent the last Sunday with friends talking about funeral tolls, because Cometa had refused to change the term "death knell" in a translation he'd done of my story, "Els alegres funerals dels parents de Bordeus" (The Merry Funeral of The Relatives from Bordeaux), when I had suggested "funeral toll." He said the term was bullshit, and we discussed it later over a long lunch in the town of La Floresta, at the home of G. and A. who, as always, agreed with him. It's striking that, on the Friday in question, I bought Coetzee's novel *Disgrace* (which in Catalan is translated *Desgràcia*, misfortune). But that's easy to explain—I'd heard a critic I trust recommend it that morning on the radio. I never buy books people recommend, and yet I bought this one. Needless to say, this critic doesn't recommend books that bear the title of *Misfortune/Desgràcia* every day. It's striking that after working on his book for more than twelve years, Cometa assured me in September that it was practically finished. It's striking that the present he promised me became not a gift but an inheritance. And it's interesting that he speaks so much about death in his book, and that during our last summer, in Corsica, he would announce, "This is the last swim of my life!" However, that could easily be translated as one of his jokes, especially given the fact that he hadn't swum in many years and could, therefore, have believed that he wouldn't swim again.

It's also striking, when you consider that we never read the same books, that last summer we were both rereading at the same time *Chronicle of a Death Foretold*, by García Márquez, and *Farewell Waltz*, by Kundera, though that was for the simple reason that they were the only decent books we could find at the village newsstand. But then he also read *Lawrence of Arabia* on his own, and I read other books on my own.

Striking it is. But at the same time, why should it be so extraordinary to have forebodings of death? What is strange is that we don't think about it all the time. It's also possible that we know things that we don't realize we know, or—as in Poe's "The Purloined Letter"—we don't see certain things because we're blinded by everything around us and fail to notice what should have captured our attention and is right before our eyes. Thus, I'm not in favor of searching for explanations in patterns. Why shouldn't the events that shape our destiny also follow more or less orderly patterns, as in nature, which creates forms based on surprisingly regular blueprints?

And yet, at first, I was astonished by the profusion of coincidences. But I didn't scrutinize them in search of interpretations—I've never done that. It was simply that I found it striking, in the same way that I find striking the crop circles in the county of Wiltshire with the astounding designs that the wind—or something or someone—has drawn in the fields.

Daily events also evolve toward less painful avenues, not because time passes, but because the passing of time is accompanied by multiple and infinite repetitions of painful events. I go to dinner parties I used to attend with him. I go to dinner parties I never went to with him; and he's not waiting for me at home to play, as we often did, the game of seeing if we could make the account of the event more interesting than the event itself. I've also returned two or three times to our house with the three doors. Returning to houses is terrible. Especially when you only go there occasionally.

The photographs are also growing less poignant, just as I feared. That's why my daughter and I swap them around, so that we always have fresh ones, and in that way we make him change his gestures. Nevertheless, I have kept his voice as a last recourse. The first days, I listened many times to a tape of him reciting poems by Rubén Darío on a night of wine and roses. And also to tapes that students had recorded of his classes and had given or lent me. But, keen not to wear them out, I put them away almost immediately in one of my keepsake boxes. I bought the boxes, in a variety of sizes, with the idea of being able to locate any object, in any moment of need, in the shortest possible time. One for each keepsake: photographs, small objects, notes he left me, recordings.

But today, as I was tidying up a bookshelf, I came across a misplaced tape. It's labeled: "Bagpipe Lunch." Straightaway I recall a meal with some colleagues to which we had also invited two students, jazz lovers, good saxophonists, good bagpipers. It was at Ml.'s house in Vallirana, an essential place during our falling-in-love process. At the time the tape was made, I was taking a postgraduate course in discourse analysis, and conversational analysis interested me. Supposedly, if you're a conversational analyst, you go around recording conversations and fragments of conversations in order to collect material. This explains how I now stumble upon this tape that suddenly offers the hope of finding what, in these moments, is a treasure of incalculable value to me: his voice, once more.

And so I listen. For a long time I hear only our voices, not his. Almost all the members of what was then our group have moved away and we haven't seen each other again. But what most impresses me is the change in our voices: Those distant echoes from the past exude a sparkling lack of concern, a lightness that is totally missing in the tone of our present conversations. We're accustomed to examining pictures and exclaiming, "Look how young we were—and now, wrinkles, receding hairlines, bags under our eyes . . ." But the voice, the voice is a completely different matter. Strangely enough, we tend to keep and restudy images, instead of keeping and re-listening to voices. But a voice is more alive than an image, and it offers the gesture and the gaze and the precise state of mind.

Bagpipe Lunch. The voices are cheerful, scintillating, jovial . . . At least ours are; I don't hear his—he must have been having one of his taciturn days. I listen for a few minutes, hoping to catch a word from him, a cough; I know I'll immediately recognize any sound coming from him, no matter how tiny or faint. Not a thing. We talk, we laugh, we make noises with our cutlery. Then, suddenly, hope. A friend calls to him, requesting a bolero. A couple of times she says, "*Por favor, un bolero.*" In the distance, impassive, his only response is to order coffee. The friend again pleads, "*Venga, hombre, por favor, un bolerito...*" There's no answer. And no bolero.

Someone opens a bottle of cava. A few minutes later, having given up trying to convince him to sing, we begin a discussion about fish: the typical question of whether the *seitó* is a variety of anchovy or is exactly the same as an anchovy. The friend who requested the bolero now asks that Cometa pronounce himself on the matter:

"So, what do you say?"

Finally, his voice, in the distance, "The truth is I don't know."

"We'll have to vote then," the friend says. "For the time being, we have one undecided vote." And now we do hear his voice, strong and indignant:

"Undecided? Absolutely not! I've unequivocally decided to maintain that I don't know!" Laughter. Noise. Bagpipes and the singing of a Galician *muiñeira*. Again the sound of bagpipes. The tape ends and I put the treasure in the box of voices.

Finally, the self-destructive thoughts and suicide plans contemplated with varying degrees of seriousness also begin to vanish. And then, one fine day, you think: Why rush things? Which reminds me of the time I had a renal colic. After several hours of intense pain, I suddenly thought: *I'll just let the pain flow, as if I'm not here; just let it flow, while I wait, I wait.* No, there's no need to precipitate matters. No potassium injections, no head in the oven, no need even to become a war correspondent. It's enough just to wait. Nowhere do I find this idea better expressed than in my rereading of Juan Rulfo tonight. This sentence from "The Burning Plain" will be my North Star:

"Eventually night will come. That's what we thought about. Night will come and we'll get some rest. Now we have to get through the day, get through it somehow to escape from the heat and the sun. Then we'll stop—afterward. What we've got to do now is keep plugging right along behind so many others just like us and in front of many others. That's what we have to do. We'll really only rest well when we're dead."

It's a dark consolation that's profoundly comforting. Not all consolations are bright; some are cool shadows of poplar trees in the blazing midday sun, shady and restorative. This is one of them. One step after another, like that first day when I walked along our street to the restaurant where his family were having lunch after the funeral. With the book still open to the same page, I suddenly think: *Today is the beginning of the rest of my life.* That's how the lives of survivors begin. One step after the other. Mechanically. And then you get on with whatever is left, with the rest. There's an advantage to dealing with "leftovers": You don't expect anything of them. Everything seems excessive, everything is an unexpected gift. The rest only comes when you believe that you have already experienced the things you most wanted—regardless of whether that time was long or short—and that only what never particularly interested you (for you didn't need anything else) remains. And now, suddenly, the rest is here. You can toss it out or simply resolve to get through the day as best you can. One step after the other.

When he died, I stopped writing in the diary I had kept since I met him. I thought I would resume it later. But now I realize that it's a definitive interruption, and this validates what I've just said: It has to do with what remains. There's no need for a diary now. Across thousands of pages, I felt the need to record every event that occurred during these sixteen years together, much as one takes snapshots of moments you think you'll want to remember. But duplicated life has no meaning now. The life that looks itself in the mirror and marvels at its own quality no longer exists. A diary—in contrast to a novel, which is undertaken in order to distill life—is a chronicle that attempts to copy life. I have enough with the original now, enough, more than enough. I don't need a copy. Finally, I need nothing more than the present in its purest form. Not to need anything makes you immune.

Immersed in this sweet Rulfian fatalism, I feel myself permeated by a sense of serenity that emerges after the shipwreck, and I prepare to begin the rest of my life with an optimism that until recently I found only at night. But suddenly an untimely phone call shakes me out of this sweet state of mind. I'm taken aback because calls too are less frequent now. The phone doesn't ring as often as it did during those first weeks, and there's only the odd person left who has just heard the news or who hasn't phoned because of some particular circumstance. Such is the case of the person who rings tonight. He's a neighbor in the village where we spent the best and most productive part of our summers, near the town of Poblet. He was married to T., who died a month before Cometa.

A6

The Open Door

Teresa died the month before Cometa. Her zestful, energetic charm had pleasantly disturbed the peacefulness of the landscape of olive and almond trees in the village where the two of them spent part of their summers. She lived next door and on her way to work she would stick her head over the hedgerow to say hello to Cometa as he read in the garden in the near dark. They would exchange a few words, and, for a brief moment, Lot would awake feeling that the world was a perfect place, before going back to sleep. Some time later, the neighbor battled an illness for seven years. She died in September.

Lot and Cometa went to the funeral. They had a tradition of combining these sad occasions with some form of gastronomic compensation; and, so, before the funeral, they had lunch in a restaurant in Coll de Lilla that they had often frequented during their first years together, though they hadn't been back in ten years. They found themselves having a long conversation about the burden of the past on the future. It was a moment of communion. After lunch, they went out for a view of the countryside. He phoned his Friday lunch friends to say hello. They knew he was at a funeral. "Paco?"

Cometa asked when his friend picked up. Then, he burst into laughter. His friend's very Basque sarcasm always put him in good spirits. While he was on the phone, Lot moved farther way and occupied herself by stepping on and off a rock. When he ended the conversation, she asked:

"What did Paco say that was so funny?"

"He said, 'So, you got the stiff in your line of sight yet?'"

He was almost in tears from laughing so hard, and added, "Promise me, when I die, those will be your exact words."

Lot was not amused.

"Come on," Cometa insisted brightly. "Promise me those will be your words: '*What a stiff!*' Please?"

"I don't think this is funny," Lot said, though in reality she did. And, in the end, she promised (she wouldn't keep her word a month later, but that's understandable). She would have promised anything that day to be able to carry on with her little speech that had been interrupted by the call. Standing atop the stone, she continued to declaim before the sunlit valley. She felt herself touched by inspiration: Concepts linked up with clockwork precision; all her reasoning about the perfect and imperfect past fit together with crystal-clear, astonishing logic.

Cometa was suddenly moved and embraced her. "Ah, my philosopher queen," he said, squeezing her tight as she continued with her peroration. Cometa wasn't fond of public displays of affection; he said they were for adolescents or degenerates. He was extremely modest. But this time, this time, he held her and rested his head on her chest (he was tall, and his chest was usually level with her face, not the other way around).

As she stroked his perfectly shaped nape under his soft brown hair, she fell silent, seized by a newfound euphoria: He had proclaimed her not a princess, but a queen! It mattered little that his comment contained a dose of tender irony, what mattered was that, though he didn't recognize her philosophical disposition, at least he had acknowledged her vocation. Receiving some form of recognition wasn't bad at all, considering that he'd been so often annoyed with her for disrupting his sense of *Logos*. He used to tell her, "No chance in hell you would have passed my course!" Which was a fat lie, for he gave everyone a passing grade, and when he couldn't, because it was simply impossible, he'd give the student two, three, ten tests, until finally, out of desperation or nervous exhaustion, the student would pass.

For a few hours on that splendid day, they managed to forget about the funeral, which didn't actually make too much of an impression on them because their friend had been terminally ill for a very long time. Lot could see that their exchanges continued to be as lively as ever, and this gave her an immense satisfaction, which was augmented by her lucid pontifications atop the rock. The moment had reached its climax with his unexpected embrace and her sudden coronation. No—the routine forced on couples by family life had not succeeded in undermining the interest each had in the other's monologues. From time to time, they still had glory days, recently-in-love days that welcomed long conversations, inexhaustibly monologic in their nature. She enjoyed feeling there were still things to be learned at his side. For finally, nothing was more satisfying to him or more moving than his teaching vocation. He was a vocational teacher.

His dedication was absolute, and students returned the passion he injected into his performances with accrued dividends: His ability to perform never left them indifferent. Perhaps precisely because it wasn't exactly a performance: He wasn't acting out the part, he *embodied* the characters. "Our being is manifold; this has been repeated *ad nauseam*. But few act as if this were true," he wrote in the book he never seemed to finish. It was clear that he took the idea of being manifold quite literally. He was tireless when it came to deploying his vitality and analytical ability, and he easily captivated his listeners. Though he maintained that the spoken word was messy, though he said he was tired, bored with teaching, in reality he could not have lived without those avid eyes on him, to such an extent that, on days when they failed to light up, he seemed out of sorts, like a dog in need of petting: He wasn't accustomed to it.

And, yet, the work situation had changed dramatically and it had affected him deeply; the teaching profession had been radically transformed. Practically his entire career had unfolded during a time when education still aspired to the transmission of knowledge, and being a teacher did not consist of the strange mix of bureaucratic, correctional, and entertainment functions it had now assumed. In those early days, the relationships that flourished between professors and disciples were different. In those days—a period that encompassed almost his entire professional life—Cometa could afford to begin his course each year by addressing the students and showing them the door: "You should know that you have all earned a passing grade. Let us be clear on that. Whoever wishes to attend class may stay; whoever wants to leave is free to do so. The door is right there, always, when you feel like leaving, when you want to, if ever you are bored, or sick of being in class." He knew almost no one would choose the door; more than likely, a couple of outsiders would join them, and often classes would stretch beyond their official time slot—neither he nor the students were in a hurry.

It was his vanity. He couldn't tolerate the thought of someone being with him, even for a moment, out of any sense of obligation that did not stem from the devotion engendered by his words. It was the same when it came to love; it was as if he were constantly inviting you to leave, making you sense that you were superfluous for the sole purpose of making you feel free, comfortable, hungry for his presence.

Lately, however, he admitted that he was tired, truly tired of teaching. He felt a deep chasm opening between himself and the younger generations. He'd say that the time had come for him to quit, that he no longer enjoyed it. He'd say: "I'm sick of it." "I'm getting old." "I don't enjoy this anymore." But time and again, he would leave class with the air of someone who had just conquered a tough crowd. Twenty-four hours before he died, Lot heard him say, "I haven't enjoyed a class this much for a long time!" His class met at eight in the evening. Ten minutes before it was to start, he felt a sharp pain in his arm and said, "I might have to go home." Five minutes later, "I'm fine." He went up to teach his course and when he came out, he told Lot, who was waiting for him, "I'm glad I did. I haven't enjoyed a class this much for a long time, and they did too. I could tell by the look in their eyes, I could see it in their eyes . . ." A furtive tear (one of those that Lot would examine, as he barked, *Scram!*) shone in his eye. Nothing in this world—other than the epic scenes of a John Houston film—was more moving to him than recognizing in the eyes of a student the light of knowledge striving to be kindled. And it wasn't imperative that they be students in the proper sense of the term: When vocation called, anyone would do, anyone who was in front of him and could spontaneously serve as pupil.

One winter, it snowed three days in a row, and the roads were impassable. For three days, they didn't go to work, and he didn't leave the house to meet his friends. On the second day, about the time his class would have started, he entered the room where Lot was in bed writing (wrapped in a pile of comforters because the heating had broken down and it was bitterly cold) and, with the excuse of announcing the dish he planned to cook for dinner, he began to teach the class. And he carried on until he had given her a two-hour lesson—the one he would have taught had he been at work, point by point. He taught wherever he found himself, it was his destiny.

Nevertheless, the things that Lot learned at his side were not the fruit of any class or lecture: At some point, she would simply become aware of a certain trait of his that intrigued her, and she would begin to investigate. For instance, she realized that he never felt indebted for what he received, whether affection, invitations, or gifts. Conversely, he never expected any compensation for what he gave. When she brought this to his attention, he volunteered a piece of advice: "Never give anything you can't spare." She stopped to consider the things she had that might be considered superfluous. There wasn't much. But he, who gave so much, who was generous with his time, his money, his affection— was it because he had more than enough of those things, and even some to spare? From that day on, she started experimenting and, to her surprise, she found that the more she gave, the more she had.

On another occasion, she noticed that when he interacted with someone, he always gave the impression that it was a new relationship, thus affording his interlocutor a fresh opportunity every time they met. Generally speaking, when someone who has been labeled a bore approaches us, we tend to think, *Here comes that bore,* and we may even unconsciously treat the person as such, not allowing them to sidestep the role we have hitherto assigned. Consequently, they behave like a bore. If we encounter someone who doesn't know how to listen, an automatic response immediately springs up and is replayed—*he doesn't listen*—and as a result, we won't share anything interesting with that person, which only makes them pay even less attention. But Cometa seemed to have no use for this type of before-the-fact filtering. And this stance allowed others to showcase their intelligence or dullness, their caution or temerity. For someone who is a bit of a moron, this attitude can be quite pedagogical. Let's say I'm a moron: Everyone around me knows this, and when I approach people, they won't allow me to behave as anything other than the moron I am. But say I come across someone who, as though oblivious to it all, allows me to ramble. And as I ramble, I become aware of certain aspects of my moronic nature, and in consequence these traits diminish. Whatever the interlocutors' attitude, Cometa's presence brought out the best in them, precisely because of his lack of prejudice in dealing with them. When Lot brought this to his attention, he said it was because of his bad memory. It was true that his memory was occupied with so many other files that he didn't register a priori notions regarding others. He never harbored "the dark flower of resentment" and, when in doubt, he always asked. As far as he was concerned, the door was always open. And so, in

173

his presence, the arrogant frequently behaved humbly, and the highhanded postponed their display of showiness. Starting that day, she began to test Cometa's approach. But it didn't come easily: She would need to lose some of her memory.

Another day, she realized how little he cared about what could be termed the opinion "of others," of those who are usually referred to as "acquaintances." And yet, he was extraordinarily particular about the image he projected to strangers, to those for whom he was completely anonymous. Apparently, his only concern was feeling comfortable in his own skin, not having to ever regret anything, leading a life, as he put it, "worth living." And he seemed to succeed. Or at least to get on rather well. When she mentioned this to him, he responded that he preferred to be scorned for what he was than to be loved for what he wasn't. She found that interesting: The opinion of acquaintances had never much mattered to her. The problem was she wasn't troubled about those of strangers either. From that day on, she made an effort and began to concern herself with the latter: Forevermore, she wished to behave as though a thousand eyes were watching her, or, to put it differently, not to engage in any action she wouldn't be prepared to publicly defend with absolute conviction.

Another day, she detected in him an odd mixture of utmost discretion and extreme exhibitionism. On the one hand, he never hid anything: If necessary, he would put his entire person on display, unadorned, and in this way, he easily transformed a weakness into a strength, a flaw into a virtue. On the other hand, he never made confessions and rarely spread news, gossip, or announcements. When she mentioned this, he again said that it was his bad memory: He never seemed to remember comments of that sort. So, he never allowed private conversations about other people's lives to slip out; and people must have known as much, because they often confided in him. And yet, he detested the phony discretion that is so common here. Especially given that he was incapable of hypocrisy, utterly useless at feigning. From that day on, she tried to practice that kind of frankness. She was rather good at it. She decided to eradicate all secrets from her life.

Another day, she realized she'd never seen him express any fear of the things she was scared of. She'd never seen him be cowed by an argument or a verbal aggression. Certainly, in this regard, he had a sharp weapon at his command: his talent for oral improvisation, his ability to deliver difficult-to-rebut verbal onslaughts. When words weren't an option, however, he displayed the same courage. He didn't back down one millimeter that afternoon when a wild teenager charged toward him with an iron rod that landed right on his collarbone. His was a peculiar courage, for some things—often the most absurd and trivial—were enormously debilitating to him. Something as banal as going to the bank could prove devastating for him. He became irritable, exasperated, transformed, wishing only to escape or to sign whatever paper was put before him and flee. The reasons for such an aversion, which he practically somatized, were inscrutable, though probably associated with his peculiar moral dilemma regarding money and the institutions that manage it. Fortunately, in most matters, he and Lot enjoyed a complementary form of synchrony: She found the cold, neutral fluorescent lighting in such places to be a balm to her fiery spirit. When she pointed out that they could give each other mutual and complementary lessons in courage, he expressed no interest in getting past his aversion: Dealing with the practical aspects of real life was her chore; there was no need to duplicate efforts. His kind of courage was more difficult to imitate. The epic points-of-reference that punctuated his life had never left their mark on hers. In any case, she wasn't concerned about it. She soon dropped the issue of heroism without any regret: Some lessons were meant for her, others were not.

Some of the things he had taught her, she was getting better and better at. Others, she would never learn. Still others, she didn't master until he was no longer by her side.

B6

The Inconsolable

"I was an indomitable creature, and then I was tamed," says Z., a former student who has come to see me. Spring has arrived. Outside, the afternoon grows longer and longer. He seems uncomfortable sitting on the sofa where his teacher and friend used to read. I only know him from having seen them together. He knows me even less. He doesn't know how to commence this unexpected intimacy with me. He's tall, heavyset, shy, extremely polite, and he starts like this, somewhat abruptly, "I was an indomitable creature, and then I was tamed." After this, his story unfolds easily.

Z. is a tremendous guy, of uncommon intelligence. When he was younger, he ate a classmate's ear. Or, to be more precise, he bit off a piece of it. He was always at odds with the system. A teenage rebel, he raged against anything he deemed unjust. After the incident with the ear, he became, naturally enough, *that student who ate someone's ear*. He was expelled. Several years passed, and the student returned with a new disposition. He was no longer fifteen, but nineteen. That's when they met: "I came back to get one of those little diplomas they give out, so I could study physics at the university. That's all I had in mind. But my life changed forever." The teacher noticed the kid's unusual talent; he was a voracious reader of literature, philosophy, and science. And one day Cometa asked him if he wrote.

"'Do you write?' he asked me. 'Some,' I said. The truth is I'd been writing all my life. And then Cometa said, 'I'd like to read some of it, if you want me to.' I dug up my best writing and tried to improve it. I modified adverbs and adjectives, I searched for the right words, I used all of my ingenuity to impress him. Finally, I handed it to him."

He pauses. Lights a cigarette. Smiles.

"A couple of days later he hurled it back at me: 'This is a pile of crap!' he said. I was shocked. A few days later, he said, 'Do you have anything else to show me?' That's when I realized: He'd given me the exact number of days I needed to reflect on it, not a day more, not a day less. The rascal knew what he was doing, I thought. And I knew I'd finally found someone who made no concessions. Later, we became friends. After that, there was only one criticism he leveled against me: 'Too much rage,' he'd say. 'There's still too much rage. Watch your anger, be careful . . .'"

I've read some of this young man's stuff. It's good. Not only is he a good storyteller, he's demonstrated his excellence throughout his degree in physics, which he finished two years ago. I ask him if he's lonely, if he's comfortable. Cometa and I had spoken of him recently; my husband wondered if Z. would be able to adapt to the indignities of academia or if he would end up squandering his considerable talent. And, certainly, seeing his sensitivity, combined with a refined taste and such uncommon gifts, I wonder what kind of time bomb he carries inside him. How many rungs will he have to descend, how many beautiful things will he be forced to abandon, how many just things will he renounce? He's still young and tender, and he rebels against those who treat him as a prodigy: "Unenlightened adulators," he calls them. "However much I may love them, I do my best to do without their services." He rebels as well against friends and acquaintances that "adopt a look of incomprehension and look at you as if you were talking about banalities when in reality you're referring to such parochial matters as beauty, loyalty, or friendship . . ."

"You see," he says, "I only feel on the same wavelength with the others he taught during those years. I have friends from that period who are fully part of the system—mortgage, business, children, marriage. They may have never again opened a philosophy book, or perhaps they have. But when we look at each other, we sense there's something that unites us, something we truly learned: to live with our eyes open, to always be alert . . ."

He has trouble with beautiful words, because his teacher had trained him to demystify teachers, instilling in him the conviction that there are no unassailable oracles or thinkers. "I needed to say these words," he adds. Both of us are orphaned now, both of us are pupils who have been tamed, he and I have things in common. "And I've enjoyed hearing them," I reply. "I would have liked to say them to him, but I'm too late. I'm always late," he says. A few years ago, when I lost my professor from the City of Fog, I, too, had that same feeling. Until, finally, with time, I reached the conclusion that being late is part of the appeal.

"Everything you've said here . . . you'll someday repeat to my daughter, won't you?" I say, knowing he'll probably be late—or she will.

"You can count on it," he says, with the timid resoluteness that characterizes him.

Before he leaves, we reminisce about the last day the two of them spent together. He remembers seeing his teacher arrive; I remember seeing Cometa leave. They had arranged to meet near the train station.

"Do you remember what you talked about?" I ask.

"About the telescope he'd promised to make for your daughter. And about the moon."

Before he goes, he adds:

"For years, we only talked about philosophy and physics. But recently, we only talked about the moon."

This afternoon I went to see a friend of ours. She's over seventy and enjoys an enviable vitality. In many respects, she's the one who was a teacher to him, and I tell her as much. "Yes, but over the years," she responds, "the roles were reversed, and he taught me something fundamental that no one had ever taught me before: to apprehend the world. What little ability I have to think, he taught me, no preaching, no lectures, no foolishness." As we sip our whiskies, her eyes flicker, and suddenly she sighs and adds: "Life is curious . . . Your husband taught me how to think, my husband taught me how to love, and the man I met after my husband died taught me how to fuck. And when I finally knew about everything . . . that was it."

"That was it?" I smile, "What do you mean by that?"

But she refuses to offer a translation, such as *when we learn how to live, life is over*, or something to that effect. She's very matter-of-fact, and simply concludes:

"That's all I mean: That once I knew everything . . . that was it!"

Yes, having a good teacher is good. Life doesn't always offer you this opportunity. The problem is that, one day or another, luck always runs out. And then you have to shape up, take the tools your teacher has given you, and make them your own—in order to carry on with them, or to make something new of them. And you must reclaim your own skills and do something different with them. A strange combination.

"There's so much you've never done!" says my friend, the advocate of intravenous potassium. Anxious to see me create a world of my own, she encourages me, "You still have a long list of things left to explore!"

Indeed, there were countless things I didn't do when I was with him—nor did I need to. But I can learn to adapt. With an added advantage: In the rest of my life, there'll be no more fears. Except for those concerning my daughter, I've shed them all. So I'm prepared to launch into a life of action and novelty.

If I stop to think about it, there are many things I've never done but always thought it would be interesting to try: horseback riding, singing in a choir, growing hydrangeas, having a dog, taking antidepressants, getting a massage, visiting New England. But this spring—a period of transition after the explosion—is strange, the days uneven. I start with a visit to the spa, one of the many things my close friends have organized for me.

There is no blood bath at the spa, not by a long stretch. Quite the opposite: The repossession of my body commences. For a long time, it's puzzled me that my emotional pain wasn't accompanied by physical pain—I would have preferred it. But my body was healthy and felt nothing, aside from a few twinges in my stomach caused by my mental state. I suppose my body had gone astray, in an attempt to follow him. Now, suddenly, at the spa, I find myself inside a body I had taken for granted and ignored. I give up my hunger strike. I rest. I feel the snowflakes on my face as I watch my daughter in the pool, squealing with our friend's children because it's snowing on the warm water, the day growing dark. Cold, hot, hot, cold, little by little I reenter my body. Under the effects of massage and Scottish showers, I feel myself slipping into my own skin as though getting into a tight dress, slowly, like water filling a balloon with lots of protrusions; first one, then another—plop, plop—they all fill up.

Rome, on the other hand, is an altogether different story: A painful trip, the memory of which is, nevertheless, inimitable and intense. Even though I never visited Rome with him, it doesn't matter. Because Rome shatters into a thousand pieces, and it becomes an inexhaustible constellation of nooks, street corners, skies, rains, lawns, sidewalks, cobblestones, and bar tables that I have shared with him. A sudden downpour falls on the domes of Santa Maria Maggiore, and Rome is no longer Rome, it is Salzburg (Salzburg, drenched to the bone, still no child, the first bar in which to shelter is in a hotel, a glass loft overlooking the rooftops pelted by rain). While we wait for the menu, an eye comes to rest on an empty wine glass turned upside-down and Rome is no longer Rome, it is Zurich (there's a wasp inside the glass, we're with some friends in a restaurant near the station waiting for the train, a friend traps a wasp in a glass to stop the buzzing, the sight of the wasp inside the crystal bubble makes him uncomfortable over lunch, he frees it, the friend protests). A ray of sun falls on the damp cobblestones of Piazza Navona, and Rome is no longer Rome, but Prague (a leisurely stroll along a street after we'd abandoned the idea of visiting Kafka's house because six people were waiting in line). Each spot seems to have its counterpart, seems to evoke a referent, and Rome becomes the dozens of cities we visited together and were happy in: No detail is lost on the pain. When a place conjures a sudden image, the pain is intense because it's unexpected. And, when you're far from home, pain is a dangerous thing.

We are not far from home, however. We are with our friends, G. and C.: teaching me how to send a text message in the Villa Borghese gardens; all five of us laughing as we struggle to maneuver an impossible bicycle; my daughter protesting for having to walk *so much*, her *gelato* precariously teetering amid the crowds. It would have been a terrible mistake for the two of us to go on this trip alone at this time. But I behave: I allow myself to be loved.

The day after he died, my friend MI., with whom we are now traveling, said to me, "I ask only one thing of you: Allow yourself to be loved." It was almost a plea, but spoken as if addressing a cactus or a prickly shrub. She knows I've always wanted to call the shots, to be the one who does more of the loving, and for it to be reciprocated only to a reasonable degree—one notch beyond that and I'm overwhelmed. But in that moment, I decided to listen to her.

All through the spring, I've socialized nonstop. Parties, dinners, lunches, and cocktails, almost all connected to literary circles. The people I run into exclaim, "But you never used to go anywhere!" Naturally: I was just fine at home. But things are different now. No need to get carried away, though. I'm so lazy, so accustomed to entertaining myself alone or in tandem that, for me, going out to "have fun" is the equivalent of some kind of mandatory therapy which entails accepting all the invitations I would have previously refused. That is all. Not much in the end, but I've met more people during these months than over the course of my entire life.

Yet the harshness of this spring hasn't diminished, though, aside from him, I lack nothing. Not even a special friend. In June, I sneak away to Paris on a furtive getaway with a charming friend, a man who has decided to look after me with a steadfastness and determination I find disconcerting and moving. Disconcerting because he has many other things to do in life—more interesting in my opinion—so his obstinacy in clinging to this relationship is difficult to understand. Moving because it's always moving to see someone who insists on caring for a prickly shrub. (*Allow yourself to be loved*, said MI., whom I've designated as my principal adviser. And so I do.)

And yet, nothing seems able to prevent the nosedive my mood takes this spring. One morning in Paris, while my friend is at a meeting, I go to the cemetery in front of the hotel—Montparnasse cemetery—in search of an atmosphere that will provide a measure of solace. I like epitaphs, especially ones that have a certain charm to them. On a tombstone, I read the following: "*Il m'attendait et je suis venue.*" It's Marfa's epitaph. She shares the tomb with her husband, who died thirty-five years before she did. When did Marfa think up this epitaph? Perhaps when her husband died, not knowing she would survive him by thirty-five years? Perhaps she wasn't the one who came up with it? In any event, if it was her, it shows that she was endowed with a magnificent sense of humor. Or steel-plated optimism. "He waited for me and I came," Marfa says.

184

I think I've kept the pain more or less under control until now. I've lived through the mourning process with a certain serenity. *I have my whole life to do this*, I thought. *There's no need to exhaust its course in a couple of days.* Sometimes, when I have needed to forget a lover, I've been in a hurry, and perhaps the haste made the pain more intense. With this bereavement, however, I am in no rush; I do not want it to end; I can devote my whole life to it.

But right now, all of the consolations I have compiled into a list seem worthless. "Nothing will work if your serotonin levels are low," my doctor says, and my expert friend agrees. I balked at the idea of chemical helpers, always holding back in case I might need them more in the future, at a worse time. "Worse?" asks my friend. "Worse than what?" My mood has always been so volatile that, if I wait long enough, invariably I rebound without the need for chemicals. I'll wait. But only a little longer. Someone else, wanting to dissuade me says, "No, no. No chemicals." She means synthetic chemicals, obviously, because she uses natural remedies, and she doesn't seem to mind that the molecules distilled in a laboratory are in many cases identical to those extracted from a plant. What she really likes is the plant itself—even if it poses more dangers than the laboratory product—because it's natural. For a while, though, she was on medication, and seemed quite happy. I ask her why she stopped. "I didn't feel like myself," she says. "Now I'm myself again." I wonder how in the world she determined that *this* is her real self and not the other. In any event, I don't find this a deterring argument. I'm willing to try anything. But for now, I want to continue on my downward spiral, lower and lower, until I know what lies at the bottom.

Today I went out for lunch, and as it's Friday, when I got home I suggested to my daughter that we watch a Frank Capra comedy suitable for us both, *You Can't Take it With You*, in which the multigenerational, charming, and lunatic Sycamore family meet the granddaughter's much more conventional boyfriend, Tony Kirby, played by James Stewart. And when the grandfather asks the boyfriend's presumptuous father, Mr. Kirby, Sr., why he wants so much money:

"You can't take it with you, Mr. Kirby. So what good is it? As near as I can see, the only thing you can take with you is the love of your friends."

. . . I find myself captivated by the line, as I often was during the first weeks of mourning. But this time, the feeling isn't a pleasant one. And only Cometa's sister's luminous, almost daily visits can shake me out of this state, but only momentarily, until she leaves at dark.

For the first time, night no longer brings consolation. At dinner, Píulix puts on *The Magic Flute,* for a school assignment, and when she goes to bed she leaves me with the end of the first act. Art has the peculiarity of always being extraordinarily apropos. Haven't you noticed that you play some music and it's about *that,* you open a book and it's about *that,* you read a poem and it refers to *that,* you look at a painting and discover *that* in it? This is my experience. Or maybe this is just one more thing we writers have in common with paranoids. Now that, for the first time in months, night no longer comforts me, I hear Tamino sing: *O ewige Nacht! Wann wirst du schwinden? Wann wird das Licht mein Auge finden?* And the response: *Bald, Jüngling, oder nie!*

"Oh, eternal night . . . when will you end? When will my eyes rediscover the light?"

"Soon, young man. Or never more!"

The worst part about nights of mourning is that they are infinite. Is this what lies at the bottom, an eternal night? I prefer to dwell on the last phrase: Soon or never more.

The problem is, I don't have much patience for never-ending nights.

A7

The Only Thing You Take to Your Grave

Some men come with mothers attached, some with ex-wives, others with dogs. He was a man with friends. Lot realized this from the start, and she respected it. She couldn't imagine being with him in any other way: His true family wasn't determined by blood. He was a man-with-friends—it was a package deal. Take it or leave it. There was no room for negotiation, but neither was there any obligation to socialize with them or even meet them. Cometa offered Lot more freedom than she would ever have wished for. But the time he devoted to his friends was nonnegotiable. For Lot, who was appalled by the kind of social obligation that forces one member of a couple to become acquainted with the other's social milieu, things were easy this time. Loving his friends was easy, just as it was to love the rest of his family, or even his street: They were such an inextricable part of him that it was inconceivable to love him without loving the rest.

He was sociable by nature. While his exacting tastes and conversational rigor might have condemned him to a certain existential solipsism, his nearly constant need to communicate prevented this. A need that wasn't about sharing one's life story, but about being surrounded by friends, conversing vaguely about the world, feeling alive and experiencing companionship. This sociability was nevertheless limited to the three worlds in which his friends moved, three very different scenes, governed by different types of music, relationships, and modes of interaction. Cometa was a different man in each. And he didn't like to mix those three worlds. Lot established a different rapport with each. Whereas she'd been fascinated by the world in which she had first met Cometa—seated at the bar—the one that coalesced around his metaphysics-inclined friends instilled in her a sense of calm and serenity. The one from his childhood, meanwhile, linked her to an atavistic past in the City of Fog; whether it belonged solely to Cometa and his friends or she'd also been a part of it, she no longer knew.

His childhood friends, brought up in large families during the Franco dictatorship, were deeply humane individuals. In the days when they roamed freely through the reed beds and put their lives on the line by the canal or on the train tracks, Cometa must have been the source of many valuable ideas: judiciousness, restraint, solutions delivered at critical moments. But his friends also contributed their share of lessons—austerity, strength, vitality—ones that Cometa would always carry with him. The commonalities between his family and his friends' were few. Cometa's father was left-wing and pro-American, not an infrequent combination in the fifties. His home was a place where things were done differently: the home with an American-style refrigerator, where the kitchen wall had been knocked down to facilitate simultaneous cooking, dining and conversing, the home with a Christmas tree instead of a crèche. The parents of all the friends shared one particular trait:

honesty and civility toward others, values which they passed on to their children and which took precedence over all others.

With his friends, Cometa devised pranks or put a stop to them; with them he played soccer on sunny fields, using makeshift balls crafted out of rags and strings. With them, he shared the Great Apple Tree, an old tree that was so immense that everyone had their own branch on which to spend long periods of time. They learned everything together; they fell in love together; they left town to study at the same time. Later, life scattered them across the map. But they never stopped seeing each other. Every Christmas, every summer, they gathered and, with renewed enthusiasm, conjured up memories of their adventures. They spent Christmas holidays together; they lunched in the countryside or barbecued at Fernan's country house among apple and peach trees; they played card games on perennially foggy Saint Stephen's Days, and they spent the rare afternoon of glory at the local soccer stadium. Together, they rang in the New Year. An entire night of songbook repertoire at the house with the three doors, everyone seated around the dining-room table, while the children had supper in the kitchen, and guitars were brought out: *havaneras* and *corridos*, *milongas* and *garrotins* until they couldn't go on. The effects of repetition and aging would inevitably cause someone to forget a line, another to sing out of tune, but there were also magical instants that salvaged the night: Alvaro's *milonga*; Palestrina harmonized in a duet with Pepe; Fernan on the guitar, launching into a beautiful song he'd been practicing; Cometa singing "La chancla." And, fuelled by the last emanations of alcohol, there was also that ominous moment when a fan of Joaquín Sabina would insist on singing one of his tunes for the sole purpose of provoking Cometa, who in turn would

191

inevitably end up giving a rendition of "The Internationale," the Foreign Legion Hymn, or a Wagnerian aria—which were, in any case, interchangeable—or else threatening to storm off to sleep, or something worse. There were always twelve of them, like The Last Supper. And often, judging by the apocalyptic atmosphere of the final minutes of the evening, it was indeed the last supper.

Lot always found the following day a particularly pleasant one: staying in and clearing away leftovers, cigarette butts, glasses, ashtrays, and bottles. After days and days of milky grey skies, the first of January was usually sunny, and the stores were closed—the perfect day to turn in early.

For some reason, Lot and this set of friends shared a special affinity. Their gatherings had a certain whiff of eternity. Even friends who had left the fold as kids, whom Lot had never met, seemed present. And it was clear that it didn't matter which of them had left early, later, or who was present and who was missing. As long as one of them remained, they would all be there, always. And she wanted to be near.

The second of these worlds was that of exquisite metaphysics, of the friends he'd made during his school and university days, those for whom philosophy was the foremost passion in life. For many, many years, they met for lunch on Fridays, over books that served as pretexts for detonating clouds of fresh, fertile ideas. Whatever their chosen topic was, when they latched on to a concept, they knew how to radically sever all ties with the outside world, and in so doing, they became immune to the seductions of cliché. Cometa practiced this way of speaking whenever possible, but precisely because it was uncommon, he was only in his element when he was with this particular group of friends; only in their presence did he experience the serenity that comes from not having to struggle against those unable to debate with finesse, who were many and well-loved.

The third of these worlds were friends from the town where they lived. It was a motley group: people of independent means, big business owners, and clochards. The other two worlds in which Cometa moved were rather conventional in their affective and familial arrangements, but the bohemian lifestyle of the sixties had firmly taken root and successfully installed itself in this third domain, giving rise to a large, more or less convivial family, where rich friends helped poor friends, poor friends didn't feel indebted to their rich friends, ladies fell in love with vagabonds, ex-wives were close friends, and offspring from different provenances and stages in life went on excursions together. Feelings such as jealousy were expunged from relationships, and words such as "marriage" did not figure in their existential dictionaries.

This was the world Cometa abandoned most abruptly when he moved in with Lot. In part, because of Cometa's renewed passion for the City of Fog, where they were spending more and more of their weekends. In part, because these friends belonged to a nocturnal life, a life lived on the screen that was, generally speaking, incompatible with life in the stalls.

And yet, he held this part of his past in high esteem. Aside from childhood, his most intense moments had been with them. And though he never seemed nostalgic, had he longed for anything, it would have been for this—what he referred to as "the call of the wild." When "the wild" called—that is, alcohol, jazz, nightlife—nothing in this world could have held him back. "I would never have imagined that anyone could restrain him," a friend of Cometa's told Lot soon after he migrated to an orderly, diurnal life. The comment, of course, referred to her. The friend had uttered the words with a mixture of surprised admiration and veiled recrimination for depriving them of Cometa's presence during those magical nights on the town. His friends declared her the levee, him the surging wave. Quite frankly, between a cement dike and a wild wave, there is no comparison. But she was to be the levee. Nonetheless, he was the one who had chosen to be contained, and he never questioned the decision: Cometa knew no regrets. Nor did he know the meaning of nostalgia.

"I don't think I know what nostalgia is," he told Lot one day. "Can you explain it to me, since you're an expert in these matters?" But when she finished, despite her effort to establish some kind of empathy, he responded, "No, I've never felt anything like that. When I think of the past it's always with a pleasant sense of melancholy." But one morning he said, "I had a dream today, and I think I felt what you call nostalgia for the first time: I was young; I was leaving El Mesón after lunch, surrounded by friends; there was a beautiful woman; we were riding around in a convertible filled to capacity, my legs dangling out, and I was intensely happy. And yet, for a moment, I felt a kind of pain, in the dream itself, when I realized that that was the past." This was the closest Cometa ever came to feeling nostalgia. And it was a dream.

How could one not yearn for a world filled with alcohol, ideas, women, dreams—a world where life was lived to the fullest and each encounter yielded the unexpected? Alcohol was an essential part of this. Cometa, who was born at the foot of a vineyard reminiscent of Brassens, had a deep veneration for alcohol. Experimenting with it, he had at times tested his own limits, and he was lucky to have reaped from it the best and escaped the worst. He never gave up alcohol. And he never adopted the role of the *enfant terrible* who tries to pass himself off as more degenerate than he really is: He had lived to the fullest, as much as anyone could, and yet he constantly sought serenity and judiciousness, and he radiated both. When a friend whose doctor had forbidden him to drink reported the dismal news, Cometa cheered him on, "We'll get drunk on conversation, or gazing at the moon!"

For his part, he had consumed alcohol in moderation for years, and whenever he allowed himself to be completely frank, he would always express his infinite gratitude for the fruits of Bacchus. "It's true," he would say, "that I've wasted a lot of time drinking . . . but it's also true that it has given me what nothing else, no one else, has ever been able to provide—not women, not books, not my most glorious experiences, perhaps not even music. It's given me so much. How could I not be grateful?" When Lot heard him talk like this, she wondered what magical instants, what unfathomable and extraordinary highs he was referring to. She, a more prosaic consumer of alcohol, hadn't a clue.

And so it was that he transitioned without nostalgia into diurnal life, and he adjusted to Lot's Danish schedule as if it had been his own, turning nighttime forays into an exception. From that world, he maintained one constant: the company of his most gentle friend. The friend he went to the market with and cooked with, the friend who always waited for him, who always accommodated his schedule to

Cometa's, who followed him into his diurnal schedule. If Cometa no longer went out at night, the friend went out during the day. Together they hunted for wild mushrooms in the fall, went tuna fishing in the spring, watched soccer matches, had breakfast together, and allowed themselves to be swindled by the fishmonger. Lot had sometimes wondered what would happen if one was left without the other. When they were younger, the two of them had lived together for a long time, in a veritable alternative version of Neil Simon's *The Odd Couple*. They roomed together whenever they were separated from their women. And when one of them lived with a partner, the one who was alone became part of the other's family. During the sixteen years Cometa was with Lot, the two of them regularly had Sunday dinner at the friend's house in La Floresta. The gentlest friend looked a bit like Tintin's Captain Haddock, in a gentler incarnation. Lot and Gisèle, the friend's partner, jokingly called them "the happy couple," as they watched the two men bickering over a paella or a shoulder of lamb in the garden of the house in La Floresta, the women never lifting a finger. They had never learned to cook (whatever for?).

Each of these worlds had its own musical and beverage pairings. Jazz bound him to his friends from town, a relationship built around nocturnal distillations, in an atmosphere in which breaking down boundaries was common, and conventions were ignored. In a very different milieu, traditional folk music accompanied the parties with his childhood friends in the City of Fog, an association founded on memories, tender affections, and leisurely *carajillos*—black coffee with rum—savored as they sat for hours at the village café. And finally, classical music accompanied him and his philosopher friends in a fellowship built on intellectual complicity and bottles of Nuits-Saint-Georges and Chateau-d'Yquem imbibed with the consideration they merited. In the abstemious solitude of his diurnal life, classical music—Schubert, Bach, Haydn—played at all hours of the day. Lot awoke every morning to the sound of those angelic allies, and knew that everything was in its rightful place, that order prevailed in Cometa's universe. Music was to him an unmitigated provocation that should be avoided in the interest of preserving domestic peace. Whether he detested or adored a particular piece of music, Cometa's eyes could suddenly cloud over and turn belligerent if he wished to malign it, or else seek out friends with whom to share his unbridled passion and cause a formidable scene. Lot had often been captivated by those scenes. But now she had become the designated levee, and the function of levees is to hold back the waters; it is their job. And it wasn't easy, because his radio was always tuned to a classical station, which meant that a diabolical ally—such as Wagner or Charlie Parker—could turn up on the air at any moment, and she had to be prepared to act as a circuit breaker, if necessary. The summer broadcast of the Bayreuth Festival was a particularly dangerous moment. She had joked about it with their daughter the previous summer: "Help! Isolde's death is coming, change the station. Quick!" She trusted that Píulix would learn that Isolde's death was dangerous for Papà. But it didn't turn out that way. Instead, the child soon became Cometa's partner in musical passion: His indescribable exclamations of pleasure drew from her enormous peals of laughter, and his passionate scenes triggered an acute musical curiosity in her. With the exception of music, there was nothing for which Cometa was not prepared to make concessions. No charged political discussion with friends, no soccer-themed bull session ever lessened his tolerance; it was, precisely, the defining element of his personality. But music was a different story.

There was, however, a fourth dimension, comprised of rarely seen friends, of half-forgotten rendezvous that he almost never mentioned. One morning, an acquaintance gave Lot news of an old friend of Cometa's, "Tell him that my father mentioned Juan the Mexican. He's somewhere in San Luis Potosí." She conveyed the message to Cometa and asked, "Who's this Juan?" "A friend, a friend I lived with many years ago, when I was a student, someone I haven't seen since." Cometa was never much of a raconteur, and no story ensued. But a few weeks later, Lot joined the philosophers for coffee, as she often did on Fridays. She usually arrived as desert was being served, just as they were abandoning Kant or Heidegger to devote themselves to the pleasures of table talk. They had listened to Gardel tangos that day, and were wrapping things up with Trío Calavera, a band that had just brought out a song that Lot had occasionally heard Cometa sing or whistle.

When they left, she couldn't get the tune out of her head, and started singing it in the car: "*Han nassido en mi rancho tres arboliiitos.*" He would usually let her go on, but at other times, such as this, he corrected her: "It's two—two little trees." She continued: "*Dos arbolitos que paressen gemelos* [two little trees that look like twins . . .]" and he joined in, whistling the rest of the tune. When it was over, in an uncommonly melancholic tone, he said, "Many important people in my life have disappeared and I've never heard from them again." Then he told her about Juan the Mexican.

"It was a period when I was living with Javier the Peruvian, Fred (a friendly Canadian architect we nicknamed Kas Manzana, after the soda drink), Juan the Mexican, and Pano Paluria, an Argentinean guy who wrote prologues and is now a well-known intellectual. Back then he wrote prologues, always prologues. He also kept files of index cards with notes, lots of notes. Juan was like an American Indian: straight black hair, deep black eyes, aquiline nose. Learned. So learned that his head couldn't hold everything he knew. You could have an in-depth discussion with him about Shakespeare, Mondrian, Bacon, about anything really. He made me see the 'hole' in Renoir's *The Swing*, a hole you don't notice at first, but through which the forest is visible. When I returned to our apartment one day, he'd shaved his head; this wasn't at all common then. And he was behaving strangely. He stammered: "Tie me up, tie me to the bed right now before I jump out the window."

With a lump in his throat, Cometa explained that he found a sheet, ripped it to pieces, and with the torn bits tied Juan to the bed. Javier the Peruvian, a great guy, helped him.

"But Pano Paluria," he continued, "was horrified. 'What are you doing? What's going on?' he screamed. We made him shut up. Intellectuals panic so easily; they can be cowed into submission with a few shouts and one suck-my-dick. Juan the Mexican spent three days tied to my bed, without moving. I slept beside him and fed him like a child. On the third day, he said: 'You can untie me now, it's over. I'm done with wanting to jump out the window.' I untied him, and we hugged."

In an attempt to quell his emotions, Cometa went on musing about those strange days, a time when people made a living doing bizarre things. Or doing nothing at all. Javier and Cometa were students; Juan had no occupation at all; the Canadian architect experimented and experimented; Pano Paluria wrote prologues for the sake of prologues. You could almost say that many of them lived off the air. "A whole theory," Cometa said, "could be developed around those intense, and at the same time fleeting, relationships, connections and disconnections, separations that weren't experienced as such."

Juan the Mexican returned to his country. Soon afterward, he was found lost in a forest in Huatulco. He was looking for a sock. Cometa learned all this through a phone conversation with a friend whose father worked at the Nicaraguan embassy in Mexico and had kept up with Juan through a mutual acquaintance. Among other things, Juan believed that someone had implanted microchips in his brain; *unos aparatitosss* [some little gadgets] he called them.

"An extraordinary fellow," Cometa concluded. "Kind, noble, learned. He knew too much, Juan the Mexican. He just couldn't handle it."

Lot never forgot the story, even though a week later she was again singing *Tres arbolitos* and Cometa had to say: "It's two, love—two trees!"

Cometa never saw Juan again. The opportunity never presented itself. But he wasn't much in favor of reunions anyway. Perhaps he was thinking of Juan when he wrote in the book he never would finish:

The hunter is inaccessible; for that he must limit his contact with the world surrounding him, avoid leaving his mark on anything or anyone. The hunter does not use the world, does not use people, does not use living things. He takes what he needs and moves on. And we can apply this to everything, including love. Wretched is the love that traps, oppresses, and sickens the heart, wretched the possessive, feverish passion that shakes the love object until the comforting affirmation of feeling oneself corresponded falls from it. Wretched is the love that marks its territory again and again, pissing on what is loved until its stench permeates it completely. Amorous moth, learn from Lancelot, the Knight of the Cart, who forgets his condition and exposes himself to shame and disgrace in order to save his loved one!

This also applies to fortuitous encounters that spawn some kind of affection. A heroic way of squandering that affection, leaving it faded and spent, is to force reunions and dig up the vicissitudes that both have encountered in the meantime (How did it go for you? What became of such-and-such? What are you up to now?), when often those who cross our path but once and vanish forever leave behind an inimitable, indelible fragrance (and often this encounter leads to a slight, but fortuitous change in the course of our lives).

The course corrections introduced in his path by friends (both permanent and occasional) were forever. They could be found in the words, turns of phrases, and expressions that he passed on to Lot and their daughter, to the rest of their friends and family, and to everyone around them. In the end, they all inherited Cometa's friends.

B7

A Cobalt-Blue Sky

"Do you think *Papi* would have come?" asks my daughter as she drags her luggage through the airport terminal. "Well, I'm not sure. What I do know is that he preferred other places, or even staying at home. And Boston probably wasn't among his favorite destinations. There are plenty of things we would have done if he were with us, and plenty of things that are completely different from what we would have done with him. This is one of them."

We are en route to New England, where we'll spend a month in a tiny village in Maine, in the company of several complete strangers. But before that, we'll have a few days in Boston on our own. I hope none of the skies in Maine will remind me of a sky I've seen before, and that the places we stumble upon, unlike those in Rome, won't crumble into shards of familiar places. For that reason, I've chosen a very different destination. I could have chosen somewhere even more different, of course. Of the choices I had, however, this was the one I felt I could handle. When you leave home and travel to distant parts, you take risks. Each departure (as well as each arrival) causes deep pain and an intense rush of memories, both old and recent. You enter into a different logic, where it's easy to lose touch with reality and find yourself in a crisis.

I soon realize that we haven't made a poor choice. In Thomaston, Maine, everything seems new: the lighthouses in the vicinity, the white houses and their shiny red and blue doors, the great meadows and endless forests. And, especially, the people. Everyone seems new. Nobody is from here. The town constantly welcomes new residents. Everything gives the pleasant impression of being a place where you can settle, where you too can become new, and acquire new friends, acquaintances, neighbors, and landscapes. You enter a home and start to imagine that family's past, as you observe the furniture and bibelots, and then you suddenly learn that they have only lived there for six months and that they bought the house with the pictures of the former owner's relatives on the walls. This is the case of the house where we sleep. Together with the pictures of the extended family, presiding over the house is a photograph of President and Mrs. Bush, its frame decorated with a garish ribbon. A couple with their children receive us at the house where we spend the day (we have a place to spend the day, but sleep in a rented room in another house). An open-minded family—as is often the case in states with a long democratic tradition—whose appearance suggests that they just disembarked from the Mayflower. They are also hosting a refugee Tibetan monk who witnessed the killing of his entire family, and a Korean man who, after surviving in the jungle on snakes and rats during his childhood, became a poetry editor in Korea and now ekes out a living by teaching at Harvard. The neighbors we gradually come to know are also newcomers. Marianne moved from Switzerland for love. Love ended, but she stayed. Erika came from Seattle to care for her sister. Her sister died, but she stayed. The owners of the house, our hosts, were born in Ireland, and after living in five different countries decided to raise their family here. Everyone is from somewhere else. That is what I was looking for. When you're young or are a student, it's easy to find places where no one is a native and everyone is from somewhere else. But things are different when you're older. And if, for whatever reason, you feel the need to go to a place where everyone is a newcomer, it's not that simple. Older people always maintain their roots, especially in Europe. With the exception of a few permanently displaced communities, in Europe we have always been accustomed to being from a given place.

You need two things in order to create the illusion of starting a new life, even if just for the summer: Everything must be a novelty, yet, at the same time, sufficiently familiar. This means I couldn't initiate a new life—not in the way I'd want to—in Patagonia or the Madagascar jungle. It needs to be a place that, though new to you, has sufficient points of reference to afford the impression that (again) you have the opportunity of inaugurating not *a* life, but life itself. And when you need such a place, Thomaston, Maine, is just the ticket. The impression I have here is the opposite of what I experienced the day I returned home without him. That feeling that the town where we had always lived was deriding itself—that the town I'd known so well had turned into a stage set.

Here, I am flooded by the opposite sensation, a pleasant one: an unknown town that, nevertheless, soon feels familiar, though you are always aware that it is new to you. A town where you feel anything but a stranger. It helps, I suppose, that you find people with whom to interact on every corner. Here it would be inconceivable to stand next to a stranger waiting for the bus without speaking. It would be unthinkable for the neighbor you've just met—when she sticks her head over the hedge—not to offer to lend you her bicycle the very first day she lays eyes on you. Conversations, it is true, seem rather perfunctory. On the long but rather solitary trek from where we have gone fishing to the house where we sleep, my daughter has counted the question "*Caught any fish?*" five times, spoken by the five passersby we met along the road. "Caught any fish?" asks an elderly couple walking a greyhound that Píulix (who's hoping to get a dog) immediately falls in love with. "Caught any fish?" asks a heavyset policeman who seems to have been lifted from a police procedural television series. "Caught any fish?" says a young guy as he strolls by with a bagful of bagels (not even a full mouth could hold off the question). And, finally, when we arrive, both our neighbor and our host ask the same question. And, for the fifth time, my daughter answers that, no, she has not. She leaves the fishing rod in the garage and says:

"I've made a fool of myself enough for one day."

"No, darling, it's just a way of making contact," I tell her.

Making contact. What contact? I've always believed that any contact not destined to last until the end of time was superfluous; I have never had this kind of superficial, pleasant relationships. So now, this too figures among the things that are new to me: superficial, pleasant relationships. This is precisely what I need now. What we need.

It is a curious summer. A summer of newness. It's my debut with a courage that is unfamiliar to me. My daughter does things that would have made me uneasy before, that I would have tried to avoid simply by not coming to a place like this.

I allow her to swim in the charcoal-grey ocean despite the icy waters. I let her go boating in a canoe without a GPS. We go fishing without fearing that the guy we catch staring at us on this lonely tract might be a psychopath. I allow her to go horseback riding for the first time without worrying that the arthritic horse I have chosen for her might unexpectedly recover its strength. We take excursions in the woods of Maine without fearing that we'll get lost or that an elk might attack us with its antlers; and to make the experience more exciting for her, I conjure up witches and trolls, as my grandfather used to do on our afternoon walks through the forests in the Montseny Mountains. We go whale watching one windy Sunday without fearing that our small, rickety boat might capsize. I allow her to play with the children of my neighbor Terry, whom I barely know, watched over by a Japanese babysitter whose references I haven't checked. Experiencing a new life imparts a certain sense of tranquility, similar to what you experienced when you were young and felt invulnerable. I try to re-walk the corridors of my childhood, that period in my life when I had no fears. To walk them now with my daughter and experience them anew.

I also decide to try some pills for the first time. It was a friend's wonderful idea, and she delivered the coup de grâce that forced me to stop pondering the matter and make a decision. We tend to think that being on medication is some kind of panacea, something that will bring us into contact with surprising aspects of our personality or make us feel unbelievably good. What I feel when, halfway through the summer, I decide to start medication, isn't anything special or even new, but rather a tiny increment of serenity that provides a sense of well-being: The crises I experience aren't as deep, my highs aren't as lofty. The volume of tears is reduced by fifty percent. As my serotonin levels have never been high, I assume they will now fall within the normal range. As the intensity of the pain abates, I am able to press on with a project I vowed to fulfill at the time of my loss: not to banish any memory, no matter how painful.

We leave Thomaston with the Korean editor and arrive in Boston, where he has his home and where we will be catching our flight. We spend our last days in this city; I will always remember it as the place where my daughter and I forged a new bond, a stronger one, built on complicity and appreciation. I am profoundly grateful to her for being, from the very beginning of the trip, a cheerful, attentive, and solicitous traveling companion. She is profoundly grateful that I, in return, have allowed her to trot and gallop on all fours through the interminable expanse of carpeted halls between the Prudential Center and Copley Place. Her passion for trotting and galloping is considerable. And every day while in Boston, in order to circumvent two kilometers of wide, inhospitable avenues to get to the center of town, we have strolled the full length of the Prudential. Every day she would ask with a pleading look, "May I?" and the transformation would begin: walking, trotting, galloping, neighing, snorting, kicking, and, with an unmistakably equine turn of the neck, stopping to assure that I'm still behind her, waiting for me as she swats away flies with her tail, tosses her mane, and trots off again. Never before had she (who gallops wherever she can and whenever she's allowed to) had the luxury of two kilometers of urban carpeting to trot and gallop on. And, observing the constant, bemused, and tender looks from passersby, I couldn't help but wonder what those looks would have been if I had been the one trotting along, especially as I often experience a nearly irrepressible urge to imitate her. What would the looks have reflected if she had been twenty years old? It is not improbable that one day, when she's twenty, she'll happen upon a similar place one day and feel this same urge. And act upon it. What would the looks be then? Or the consequences. Our collective fondness for small creatures has always struck me as rather sinister. But she is not twenty, nor do I give into my urge, and this allows us to place Boston on our list of benevolent allies, despite having trotted and whinnied all through the Prudential Center.

For these reasons, my reencounter with Boston is gratifying. On this last day, when I gaze at the sky one last time, I find that it has bestowed on me a parting gift: a remarkable cobalt-blue sky as I had only known in some of Poe's short stories, never in real life. While I am observing it, it turns greenish, as if an emerald filter were slowly being interposed between us, and then a storm breaks out, so violent that I have the impression of being atop a high mountain, not in the center of town. And this makes me happy.

Trips have always seemed a bit like going through an enormous automatic car wash, and the downpour on our ride to the airport is the final rinse. When I travel, I completely disconnect from my daily life; nothing binds me to my usual routine, not even literature. I never take notes. I think, *If it is worthwhile, it will stick*. Often, much more so now, I travel with a nomadic spirit of sorts, a willingness to allow myself to be captivated by my surroundings and, if necessary, to stay there forever. But I never do.

On the contrary, when the trip is over, I realize more than ever the significance that friends have acquired in my life. The bonds established through him and on my own (the friends among whom I count my family, or perhaps I should say my family that includes my friends) have become part of my life in a more definitive way. I wouldn't say they have become more important (I have always valued them deeply), but they have become more present; they have found their way into a home that I had tried to make impenetrable. With this change, I have lost that singular feeling of warmth and den-like safety—my shelter, my sanctuary, my cave. He appreciated the cave, but not as I did, not by a long stretch. Only those who are inherently unprotected (he never belonged to this caste) can fully savor the unparalleled sense of security that a cave can offer. I know I won't experience these feelings again, among other reasons because those of us who have found protection can never again do without it. We cease then to belong to the caste of the unprotected and, in consequence, no longer feel that powerful, glorious sense of shelter we had known before. In exchange, however, I have other things now. My new home has gained numerous, diverse affective paths, which course through our home like a breath of fresh air.

At the end of the trip, then, I realize that the idea of settling temporarily in Maine, among strangers, had been more a long-standing obsession of mine than a true desire. A desire that has lost its meaning now. I realize that the landscape that interests me is composed of affections, not forests or buildings, or anonymous beings. Almost a year has gone by, and the scene I see taking root is another: Some of the friendships we inherited have blossomed into something colossal. Others have remained the same, reinforcing their position with each new vicissitude. Still others, very few, have faded away because of a lack of shared interests. Other relationships have taken a curious turn. Almost all of my friends have given more than I am capable of assimilating, more than a cactus or a bramble ever could. In sum, the gains have been considerable. Old and new affections have coalesced into a new composition, and they have changed us.

It is always curious to corroborate this: You move a human piece, and not only does the general composition change, but each of the pieces changes.

A8

Skating in Central Park

Lot suggested once that they spend Christmas in New York. She and Cometa had been together for three or four years. He craned his neck out from behind the shower curtain to exclaim, "New York! What the hell would I go to New York for!" Good question, to which Lot improvised an answer he must not have liked, because she sensed that he was stewing under the showerhead. Finally, he announced that he'd sooner commit hara-kiri than visit New York. Lot was offended. She pointed out that he'd never traveled, but if he did he might discover things he'd never even imagined. "*Aletheia, aletheia!*" he shouted as he got out of the shower. "You must be one of those who think people can suddenly change, like Saint Paul when he fell off his horse!" While he was grumbling that he wasn't the kind of person who appreciated falling off horses and making luminous discoveries, Lot was wondering if *aletheia* was Greek or Latin; she decided it was Greek. "You are sorely mistaken if you think you'll turn me into a traveler!" he said in a surly tone, as if she had proposed that he become a TV addict, a legionnaire, or something equally bizarre. "I am not interested," he said.

He had always refused to travel. Naturally. Comets pass by, steady on their trajectory, immutable. Comets don't *do* tourism. They don't take excursions. With a nomadic spirit and a sedentary body, his territory was reduced to a small triangle demarcated by work, home, and bar. Occasionally, friends had dragged him on lesser adventures. The mountains of Camprodon, Soria to visit his roots, Galicia, the Basque Country—trips of that nature. Short and sweet. There had been other, more adventurous jaunts, such as voyages across the Cap de Creus with his sailor friends, where he became acquainted with the seaman self he'd carried with him since reading *Moby Dick* as a boy. All things considered, he'd only traveled when he'd been dragged into it. Forced to.

"And I will never change my mind," he concluded, stepping out of the shower.

And he never did.

But travel he did, and a lot. The Grisons. Alsace. Normandy. The Grisons again. Cornwall. Burgundy. Périgord. Périgord again. Bavaria. Jutland. The Rhone Valley. The Grisons again. Provence. Normandy again. The Baltic. The Austrian Alps. The Massif Central. The Grisons again. The Danube, up and down, and down and up again. Regional roads of all stripes and conditions. For years, Lot made him cruise the whole of the European geography. The narrative of their love story was to be built through travel, because only on trips was Cometa truly hers and no one else's. She'd followed him in his social and family life. It was his charge to submit to the travel plans she laid out for the summer. "Traveling is your desire," he'd finally accepted. "We'll do whatever you want. You decide where to go the month we have to travel, I will accompany you," he would say, with the air of someone about to self-immolate in saintly sacrifice. Whenever a trip was in the cards, he'd accept it as the cross he had to bear for having the wife he did. And no matter how much his traveler friends exclaimed over his good fortune, no matter how often they told her, somewhat moved, somewhat in awe, "He has discovered the world through you," he *would not change his mind.* She enjoyed challenges and went to great pains to plan everything to the last detail, knowing that he disliked travel and any small inconvenience on the road would perturb him. It was no easy task to ensure that his feline self didn't feel deterritorialized, or that some unforeseeable event or misunderstanding didn't leave them without dinner or reservations, or that they didn't arrive at what was supposedly a wonderful restaurant only to have to endure Los Indios Tabajaras as background music. On the other hand, he possessed very solid literary references for nearly all the places they visited, and seeing the actual places could only diminish and degrade them. He did not discover the world through her. He had already seen it, and with greater clarity. What could the Baltic or Davos of the nineties offer him, compared to the Baltic of *Buddenbrooks* or the Davos of *The Magic Mountain*?

He had always practiced a nomadism built on curiosity and reading, through which he had formed a personal universe. He had no desire to supplement the knowledge he'd garnered through the world of books and fiction with the so-called "real world." Curiously enough, traveling with him procured for her a wealth of referents to which she had access solely through him. He always knew what a specific dish or condiment consisted of, and if he didn't, he knew to ask. So, if they went to a restaurant he knew what to order, if they passed a market he knew what to buy. Through books, he had become a true man of the world. Lot, on the other hand, was a restless traveler, constantly searching for new emotions and, especially, memories. She was a bit like those people who always have their camera on them, and only look at the scenery through the lens. She was like them, but without a camera. She had a mental camera that made her see everything as though she were viewing the past of a hypothetical future, thus allowing her to select the best scenes with which to recreate her own story while she was living it.

Perhaps because of this, for their first long trip together, she chose a particularly trite scene, one that stemmed from her most basic romantic reference points, cemented during her childhood and adolescence: Manhattan—the Paris of her generation. When she was ten years old, the couple in *Love Story* that skated on the frozen pond in Central Park had made her swoon; and when she was twenty, the couples in Woody Allen films that strolled under the Brooklyn Bridge had been her romantic role models. Manhattan seemed an essential place to spend a few days with the man of her life. She'd never been there, no doubt because she was hoping to go there with the man of her life. And he resembled that man. Of course, she didn't mention any of this to him on that day when he was shouting *aletheia*—she would never have heard the end of it.

But they went to New York City.

Naturally, they did not go skating in Central Park. But, once again, Cometa surprised her by giving her a few unforgettable moments. Had he not chanced upon Dubuffet's cow at the Metropolitan Museum of Art, Lot would never again have thought about the museum (it would have been like so many museums where one views an endless succession of paintings, one after the next). It was a glorious encounter. First she heard his greeting: "Holaaaa," he went, in his strong accent from the region of Segrià. The cow returned the salutation. It was a moment of mystical communion that foreshadowed other encounters with successive cows during the course of their life together. One evening, five years later, on a farm in the Loire Valley, they were strolling in the countryside after an early dinner when a connection occurred similar to the one with the magical cow at the Met. But this time it was a real, flesh-and-blood cow.

Later, Cometa wrote in his never-ending book:

Dubuffet's cow lives a painted life inside an enormous canvas, isolated, without scenery, without meadows, without grass, without any kind of background; it is only her. She gazes. She is not a cow, but, indeed, the cow. It is a remarkable experience to come across this painting; one feels compelled to greet her— "Hello!"—to somehow address the animal. The painting achieves in the onlooker an immediate and inevitable approximation to his own animal nature. The museum explodes, shattering into tiny pieces. It is a joyous experience, a luminous instant in the somber, grueling cultural parade.

Lot was pleased to learn, on reading this, that he didn't find everything about their trips tedious, though he often grumbled and his views on travel never changed. Sometimes, the yammering itself was transformed into merrymaking. For instance, on New Year's Eve in New York. They had made the trip with another couple, and that night the four of them dined with a friend of Cometa's who was a sculptor living in the city. He was involved with a woman who worked at the UN. She was having a party at her place, and they were invited. When they arrived at the party, at an apartment in Murray Hill not far from the hotel where they were staying, the sculptor's partner was already banging a large spoon against a pot to ring in the New Year. About forty people, mostly from the UN and the New York art scene, were standing around, champagne flute in hand, or introducing each other. After a while of greeting strangers and observing a group of Catalan expats engage in an impossibly shallow and staid demonstration of folk patriotism, Cometa started to show signs of impatience. He didn't say anything; he was perfectly polite; but he seemed uncomfortable. Lot and their friends had nothing better to do, but sensing Cometa's discomfort, they suggested leaving, and he happily agreed.

He probably wouldn't have made any comment about the party, but Lot provoked him with an "It wasn't that bad," and he exploded. They were walking up Second Avenue, unable to find a cab, and Cometa launched into a comical show of perplexity that what they had just witnessed could have been termed "a party." Neither the cinematographic views over the East River from the fabulous apartment, nor the company of his sculptor friend could dislodge his impression of the coldness and banality of the gathering, compared to his opinion of what a memorable evening should be. "Party?" he repeated in outrage, recalling the circumspection of those individuals with their champagne glasses. Doubled over with laughter, the four of them strolled along to the rhythm of his invective against the ridiculous way of toasting at the party, followed by a celebratory account of the orgiastic parties at the old Bebop Bar, where whiskies were measured by the bucket and sensual moments by constellations. And Cometa walked on, too, taking long strides (*rapidly-moving calamity*, Lot called him), stopping every now and then to give someone a light, replying easily to the *happynewyears* from passersby before returning to his tirade, never skipping a beat. They had more fun that night just walking up Second Avenue and winding down at the hotel bar, the four of them, than doing anything else, and it was thanks to the first-class revelry that often ensued from Cometa's outbursts.

Like all good felines, he was out of sorts when removed from familiar territory. He felt lost when he first arrived at a new place, a bit sad and disoriented—a feeling that would wane a few hours later. The following day, however, it was as if he had always lived there, and after that, he was the local showing his newly arrived companions around. In this way, he managed to thoroughly enjoy their trips. But it didn't alter his opinion that small adventures were superior to great ones, and short distances more fertile: "Isn't it more fun to cross the street and talk about it with the same passion as if you had traversed the Amazon, and not the other way around: to cross the Amazon and not be able to provide a decent account of it because the leeches on your skin kept you from capturing the essence of your surroundings?"

"Maybe," Lot would mumble from behind a pile of maps and books, forever planning some trip or another, usually a long haul during which they would see only charming hotels and restaurants (as if they had been commissioned to produce a guide to quaint hotels and fantastic restaurants), but most of all, roads, and sometimes not even the scenery: If the roadside hedges were tall, as in Cornwall, they would only see roads. When, instead of a restaurant, they opted for a picnic, then the kilometers would add up considerably, as they searched for the perfect, most idyllic picnic spot (quiet, strewn with gentian and crisscrossed by streams), which she intended to capture with her hidden mental camera. Idyllic spots that were never easy to come by and had condemned them on a couple of occasions to lunching on a loaf of bread at five o'clock in the afternoon, while still behind the wheel.

They were opposites in the way they traveled. She enjoyed trips both in anticipation and after the fact. In between lay the present, the trip itself. Yet, once they reached a destination, it surprised him to see her turn her back on the place she had dreamed of to devote herself body and soul to planning the next goal. He, on the other hand, needed one day to adjust and two days to start to feel at ease; his level of satisfaction grew as his familiarity with the place increased. Perhaps because of his difficulty with arrivals, he never changed his mind about traveling.

She, on the other hand, did. Though she never lost her taste for travel for the sheer pleasure of moving in another direction, she came to understand other things: Under his gaze, places acquired an uncommon topography. Such as when he stood enraptured in front of *The Burial of the Count of Orgaz*—the only salvageable thing of their visit to Toledo—or when, at the Gundel in Budapest, she saw him bow to the chef and the maître d', who were touched by his gracious enthusiasm and would often stop by their table to say hello. Or when he drew her attention to the special quality of the morning light at Wagner's house in Tribschen, or was overcome with veneration as he tried to identify the rock Nietzsche mentioned in *Thus*

Spake Zarathustra, as they hiked by the lake along the path traversed by streams leading from Silvaplana to Sils-Maria, which they had taken together so many times. Like a precision tool that efficiently pulls up the particular herb one wants, Cometa's gaze would unearth the most succulent details and reveal them to her. And, indeed, it wasn't necessary for them to go anywhere spectacular; he knew how to make the most of any wasteland. "What kind of bird is that?" he would suddenly ask, pulling out his explorer's binoculars, and his curiosity was contagious. Lot slowly realized that she would get much more out of him if she accompanied him to a parched, crow-infested tract, or to a remote village in the Carpathians: Where there was nothing to see, he would uncover treasures. Forcing him to stand in line at the Uffizi on a hot summer in Florence, on the other hand, was like tossing a lit match into a haystack and expecting it not to catch fire.

Perhaps that's why they usually visited rural areas, where crowds were infrequent. All of their travels had been driven by an insatiable thirst she was never fully able to quench: the thirst for greenery. For as long as she could remember, Lot had yearned for green spaces and water. This yearning stemmed from the best moments of her childhood: the summers spent with her grandparents in the Montseny Mountains. She had grown up with a strange kind of nostalgia for rainy places and misty meadows, as if she were from Galicia or Brittany. She clearly remembered the first time she felt infinite sadness: She was six years old and she couldn't forget the place she had just left, the School of Grandma, that lonely house and school wrapped into one in the middle of the forest, where she would begin her summers by picking strawberries and would continue by inventing stories, watering massive flowerpots filled with blue and purple hydrangeas, and crossing the woods with her grandfather (who reinvented Botany just for her, answering all her questions with made-up names, as she would later discover). She adored the rain, and would go outside to sing under the falling drops while her grandparents searched for her, worried she would catch cold. Her yearning for greenery must have been an atavistic inheritance. Or, better still, one fashioned from words. Her father was from the mountains; her mother had met him there during a blizzard. Her mother and aunt had had a rather feral childhood in the southern Pyrenees area of Ripollès, a life where toys were improvised out of bits of wood, where her playmates were rabbits and hens, her enemies foxes and sparrow-hawks. There was also a homeless man who lived in a cave, whom the girls covertly supplied with eggs (of which there was never a surplus at home), and an imaginative father who, on Three Kings Day, would leave simulated camel tracks in the snow—meters and meters of tracks. Getting lost in the forest was not reserved for Hansel and Gretel, it was a common occurrence for the girls. To Lot, these experiences were the height of luxury. Having lived in a rather arid place the first years of her life, she was captivated by the illustrations of natural, overgrown British gardens full of wildflowers, and Alpine mountains suffused with purity, of the kind where cheerful Heidis lived with surly grandfathers. In a novel, the mere mention of a house on a lake with a forest of Norwegian oak trees was enough to make her immediately appreciate it. Those landscapes had always occupied a privileged corner of her mind, while the vision of an arid expanse curtailed her happiness to a considerable degree.

She assuaged a good bit of her craving for greenery through their trips to the verdant countryside. She and Cometa both enjoyed the fog and the rain—he, simply because he detested the heat. But, over time, the overabundance of greenness became difficult to digest for Cometa, who had no particular need for vegetation. Even she, who had never been able to go without it, started to sense that she'd had enough. The realization first came over her in an Austrian village where the weather was sultry and it would not stop raining, where walls were starting to smell rotten, and where they ate some disgusting potato balls served by a waitress clad in Tyrol folk costume and smelling of sweat. There, Lot finally understood that verdancy was not all it purported to be. "Maybe we should visit a different kind of place," she said. He replied, "Or no place at all." In the end, however, he suggested a few destinations, all in warmer climates such as Greece, or Castile—one of his favorite landscapes. But the pull that greenness exerted on her was so great that, given his flexibility, the following summer they would probably have ended up in the Swiss Oberland or in Asturias, had it not been for the news they received in September of a trip that would change everything—their way of traveling, and everything else.

A few years earlier, Lot had asked Cometa for a child. It was hard for him to understand. There was nothing about having children that he could find of interest, other than actually having them. That is, if ten offspring had suddenly materialized, then it would have been a *well, what are you going to do?* He was a man who accepted the fait accompli. But to "want a child," a child that doesn't exist, was beyond his comprehension, or, as he put it one day, not without humor:

"How can you want something that doesn't exist, something that is not there, which is to say, nothingness? Wishing for nothingness, now that is a strange longing!" He liked his life with Lot just as it was: intimate, filled with complicity, calm but exhilarating. Most of the reasons people had for having children were foreign to him. To educate someone? He already had his students. To tend to something other than himself? He adored dogs but had never owned one precisely because taking care of plants, animals, or children was not among his priorities; his mind was always busy, he never experienced a moment of emptiness or boredom that might have evoked the wish to devote himself to these little things. To protect someone? The possibility of abandoning another human being through an untimely death frightened him; he was over forty and he felt old: nobody in his family had reached old age. To experience love? His affective needs were covered to the point of overflowing. To project himself onto someone else? This was what he least understood: He didn't need to project himself or duplicate himself; he probably preferred not to leave any duplicate behind as his legacy—after all, they are never as good as the original.

The problem was that Lot had a hard time convincing him because she felt much the same. She had no understanding of the so-called maternal instinct. The dedication needed to care for a child seemed a waste of time; she had trouble seeing it in any other light. Taking a child to the park was not an activity that figured in her skill set. Nor was she interested in projecting herself onto another human being, quite the opposite. As for loving, she was terrified by the possibility that the fierce burden of love that she felt for Cometa might be dispersed: She believed children were to be had when the grip of passion and affection for one's partner has lessened. That was the right time. What she probably wished was not so much to have children, but to have had them; to avoid, for instance, the possibility of having regrets when she was sixty. "You can also regret having had them," Cometa would say. "But it's better to regret what you've done that what you haven't," she would respond. And so they continued to devote thought to the matter. As a baby didn't arrive, she had ample time to consider this. But, unlike many women for whom hoping to have children only increases their desire to have them, in her case, the delay served to turn the possibility of a child into an increasingly ominous threat.

Yet, despite all, she decided to pursue the possibility (in case at sixty . . .). Not wishing to associate sensual pleasure, nor having children, with any medical treatment, adoption seemed the ideal course, especially since everyone said it was a long, difficult process, so long and difficult, in fact, that with any luck it would drag on for many years, perhaps thirty, and perhaps the child would arrive fully raised, around the time of her sixtieth birthday—a felicitous gift. Lot's mother used every opportunity to take her to see adopted children, a bit like one would do with apartment listings. "You know? The pianist has adopted a precious little girl" "Guess what? The Folvias have adopted a Russian boy." And so on. Lot's mother had always had a soft spot for adoptions. For reasons quite different from Cometa's, blood ties left her cold. On the other hand, she had had a part in fostering the futurable nature of Lot's desire for children: Lot had never heard her mother say, "How lovely to have children," only "How nice to have had them." Such was the status quo when, one night, Lot, who had flat-ironed her hair all her life, saw a documentary on abandoned girls in China, with their beautifully straight hair. The very next day she made up her mind. One friend said that was not the way to decide to have children. But Lot didn't agree: She knew full well that the irrelevance of the detail that spurs a decision bears no relationship to how one deals with the situation once it materializes. In a ready example, Cometa was always irritated when he embarked on a trip, but when they reached their destination, he was a far better traveler than she was. Conversely, Lot had seen too many women experience an acute yearning for a child only to become terrible mothers.

Whatever her decision regarding the manner in which to have children, Cometa always expressed the greatest respect toward the issue. He would never have opposed her decision in such a delicate matter. Though he never said anything, it wasn't improbable that he saw it as another of Lot's projects that, once accomplished, would cease to interest to her. She might well proceed as with their trips, and once the child was in her arms, start planning more exciting endeavors and leave the child in his care, exploiting his skills as the nurturing father he had never expressed any wish to become. It was reasonable for him to think this. And she would not have put her hand in the fire that it wouldn't happen. It might, it might not.

They initiated the paperwork with a certain sense of dread, in an unhurried way. But chance doesn't factor in people's expectations, it has a wisdom of its own: The process was fast, so fast that, instead of waiting and waiting to receive a certain document, Lot often got a call informing her that the deadline to present a given form was about to expire. She picked up the final papers in person and filed them as though throwing a bottle with a message into the sea, secretly hoping it would get lost. Or that fate would decide for them and do what was best.

And fate did just that, with the perfect efficiency that characterizes it.

That day in September, after the soggy Austrian town, when they received the news that they had been matched with a child, their reactions befitted what one would expect of each: He awoke suddenly, immediately, without even a second's lapse, to fatherhood—a furtive tear, pure emotion, total readiness. She, on the other hand, was rattled. She felt as though she had played with fire and had been burned. She remained in that state for hours. And then she went to collect the faxed confirmation, a blurred paper where not even the girl's face was distinguishable. A few Chinese characters, something that looked like an eye. A name.

A radical change occurred in her. Can one paper alter so many things? The paper meant: No Turning Back. It was a "she's waiting for me." A "she was destined for me." As would happen after Cometa's death, on that day and forever after, the majority of her fears vanished. Not all of them, but the most important ones.

Compared to the trip on which they were about to embark, all the previous ones belonged to a different class. Mere preambles. He too must have believed this, because in one of the three "intimate confessions" he penned in his brief diary, which Lot secretly read, there was a line stating that their trip to China was the most important one of his life. Just a sentence and a date—the anniversary of the day they had taken the trip. It was out of character for a man who never remembered anniversaries.

B8

She is Here

She is here. Right here. An element of capital importance, both before and after his death. Excellent traveling companion, excellent fireside companion. In that she resembles her father: She is where she wants to be. She wants to be where she is. And she does not want to budge. She lives in the present and never yearns to be anywhere else. She is fully in the moment.

She is here, she and her two-hundred-words-per-minute, her rambling accounts and stories about what she is doing at each moment, what she has already accomplished, her questions about Papà, her songs from then and now, her galloping through meadows and hallways, and the echo of that laughter he called to my attention that first day at the hotel in Hefei ("Did you hear this child's laughter?").

She is here. As is her dog, whose name, taken from her favorite comic character Asterix, is Dogmatix, which seems appropriate given her dogged three-year quest to get him. "Tiiiiiiix!" I hear her bellow every other minute—the poor little hunter's name appears to have shrunk like a roll of Scotch Tape.

She is here. But I resist allowing her to acquire an outsize significance. *I'm devoted to my children body and soul. He's the center of my life. If it hadn't been for her* . . . I've always detested these expressions. I don't want her to be my entire life. I want to be light, ever so light, to learn how to tread as gently as he did (how is that done?). I don't want to be a burden to her.

Those first few months without him, my daughter posed little-girl questions. Some, difficult to answer. "Why?" "How?" "Where is he?"

Precisely. Where?

She's at that age when her classmates aren't young enough not to talk about it, nor old enough to know what they are talking about. As a result, she often comes home from school with this question renewed and with bizarre answers. Children are particularly interested in the body, and her classmates offer diverse theories on the matter. Today a girl shared with her some kind of homespun theory of reincarnation. She said Píulix's father was probably a tulip now.

"He is not a tulip!" I protest.

"Exactly," she says, "That's what I said. If anything, he's a robin or a squid!"

Goodness. I say: "It's curious how some people insist on believing that we're transformed into tulips, ash trees, or sparrows, when there is a far more evident reincarnation, which is the one that takes place with our loved ones." She knows what I'm referring to.

"Yes, I know, he's inside us, but they don't understand."

"In any event," I continue, "I'm in favor of skipping the plants and animals. Isn't it reincarnation enough that the loved ones who have left us live on under our skin and in our entrails, changing our habits, opening our eyes when theirs have closed, speaking through us? Could there be a more embodied form of reincarnation?" She asks what entrails are. "Well, entrails are,

230

say, the heart, the stomach, the liver . . . all of that's entrails, all of it flesh . . ."

But today, in the bathtub, she wants to know more. She wants to know where the body is. The bathtub is filled with bubbles, her snorkel barely visible. Suddenly she pokes her head out, looks at me through her scuba mask, and announces:

"Diana says that when you die worms eat you and your skin falls off," then she sinks back in, without the snorkel now. She takes so long to come back up (I can't understand how she can hold her breath so long) that it buys me enough time to piece together a response. When her head pops back up she says: "Is it true?"

"Hmmm, yes, but not in Papà's case. He is ashes, one day we'll all be ashes; we'll all be dust." Then, I praise the merits of dust and ash: weightless purity, etcetera. I recite Quevedo's verses—*Whatever final shadow that the shinning day may bring*—only the bits I know by heart, because I don't remember it all. I emphasize the final verse—*Polvo serán, más polvo enamorado* [Dust will be, but dust whose love still grows]—because the word "love" always catches her attention, and I hope it'll help me sidestep the issue without just changing the subject. Indeed, the issue is averted.

"Ooohhh *polvo enamorado*," she coos.

"It's the first gift I got from your father, Quevedo's complete works," I say. She wiggles her eyebrows up and down and smiles, assuming the mischievous look that the word "love" and its derivatives always provoke in her. "He recited it beautifully, knew it by heart . . ."

"By heart?"

Yes, yes—I think we're rid of the worms.

"Yes, by heart, like that poem about little Margarideta who dropped her comb while . . . the one you were reciting the other day. How did it go?"

"I don't remember," she says and sinks back in.

Her head reemerges. She's pressed the rewind button:

"Dust in love?" she says. "Does that mean that even if he has turned to dust he can still be in love?"

"It's hard to say . . . I know *I am*," I offer.

Her head bobs up again, and she asks:

"And you'll never stop being in love?"

"Impossible. It's too late for that."

"What if you fall in love again, will you be in love with two men?"

"I guess," I say. "It's never happened to me . . . (*Inbestigate!*)

But she's not done:

"Is the dust a lot?"

"No, no . . . it's about this much," I say, making a gesture with my hands.

And then comes the one question she's never asked in all these months.

"And where is it, the dust?"

"Well . . . the dust is in an urn."

"An urn?"

"Yes, a kind of vase."

She slumps back under the water and takes a while to come up again, as if she'd been pondering the matter; when she emerges, with foam horns on her head resembling Maggie Simpson's hairdo, she exclaims:

"He's inside a vaaase?"

It doesn't seem to matter, she dives back in. The hairdo dissolves. When she re-emerges, I say:

"All right, your towel is ready, and so am I."

"Inside a vase," she stammers, and lowers herself into the water. Her head appears after a while, covered in bubbles, this time in another shape, a cone hat. She asks:

"And where is the vase?"

"Good grief, girl, why would you care about a vase? There's no body any more, only the soul. What does a vase matter? The soul that animates us exists even though we can't see it. Or do you think you can see and touch the most important things in your life, such as joy, love, your fondness for your fifth-grade friend, or the distaste you have toward your snobbish friend? He's in our hearts, period."

She's no longer listening; she's gone under again. When she comes back up, she has pieced together another one of her theories:

"Do you mean this dust goes up to the sky carried by the clouds and enters our hearts through the bronchi and alveolus?"

"Exactly!" I say, delighted by such an explanation, entirely plausible for that matter. "But there's no need to say 'through the bronchi and alveolus,' don't you think? No need to be so mundane about it. But, other than that, yes, that's exactly how it works."

She finally gets out of the tub and I wrap her in the towel, while she repeats "alveolus," a word she must have learned in school, or in her books, and that she finds amusing. "It's *alvéolo* in Spanish," I say while I towel dry her hair. "*Alvéolo!*" she exclaims, bursting into laughter. We drop the subject, as she composes couplets with the word "alveolus," in Catalan and in Spanish, searching for other words that rhyme with it. Soon she's asking me about rhymes. We are done with the topic for

233

today. She'll soon be eight. I have never talked to her about death any differently than I would to myself.

It is clear to her that he's no longer here. And, yet, she knows she has him with her. She has a very precise recollection of the anecdotes. The times when he would act the clown by wearing her diapers on his head. The times he explained the heavens to her. The first time he tried to tune her violin and all the strings inexplicably started to pop. When he made her toast with garlic, oil and salt. When he cooked *kokotxas*—hake cheeks—clad in the King Arthur apron I bought him in Tintagel, as she sat at his feet, pressed against his ankles. When he lectured her on the importance of keeping one's distance from the car in front, which he considered an essential rule of driving.

She understands that his body will not come back. But she maintains some sort of tangible relationship with him through photographs. She switches them around. To renew him, she says. She takes pictures of the pictures with her camera. Today, she's put up a new photo, taken in the yard of the house with three doors, in the City of Fog, the summer she was four: The two of them blowing bubbles. Total complicity. There's a defiant air to him. He sensually puckers his lips to blow into the plastic hole, looking directly at the camera. Píulix, beside him, imitates him. Both of them sitting in the garden in Lleida, in front of the ivy, in the same spot where he read my first novel with complete attention, while I awaited the verdict. There's another photograph of him in the same pose, at age fifteen. He's beautiful. With two friends behind the fence that encircles the soccer field. A cigarette in his lips, puffed out in the same provocative, irreverent manner.

And another one: he and Píulix, the Barcelona night as backdrop, on the ferry to Genoa. It's windy. His thin, flexible body in the wind, like a question-mark-shaped reed; both of them roaring with laughter.

She often talks about the "two lives." She's ascribed to him a real life, which is now, in the present, and is a reflection of his past life. That's why she often says: "When Papà lived *outside* our hearts," meaning when he was physically present, as if the normal thing were to live inside people's hearts instead of outside them. She's made it clear that, as far as she's concerned, there are two lives: one that he lived, and another that we live for him. She thinks more about the good fortune of having had him than the misfortune of losing him (something I told her the first day, though I never imagined it could bear such fruit).

This excessive, invisible presence of her father seems to be good for her. Nothing is harmful if it's a source of creativity, joy, enrichment, ongoing regeneration . . . and everything is harmful if it's a source of sadness, destruction, or restriction of thought. She has evidently found this devotion to be joyful and enriching. Observing her determination to ensure that her father live on in this prolongation of his life, and the tenacity with which she refuses to let him go, I wonder where she found such zeal. Nobody has asked it of her. But then neither has anyone prevented it by strange looks or dense silences. She knows death is an important subject that should not be avoided; otherwise, it will crush your spirit when it catches up with you.

All of this has given her a peculiar take on death: She maintains a friendly relationship with it. So friendly, in fact, that for an entire year, she goes around singing the parts of Mozart's *Requiem* that I practice in the car. She even learns the solo parts. One thing I had always wanted to do but never had until now was to sing in a choir. Through friends, I've joined a semiprofessional one, but I don't think I can meet their demands for time and availability, or at least not for long. Nevertheless, for a year, we travel around by car intoning the *Requiem*. She, who has always loved music, has memorized it with greater ease than me. One day I ask her if she knows what the words mean, and I explain them to her. "Ah, that's great," she says. "Papà will like me singing it to him." And she goes on singing. But, then, at the end of the school year, when a close friend of hers in the sixth grade is leaving school and asks her to sing him a song as a going-away present, she says:

"I thought I'd sing him the *Requiem*." I try to dissuade her, and she's surprised. "What do you mean, it's too long?"

"No," I say, "It's more that it's not . . . well, I'm not sure it would be an appropriate farewell for someone who's going off to high school; it's more for someone who's going away for good, as I explained to you."

"Yeah . . ." she says, pensive.

"He might not know how to appreciate it," I tell her.

"Right," she says, a bit disappointed. But then, she launches into a full-throated rendition of *Quam olim Abrahae*. She has a nice voice. Joy.

Every now and then she says surprising things that at first I don't understand, such as:

"You know?" she offers while combing her hair, "Papà has won."

"Sorry?" I say.

236

"Yes, death lost. He won."

"What do you mean?"

She stops grooming herself and, holding the comb in midair, she says, "If you come with the intention of taking something, but you forget the most important thing, then you've failed: It's like if I want to steal a violin but only take the case." *Right*, I think. She continues, "Death took his body, but left what we care about the most."

"Right," I say.

That is how she deals with it.

As for him, it's maddening to think that he missed out on so many things with his daughter. He, a man without projects, one day (just one) devised a project. A simple one, one that suited him: "Next summer I'll buy a book on trees." He said it while we strolled through the forests near the town of Poblet, that last summer. As always, Píulix was at his side, holding his hand. You know what they say about girls and their fathers. She was present, intensely so, and her little voice was never quiet. Ever. When she was in the woods, she would imagine that she was walking on the seabed. She would give very precise instructions. "And now, you have to say, 'Watch out for the puffer fish, it's dangerous!' . . . Well, sort of dangerous. And I'll say, 'Okay, go behind the corals!'" And on and on they walked the seabed. He would go along with her—how exhausting! "And now you have to say, 'Careful, there, that's a shark's fin!' But you have to say it with a little voice, remember you're a baby squid!" And he would repeat the sentence with a tiny squid's voice. Inconceivable.

Nevertheless, the role he's been dealt vis-à-vis his daughter is not bad at all. In Freudian terms, if anyone is to have a symbolic life for a child, it's preferable that it be the father, who traditionally isn't much of a reference point, whereas a mother's influence has always been tied to her physical presence. No, the role he's been assigned isn't bad at all: He becomes frozen in time, forever young, while I, if nothing changes, will continue to age. I will fall prey to disease, arthritis, physical decay. He, on the other hand—the house dotted with seductive photographs of his last ten years—will continue radiant in his daughter's mind, in both of our minds. The scoundrel.

As for me, seeing her without him is the worst part of mourning. In some ways, your own mourning takes a backseat when you face it alongside a child. Often, the parent who is grieving opts for silence: A child's comments arrive when you least expect them, and they can be painful. In our case, obviously, silence was not an option. Nevertheless, I miscalculated the consequences of allowing her father to become a permanent presence. She has continued to talk about him, more frequently than I have, and I am often caught off guard. Because children don't give any warning. A child might be putting on a sock and say, for instance: "It was an excellent idea for you to find a boyfriend like *Papito*. What a great idea you had!" And you have to smile and not be evasive, because if you are, the next time she won't open her mouth. That is how she knows she can say anything and, theoretically at least, I will smile.

But sometimes it's hard to smile. Such as last Sunday. We were on the highway returning from Lleida. The A7 is where I struggle the most to conceal my feelings. The most important chapters of our lives have unfolded on the A7; it has been almost a home for us. We enjoyed life on the road, in the car. There, we had long conversations, we argued, we laughed— we sang requiems, cantatas, lieders, rancheras, boleros, and jotas. There, we listened to Camarón de la Isla, John Cage, and Renato Carosone, and later, the Smurfs and *La Rateta que escombrava l'escaleta* [The Little Mouse Who Swept the Little Stairs]. The titles of my novels were decided on the A7. On the A7, we resolved to make room in our lives for a child; that is, we agreed to it. So many things took place on the A7. We reached many important decisions in the car. I admit that it was one of my quirks. There are two places I prefer above all others: the car and the bed. It is probably a car's resemblance to a bed that makes it such a beloved mode of transportation for me: Ever since I was little, I have dreamed of having a rolling bed that would take me everywhere—a car-bed, a bed-car. The last view he contemplated, before returning home for good, was along the A7. And so, Píulix becomes especially sullen on the A7.

This is where she usually delivers her most gut-wrenching outpourings. Deep blasts that, in a way, you expect. One afternoon nearly two years after Our Loss, I see her in the rearview mirror looking downcast and ask:

"What's wrong?"

She says, "You already know."

"All right, but tell me anyway," I say. School is just out, and there are many things that could be on her mind.

In a slightly indignant tone, she says, "Have you forgotten, or what, this terrible thing that's happened to us?"

"No, honey, I just wanted to know if *something else* was going on."

And you smile. On other occasions, however, your smile tends to freeze. Two Sundays ago, for instance. Two Sundays

239

ago we were on our way back from the mountains, and I was driving along, feeling relatively content. Indifferent to anything other than the driving, I was pondering whether to pass a truck when suddenly she said: "You know what I'd like more than anything?" There was no need for her to continue, I knew what she would say. But she just *had* to verbalize it (*That when we got home the door would be open and Papà would be there and he'd hug us*), and as she did, I couldn't help visualizing that open door and feeling the most excruciating pain, which is a pain that is not your own and you cannot control—that of your child expressing a hope for something completely unattainable and forever condemned to perpetual disappointment. I was starting to plummet into an infernal chasm when, mid-fall—suspended, so to speak, before the gates of hell—I heard her voice again: "Poor pigs!"

The truck we were passing was loaded with pigs, and seeing it wiped out the perpetual disappointment, the interminable sorrow. My fall had also been momentarily halted.

That's the thing with children. They leave you with a frozen grimace while they, unstoppable, continue to spin the vertiginous, multicolored wheel of remembrance and oblivion.

The wish she expressed two weeks ago, to be reunited with her father, recurs in her dreams. She tells me about them every morning, and gets angry when she hasn't dreamed about him for several days.

"He knew how to summon certain dreams at will," I say. She then applies herself to it, without much success.

"It doesn't matter," she says, "because I put them on whenever I want to, when I'm awake."

"You put them on?" I ask.

"Yes, I click *open* and that's it. I've kept all the dreams he was in, I clicked *save* and they saved. So when I'm bored, I watch them."

Until now, her experience of these dreams has been joyful, but she's about to turn nine and finds that waking up is becoming something of a curse. They are the usual dreams one has when someone important is lost: She's given a puzzle, and when she assembles it, it's the image of her father; an angel restores him to life; I have a surprise for her, and it's him. And so forth. I too had this type of dream when I lost my father.

But I don't any more. Actually, the first time I dream that Cometa returns is during a trip to Mexico, a year and a half later. And you can't really call that a bona fide return.

A9

The Irruption of The Beast

Times were good when The Beast suddenly irrupted into their lives. It was in the form of a much feared illness. Their daughter was five. Traveling had acquired a new dimension for him, thanks to Píulix's insatiable curiosity. Waterfalls, rivers, horses, picnics, vultures—everything delighted her. Especially words. A word such as *cauchemar*—French for "nightmare"—sounded to her like "sea pig" and would bring on a two-hour-long laughing attack. A word such as *fragola*, which she learned in Positano when she was asked what flavor ice cream she wanted, could tickle her tongue more than tasting the strawberries it designated.

It had been a while since they had stopped searching for green, rainy places, because with a child, bad weather is a real bore. That summer, two months before the arrival of The Beast, they went to the south of Italy and to Megève, in the French Alps. Lot's choice of the perfect spot and hotel was hard earned: She had searched for months. Planning their trips had become even more complicated now, because they didn't like the beach, but Lot believed it was good for their daughter.

The challenge, then, was finding a beach that, in addition to being clean and quiet, met all of their requirements. Lot's radical take on what it meant to disconnect on vacation wiped from the list of contenders all the places where they might run into people they loved and who would require their attention. Cadaqués, where his friends vacationed, had to be scrapped, along with Menorca, where common acquaintances summered, Ibiza, where his sister spent the holidays, and a lengthy list of other places where they might bump into people they knew, whether loved ones or mere acquaintances. The choice also required not boarding an airplane (she wanted to avoid that as much as possible), which ruled out countless destinations, from Tunisia to the Antilles, and besides, he didn't like long hauls. The place needed to offer more than just the beach; it had to have some incentive for them as adults, such as good food, tranquility, a monument or ruin worth visiting. They settled on southern Italy that year. Lot couldn't count on Cometa to help reach a decision: "Whatever you say, I'm sure we'll have fun," was his only directive. They would visit Naples and the ruins of Pompeii. They would eat well. She recalled a trip to Capri as a young girl, and the bluest sea she had ever seen: It was imperative to see that blue again. Once their desiderata had been established, it was a matter of finding a hotel that would tick all the boxes.

She started looking in January. She soon realized that, in order to gaze again at the blue that is particular to cliff-top views, the hotel had to be in an elevated spot. That ruled out hotels at sea level, the only ones that usually have a sandy beach in front (the ones on cliffs either do not have a beach, or it is a pebble beach). It was a question, then, of finding a sandy beach below and an accessible hotel at the top of the cliff. Re-experiencing that blue was a necessity. She located a near candidate. But one important detail was missing: The beach had to be visible from the bar, where Cometa, who never swam, would sit and read. He liked to keep an eye on them and wave to them every now and then. This excluded very high cliffs, as well as hotels that didn't have an outdoor bar with a beach view.

With every nearly ideal place she found, another requirement, a new goal, surfaced to keep her looking. How she enjoyed those nearly insurmountable challenges! Never before had she faced so many conditions—multiple and even contradictory—in her search for a hotel. She was elated. From January to April, when she was finally forced to concede that she had found the place, she spent whole days immersed in her search engine, the prow pointed at expressions such as *spiaggia sabbiosa* and *a picco sul mare:* the two key conditions (sandy beach, overlooking the sea) that had become the main search criteria.

The definitive find was an isolated hotel on a cliff in Praiano, outside Positano, with a breathtaking view. It also had a small sandy beach, accessible by three elevators built into the rock and a series of tunnels that recalled the Maginot Line. There was a bar on the terrace from which Cometa could see if they were drowning. Such perfection was momentarily diminished when, arriving on the beach that first day, they encountered a large sign forbidding any swimming because of rockslides. They soon came to understand, however, that ignoring ten prohibitions a day was a particularly appreciated activity in southern Italy, one in which they happily joined in.

Il Tritone was an idyllic spot. A place that seemed intended for silence and voluptuousness, much as the ones they had frequented before the arrival of their daughter; a place that invited lengthy table talk and more hedonistic joys than could be experienced in the company of children. But southern Italians adore children, and they showered Píulix with so many compliments, so many kind words she came to relish— *bambola, bambina, bellissima, signorina*—that she also enjoyed herself immensely, running up and down in her striped dress typical of Positano.

It was a time when they were calling Píulix "Marisol, la flor de mi jardín" (Marisol, flower in my garden), because, like Marisol—the sixties Spanish starlet—she went around waving and smiling at everyone. Lot taught her the Marisol song that says life is a lottery, the lyrics of which had always prompted in her profound meditations on life.

It was in such places that Lot could almost feel the delicious aftertaste of their trips alone. And there, in Praiano, for the first and last time, she experienced a pang of nostalgia for those dinners, their passionate conversations, their intimate gazes before going to bed. And, on one of the nights at Il Tritone, for the first and last time, she wondered if they would ever have the chance to revisit that paradise alone.

Every evening after dinner, a boat would go by, a private yacht that seemed to host an around-the-clock party. A song by Renato Carosone would be playing on the boat. It was like an echo, a muffled sound in the distance. In contrast to the Capri-blue morning sea, the evening waters were misty and silvery. The entire coast from Amalfi to Positano is a cliff and, to their right, the nearby town of Positano offered an image of steeply stacked houses draped in bougainvillea. It was a moment of tranquility, the silence broken only by the distant echo of Carosone's voice coming from the yacht (*Tu vuoi fare l'americano, mericano, mericano, ma sei nato in Italy*) and the unmistakable symphony of honking SITA buses, whose drivers always strive to afford you a view from the cliff along the sea as they speed around tight curves with the temerity for which they are famous.

And so, in the evenings, bathed in that sensual peace, with half a dozen guests as their only company, the sudden, piercing sound of Píulix's whining felt like a slap in the face (playful, but still a slap) requiring some kind of response. It was always the same complaint, "I'm starving and I can't wait anymore," she would say, even after wolfing down a delectable adult dinner. She knew only two kinds of hunger: "I'm starving and I can't wait anymore," and "I'm starving but I can wait." If she couldn't wait, Genaro would bring whatever he could find, more olives, more polenta, more ice cream, more little cucumbers . . . and then Antonio would arrive, calling her *bambola*, *bella*, *bellissima*, and that would be it: There they were, surrounded by waiters, as though about to be serenaded, while Píulix sampled the food. "I'll taste it to see if I like it," she would say, adding, after two unhurried nibbles, "I'm still not sure if I like it." But there was never a case of her not liking something—whether oysters or sweet potatoes, figs or garlic soup, after a hesitant first taste she always devoured it.

There were no inebriated occasions at Il Tritone, no sensuous, intimate after-dinner conversations. In exchange, however, there was *la flor de mi jardín*.

All three of them felt a pang of regret when they left. From Praiano they drove to Champagny, in the French Alps, where they had rented a house for a few days. There, surrounded by anemones, gentian, and aster, they were treated to the greatest picnic scenery they had ever encountered. How strange that that particular vacation was so perfect. How strange that Lot would scrutinize it more closely than any previous one (perhaps because it was so perfect), as if it were their last summer, which it was not. But, in a way, it was the last summer of immortality.

That which she had always feared began one morning in September. She had always worried about cancer, the same cancer that had cut short the lives of all of his family members, those who had led healthy lifestyles and those who had not. When she met Cometa, he had just lost his father. Two years later, his mother died. And a short while later it was his Aunt Goldameier, a strong, fun, immensely generous woman; they had gone to Ibiza to care for her during the last stages of her illness. In the span of four years, three of the most beloved members of his family had passed away. His grandparents had also died young. In his family, only one great-grandmother, a relative of the Spanish poet Espronceda, was known to have reached old age, and they had only surmised as much because everyone remembered her as always being in bed and having long white hair. No one paused to consider the fact that neither of these characteristics was a sure sign of longevity— she might well have been no older than thirty. When it came to discussing people's ages and ailments, his family were rather vague; so Lot—who seemed to be the only person interested in researching the family's health saga in order to ensure Cometa's longevity—had considerable difficulty in conducting a proper genealogical study. But one thing seemed clear: Those on his maternal side were as strong as an ox (tall Viking types, blond and beautiful), while Cometa seemed predisposed to absorb the essence of his paternal side (dark, thin, and vulnerable).

She had imagined so many times that this could happen— imagined how it would all begin—that, as is often the case when you ponder something obsessively, she didn't recognize it when it did happen.

In September, engulfed in the autumn's usual whirlwind of activity, a weekend arrived at last when they would be able to relax. They drove up to Tossa, where their friend Andreu wanted to show them the beautiful house he had just bought, in the middle of the forest, by the sea. Cometa was uncharacteristically calm and quiet, but she didn't yet know why. On their way back, with Píulix, their friends, and their daughter, they stopped to hunt for wild mushrooms and had lunch in Llagostera. The following morning, she awoke feeling the weight of the new school year, in a glum mood because the holidays were over. He had been up for some time, and was reading or writing. She walked through the living room with her coffee, and though she usually had it in bed, as she read or watched television, that morning she sat down in front of him, ready to grumble about the end of the holidays. As she was about to open her mouth to complain, or perhaps she'd already started, he interrupted and said, "I think I should get a checkup." The words were so out of character that she felt as if the living-room ceiling were caving in on her; in fifty-one years he had not once made use of his health insurance card, and he had not seen a doctor since his collapsed lung at the age of twenty.

She rapidly gathered herself and, contrary to what she had always believed, this time she actually thought it wouldn't be anything serious. Completely unaware that a process had begun in which there was no turning back, she launched into action and, making use of her considerable resourcefulness, got him appointments here and there. In less than a week they had a diagnosis and a date for surgery, their only option.

The diagnosis was cancer, and the bad news continued to accumulate: It was deep, it was aggressive, it was terrible. But, after the difficult operation came a succession of positive news: It was not that terrible, not that aggressive, not as deep as they had thought. And, best of all: The chance of recurrence was so slight that no further treatment was required. During that period, any new piece of information caused a great deal of commotion. For Lot, the end-of-summer gloom was no longer of any concern. In its place, a concatenation of emotions in quick succession—blood chilling instants and moments that made you weep with joy.

That was her. He, on the other hand, took it with composure, as was to be expected. Dignified and calm, he must not have thought his circumstance very far removed from what he had expected his whole life. Death had always been a close presence. No problem. The undeniable proximity of death, however, did not leave him indifferent. Doubtless, one thing in particular brought a chill to him: the thought—which he did his best to avoid—that the two women he loved would be forced to live with his death sentence.

But that did not happen. No such sentence was handed down. Nevertheless, he did everything the doctor ordered: He quit smoking, which for him was like giving up half a life, something altogether unnatural. At that moment, only one thing obsessed Cometa: being a perfect patient. He behaved as though Dr. Behrens were about to come down the Magic Mountain to judge him, and he wanted to be worthy of the words the doctor bestowed on Hans Castorp, comparing him to his cousin Joachim:

"There's something civilian and comfortable about you, not like our sabre-rattling corporal here! You'd be a better patient than he is, I'll

wager. I can tell by looking at people, you know, whether they'll make good patients or not; it takes talent, everything takes talent—and this myrmidon here hasn't a spark. Maybe he shows up on the parade ground, for aught I know; but he's not good at being ill. Will you believe it, he's always wanting to clear out! Badgers me all the time, simply can't wait to get down there and be skinned alive."

No, he wasn't one of those people who are always on the verge of departing; he never had been and wasn't going to start now. And he wasn't about to bungle his vocation as a model convalescent, for which he'd been preparing practically all his life.

Entering the hospital system is a veritable adventure; you know when it begins but not when it ends. There were difficult moments and beautiful ones. Things become complicated when the foremost concern of both of the people involved is the other's well-being. Even after the period of convalescence was over, Lot continued to be fueled by the energy his illness had instilled in her. She had worried about his health for so many years that, now that what she most feared had shown its face, she felt empowered. She found herself, at last, in a position to attack, to face things head on. The enemy was no longer in hiding, and with that, the vague fear that had plagued her vanished. For the first time, she was able to put into practice (she had the theoretical part down pat) Cometa's way of living in the present, an attitude she was very fond of. Their present circumstance had enabled her to fully understand its meaning. She shed kilos upon kilos of fears. She savored every moment, every hour. She no longer waited for anything—vacation, travels—she wanted only to live for the day, from start to finish.

Nevertheless, it is true that her way of doing this was very different from his. Her irrepressible energy made her spend her days poring over the latest reports from the leading hospitals of the world; she knew her way around the Web sites of Johns Hopkins and Memorial Sloan-Kettering by heart. She read articles and researched clinical studies carried out with many types of medications and products. That alone had a calming effect on her, precisely the opposite of what he experienced. She enjoyed learning about statistics, findings, clinical case studies. He was indifferent to it all, completely uninterested, both in the medical advances that held the promise of imperfect futures, and in the percentages that she found so encouraging. "Eighty-two percent are completely cured!" she would exclaim with excitement, for instance. He remained silent. When she asked him if he wasn't encouraged by this, he would reply, "Let me try to explain: You're on the Titanic, and you're told, 'The ship is going to sink. Eighty-two percent of you will survive, eighteen percent will not.' This leaves me cold. All I know is that I'm on the Titanic."

But, as Lot was never fully in the present, she would simply fly over the Titanic, or swim beneath it, searching for escape routes. Out of courtesy, and because he was moved by her complete dedication to the problem, he would keep quiet and stay out of her way. He was grateful for her efficiency, her speed in dealing with bureaucratic matters or information, her medical knowledge, which grew according to the rhythm dictated by his ailments. Undoubtedly, some of this was useful to them. She was not cut out to be a nurse, however, and this she profoundly regretted. She did what she could; she was patient and meant well, but she wasn't sure-handed, and she was often inopportune. The kind of clumsy nurse who spills the patient's soup when setting down his tray, or unwittingly disconnects his respirator with a jerk.

Fortunately, Cometa was a good patient, autonomous and austere, and he never lost his sense of humor. Even in the critical moment, a week after the operation, when he needed multiple transfusions and the doctors didn't know why he was losing so much blood, he still managed to make her laugh. His sense of humor had naturally become quite dark. His family was there that day, his sister too, taking turns with Lot at his bedside. Compared to Cometa's sister, a delicate naiad born to make life pleasant for those around her, Lot was a calamity. That day, she decided to publicly acknowledge some of the qualities she admired in her sister-in-law, declaring her the best company anyone could wish for, especially someone who was sick. The sister, always Lot's supporter, protested, denied it, and was stating her admiration of Lot's dynamic, tenacious nature, when suddenly Cometa delivered the truth: "Well," he said, "there's no question that my little Lot has many good qualities, but being the best nurse in the world is not one of them." With the air of someone emerging from the shadows, a dark look in his eyes, he solemnly added, in a deep voice: "A rattlesnake would probably do a better job." The comparison brought on an incontrollable fit of laughter that might have been inappropriate in any other family whose sense of humor was not as frank as his.

For the first time, Lot and her daughter experienced what it was like to live without him for a few days. They were days of extremely cold weather. Snow blanketed the forest in Valldoreix, where Píulix's school was, turning it into a postcard landscape with Christmas carols piped through the loudspeakers in the schoolyard. After dropping her daughter off,

Lot would drive through the tunnels to Barcelona and arrive at the hospital, a true shelter where he—the awaited one—now waited for her. In the car, she played the Renato Carosone CD she had purchased on their way back from Praiano.

He left the hospital two days before Christmas. Píulix had not seen him for nearly a month, and both of them were eager to hug each other. After an intense snowstorm, it was now sunny for the first time. Two days later, they headed to the City of Fog; a frosty mist blanched the landscape in a way seldom seen in the past few years. The period of convalescence began, a winter he was able to devote to his perpetually unfinished book, his friends, his daughter. Lot would always have fond, warm memories of that winter.

She was brimming with energy and good spirits. She didn't know what had come over her. She feared nothing. She felt an incredible sense of strength previously unknown to her and the absolute certainty that the sacrifices—giving up smoking, the operation, and everything else—had entitled him to a rock-solid longevity. More than ever, she believed Cometa would reach old age. She again began making plans for the future. More long-term this time. She had never made plans for their old age, but she did now. She felt (she felt him to be) invulnerable. And yet, at the same time, she was more aware than ever that each moment could be the last.

Once the immense happiness with which he faced the months of convalescence had subsided, contrary to her, he felt acutely vulnerable for the first time. He never complained. But occasionally he seemed sullen or melancholy. After shining his shoes, he'd bring out a little tin of Valda or Juanola pastilles, open it, and silently set his gaze on an indefinite point outside the window. And then, suddenly, as if shooing away a gadfly, he'd rise energetically and exclaim with his warmest smile, "*¡Haya poder contra la Muerte!* [Let there be power over Death!],*"* a verse by Macedonio Fernández that he liked to repeat to cheer himself up.

Perhaps he was offering himself a dose of encouragement, so that he could go back to work or to the kitchen to prepare his cod dish, *bacallà a la llauna*; or perhaps he was trying to offer encouragement to those who might one day have to live without him. He would shake off his weakness and proclaim:

"Let there be power over Death."

El Ser no tiene ley, todo es posible. The Being has no law, everything is possible.

B9

Nopales, Pozole, and Escamoles

I never remember dreams. And the few I do remember aren't interesting at all. I really can't think of anyone with more mundane dreams. Almost everyone around me seems surprised by their dreams and proud of them. Not me. My dreams are usually so banal that they interfere with my daily life in a truly irksome way. For example, I might spend my night in line at the cash register trying to buy a bottle of dishwasher detergent. Fascinating. I queue in my dreams. I pay in my dreams. I bring home the detergent in my dreams. I put it in the cupboard in my dreams. Then, when I do the actual shopping, I don't buy it because I've already purchased it (in my dreams). And when I need it, and open the cupboard looking for it, I don't have it. Pathetic.

Instead of wasting time in this way, I'd much rather dream that he pays me a furtive visit, and wake up all aglow. But, no. It is only while in Mexico, nearly two years after his death, that I have a dream I can fully recall when I wake up. And it is not a pleasant one.

We're at the airport, he and I. From a loudspeaker comes the voice of Death, addressing us, "Sorry. I made a mistake when I took him away." Indeed, there he is at my side. I hug him—happy—and say, "I knew it. I knew it couldn't possibly be!" He takes issue with my excessive optimism, as he always did; he doesn't want me to be disappointed. And Death sides with him, "I made a mistake not in taking him away, but in the method I applied. It should have been slow. It should have been a long illness." I'm dumbfounded, overcome with grief. Cometa doesn't turn a hair, he takes the blow as he always did, with stoicism and humor. But I refuse to accept anything; I want to file a complaint. "Who do you want to complain to?" he says, ready to drop the issue. I study the loudspeaker and make out the logo of Mexicana de Aviación. I take him by the hand (trust me, *amor*, trust me) and we race through hallways in search of the airline. I arrive and state my complaint. But another loudspeaker behind the counter informs me that they are no longer in charge of dispatching Death; it caused them too many problems, and they had to drop it. "Try Líneas Aéreas Aztecas," says the loudspeaker. We start walking again and arrive at the Líneas Aéreas Aztecas counter out of breath. Behind it, a skeleton party is unfolding, with dancing and laughing (no doubt an oneiric evocation of José Guadalupe Posada's *Gran fandango y francachela de todas las calaveras* [Happy Dance and Wild Party of All the Skeletons] which I saw on a postcard at Frida Kahlo's house). One of them approaches the desk. But, as it gets closer, the skull turns into a megaphone and says, "It wasn't supposed to be a sudden death, but a slow death. So now, we have to redo the whole thing." My ears are ringing, and I'm nauseous. He has moved closer to the window and is observing a large airplane with feathers; I hear him say, "What kind of bird is that?" I scream, "Redo the whole thing?" and he rushes to my side. The loudspeaker says, "It was specified in the contract, in the small print. Do you have the contract, or at least the ticket or the booking reference?" "Do you have the booking reference, honey? Would you look for it, please?" I ask him. "Cut the nonsense" he replies in an irritated voice, "I'm not about to repeat anything, I prefer to stay dead." "You're only saying that because you are dead!" I plead. "You wouldn't think that if you were alive!" He smiles, then says, "There you go again, if this, if that . . ." I smile, too. "Everything's fine, just drop the conditional clauses," he says. I feel a mounting rage in my chest directed at the megaphone, which is prancing up and down the counter, dancing and rattling its bones. "Admit it!" I scream. "Anyone can make a mistake, but at least own up to it." The megaphone says it cannot, but then softens a little, and finally says, "He has to repeat the whole bit, there's no other option. And even if I wanted to change things, I couldn't; I'm just a subcontractor; everything is automated from the company's headquarters." "You see? It's always the same with these big companies that outsource their work," I tell him, implying that the real problem is the globalization of business. "It's not a subcontractor," he says. "It's another kind of bird." At this point, a deep sense of anguish finally wakes me up. One of the few anxious moments of our stay in this country.

When Píulix and I take our trip to Mexico, time no longer passes as slowly as it did two years ago, when our days of mourning had just begun. Gradually—I don't know when, I don't know how—time started moving faster, and now everything is back to the swift, rushed rhythm that has always characterized my perception of it. It seems like it was only yesterday that I embarked on this trip, but eight months have gone by. I came here for the first time last autumn, for work, and fell in love with Querétaro. The people at the Fondo de

Cultura Económica invited me to do a book reading, then invited me back, and this time I've brought my daughter with me. I take the opportunity to satisfy one of her oldest, animal-related, wishes: To spend a few days in the Caribbean swimming with dolphins, sea turtles, and colorful fish. She deserves it. She's spent her entire life lugging around her diving mask and snorkel, just in case. The usual Caribbean setup is perfect for kids, but I find it overwhelming. So every now and then, to escape the hotel atmosphere, we rent a car and take the road that runs along the edge of the jungle to the border with Guatemala, in search of a quiet, idyllic cove a few kilometers from the hotel. An easy feat. On one of these occasions, tired of watching fish underwater, Píulix sits down on a rock to inspect the sole of her foot.

"I love having these memories of *Papito!*" she suddenly exclaims.

"Really?" I say. "What memories?"

"This one," she says, pointing to a tiny scar on the big toe of her right foot. "It's from the day *Papi* went swimming in Corsica, and I cut my foot on a seashell. Remember?"

Yes, I remember, but I didn't realize it had left a scar. "It's really small," I say.

"What can I do so it won't go away?" she asks.

"I'm not sure, I'll have to check," I respond.

During the trip, for reasons I don't know, my daughter's yearning for me to reconstruct her father's presence manifests itself at every instant. "What would *Papi* do right now?" is a question she asks every hour of our stay. What would he say? Would he like *pozole* soup? Would he like this lady? Was this how he prepared kidney beans? Would he buy me an ice cream? What would he have said if he had heard what that boy just said? Would he have liked your friend Monica Sigg? Would he and Hector have become friends? Would he go swimming now? Would he like this guy as a boyfriend for you?

The questions are unrelenting, but not at all sad. The will to recreate the father she knew, to make him into an active, joyful construct, is such that I always respond with infinite patience, question by question. If I know what he would do or say, I stop to think exactly what gestures and words he would choose, and try to reproduce them as best I can. If I don't know what he would do or say, I tell her as much. And if I do know but am not sure it's appropriate to tell her, I keep quiet. Such is the case right now.

We have been atop a horse for two hours. A three-hour excursion through the jungle will take us to the ocean and, when we finally arrive, we'll go in the water on our horses. I find riding a horse rather tedious, but at least it's something new (*there's so much you've never done*). However, in the sultriness of the jungle, amid clouds of mosquitoes, it's akin to torture. Torture that I would endure with resignation if I had any privacy, but I have none. Certain Mexican males have a curious way of approaching a woman when there is no husband in sight. Often it's the first question they ask (*Where is the husband?*), and if you tell them there is none, some like to make advances along the lines of "There's nothing like a Mexican man to take care of a woman," or they offer to do you favors such as "Allow me to brush these mosquitoes away from your thighs." I'm uncomfortable around the *charro* who's accompanying us. He ogles me with gringo-green eyes as he engages me in conversation, while Píulix, who has recently become fixated on finding me a boyfriend, keeps turning around, with a raised eyebrow and a mischievous look on her face. At last I succeed in disentangling myself from the conversation and I ride up beside her. It starts to rain. The white sand covering my body (we're in our bathing suits) congeals into a disagreeable slush between my bottom and the saddle. Everything itches.

After a while, it starts raining harder, and finally, a tropical storm breaks, so intense that nothing itches any more. One can barely tell the humidity, the rain, and the mugginess apart. Drenched, we spot the beach where we will frolic in the water with the horses. I find this completely unnecessary. At this critical moment, once again, my daughter asks, "What would *Papi* say now?"

I have an answer for this one. I know it. But I keep quiet. *Stay calm.* I mustn't mention, for instance, that he would be cursing the sea turtles, because it's not completely true; it wouldn't adequately convey her father's mercurial nature. Who knows? He might be having a blast. She repeats the question because she thinks the strong rains might be making it difficult for me to hear her. For the first time, I decide to be blunt:

"What would he say? I don't know what he'd say. But what I do know for sure is that he wouldn't be caught dead here."

Píulix wrinkles her nose. She shoots me that look he would have called *defiant as a dagger's blade*, as though immediately placing all the blame on me for the disappointment I have just inflicted on her. "Why?" she says, incredulous. "I know he didn't ride horseback, but what if I had asked him to, like when I asked him to swim in Corsica?"

"Sweetheart, you need to understand that there are some things that . . . You can't expect a father to do everything just to please his daughter. You have to understand that everyone is different. For example, he didn't like to go horseback riding in his swimsuit, in the middle of a lightning storm, amid clouds of mosquitoes. Everyone has their own tastes, you always say so yourself."

It takes her less than a minute to find a justification for her beloved father:

"Of course, the lightning . . ."

"Yes, and he wouldn't have let you ride either. We wouldn't even be here."

"By Toutatis! By Belenos! How could a father possibly let his darling daughter ride a horse when there's lightning, dangerous as that is, right *Mami*?" she says, as water streams down our bodies. "Because it'll be a miracle if we aren't struck by lightning, right *Mami*?"

"Yes, honey," I say, before sneezing loudly, which again attracts the *charro*, ever attuned to our little miseries. "Did Madam catch cold?" he asks, wrapping a blanket around my shoulders; the fabric is rough against my skin, which is covered in mosquito bites.

We reach the beach. The rain has let up. Nearly everyone goes into the water on their horses. I hear her laugh, laugh, laugh, her horse in the sea, the water up to her waist. I stay on the beach with three or four other people. There's a little bar with a lemonade maker. The *charro* offers everyone a drink. When Píulix gets out of the water and off the horse, she asks for some. She's thirsty. He hands her a glass. She asks for more and he gives her a second glass. Suddenly, I have a presentiment (or perhaps I should say a postsentiment). "What is it?" I ask him. "Daiquiri and piña colada," he says nonchalantly. "With alcohol?" I ask in surprise, as my daughter gulps down a third glass. My level of astonishment must have come across as a tad excessive, because he replies, laughing, "No need to get angry, *ándele*, it's just a drop!"

I am lacking in Caribbean spirit, and the truth is that I'm relieved when we arrive in Mexico City. We're staying in Coyoacán, in a hotel close to the publishing house. But today is Sunday, and we're alone, so we visit Frida Kahlo's house, because it's close by and we don't feel like moving around. Kahlo's house and Kahlo's body, her letters and love stories, her illness and her paintings, all make a tremendous impression on Píulix. I find the house has a calming effect, and the visitors make me feel at home again: back to dark circles under the eyes and ashen complexions, prescription glasses instead of sunglasses. After being exposed for so many days to the oxygen-rich Caribbean breeze, this breath of stale air feels good.

But, once again, as in the autumn, what makes this trip special is Querétaro. For the second time, I fall in love with it.

The hospitality and charm of our Queretan friends and the magic of the city captivate even Píulix, though there are few adventures for a child here, and nothing is comparable to the excitement of the Caribbean. And yet, she is not indifferent to the city's atmosphere. Or to its cuisine, a topic that is always attractive to her. M.S. takes us again to Casa de la Marquesa, which used to belong to a relative of hers and has now been converted into a boutique hotel. She and I have coffee. Píulix and H., whom she calls Sancho Panza, feast on cinnamon-flavored hot chocolate, sugar bread, and cherimoya jam. For dessert, fried eggs with *mole*.

And yet, two hours later, Píulix announces, "I'm so hungry I can't stand it." I say, "All right, but you'll have to wait, we'll be having lunch soon." In the meantime, she keeps herself entertained by repeating delectable words she has heard or read on menus: *panquess, mamoness, rosquetess, antojitoss, escamoless* . . . "Escamoles!" she suddenly exclaims, remembering I had promised we would eat ant larvae sautéed with salt, cilantro, and serrano peppers—a delicacy. She insists, but M.S. informs us that the restaurant where she first had me taste *escamoles* last autumn is now closed. "It'll have to wait till the next time, when we come back," I tell Píulix.

When I go somewhere, I almost never think that I'll be returning with any regularity. But here, I do. There has hardly been a dark moment during the trip, other than when I awoke after that dream. Only a slight feeling of sadness on the last day. We're in the car that is taking us from Querétaro to Mexico City, and I see him floating among the nopales in the countryside, in his white shirt, searching in his pocket for a pack of cigarettes that he can't seem to find. Píulix is also looking out the window. She must have seen him too—we have an astounding synchronicity in these matters—because she suddenly says, shaking me gently:

"Heeey, cheer up, he's coming with us wherever we go."

This time, all I can muster is a weak, "Yes."

"Of course," she says, "you would like to have the soul with the body *included*, right?"

"Yes," I reply—a stronger, bolder "yes."

Then she adds, with a smile: "*Incluíído*," as they said at the hotel on the beach. She looks out the window again, and says, "That would be *padrísimo*—totally awesome."

Never were there truer words.

A10

The Last Summer

They had always spent part of their summers traveling and the rest near the monastery of Poblet. They were fruitful, placid summers. Cometa liked Lot's grandparents' house, the countryside of olive and almond trees, the climate. Everything was wonderful during those first years. The trips to buy olive oil, the hikes in the mountains with ninety-year-old Percival who revealed to them hidden grottos and breathtaking cliffs, the aperitifs in front of the monastery, the sunsets from the house with a view of the city walls, the drinks al fresco on the porch at night, the two of them talking.

Some things changed over the years: The view of the city walls was blocked by a new building. Percival died. The cheerful neighbor next door got sick. And, during the last summer, for her and for Cometa, she became terminally ill. As usual, Cometa rose at five in the morning. He went out into the garden to read, and then to write. But their friendly neighbor no longer stopped by to say hello on her way to work. That, and the fact that Lot had fallen in love with Buzy, the village in the French Pyrenees where they were planning to spend the following summer, set a less jubilant tone for that summer. And there was also the matter of Cometa's exhaustion.

Every now and then, Lot would again sense the disquieting red flags that, curiously, had disappeared since his illness nearly two years before. But it was a good summer for father and daughter. They flew a kite near Rojals, walked in the woods that Píulix systematically turned into seabed, and watered the ivy every evening; he taught her how to make Chinese hand shadows on the porch and, at night, the two of them looked at the moon through their binoculars.

Much of it was like any other summer: At night, they stayed up conversing for hours, while fireflies flittered around the lamps. They often talked about what they were reading. Or writing. About people. About the lit windows of Les Masies, the nearby spa in the middle of the black forest. About *Lawrence of Arabia*, which he had just finished reading. About a couple of books they were reading at the same time.

They also went to Corsica that summer. Ever on the hunt for secluded beaches that were geographically close and met as many requirements as she liked to impose, Lot had discovered a lovely place for them to spend a few days. Cometa had succeeded in enforcing increasingly longer stays in each place, and she had succeeded in accomplishing her dream of planning a house in a quiet mountain village. Lot spent the summer immersed in ideas for the future house in Buzy. She read books about flowers and magazines on gardening, roofing, fences, termites and termite-control products (she didn't have a house yet, or the wood facing, or the termites that would eat through the wood facing, but it was all the same: *If they ever did* have termites, she would know what to do). Everything hummed briskly along in her head. Her activity was almost feverish. She sketched all day, made gestures with her hand, opening and closing it, and took curious strides whose meaning only she understood: She was taking measurements. She had got in the habit of doing so without a tape measure, and her precision had sharpened considerably. Everything she looked at was perceived in metric terms: doors, flowerbeds, hedges, facades.

The days they spent in Corsica were the only ones of the entire summer when she stopped taking measurements. When she traveled, her desire to disconnect applied to everything, including her latest feverish project. She was able to quiet her mind completely. As usual, the hotel near Bonifaccio where they were staying had a beachfront and a lookout spot for Cometa. On this trip, he did something Píulix would never forget, something she had been asking him to do for a long time: He got in the water and swam.

Cometa's story about swimming was rather peculiar. Many years had passed since he had last been in a pair of swimming trunks. Lot had told Píulix the anecdote his family liked to share concerning Cometa's dry-run approach to learning how to swim. Their daughter loved hearing it: "He was around seven years old and still hated the water, or was scared of it, even though his cousin's house next door had the swimming pool where you swim now. He could have learned to swim there, but apparently, he wasn't willing to get in the water and make a fool of himself. So, for a long time, he would go down to the basement with a chair. Secretly, he would balance himself on it, face down, and practice the four main strokes for hours. Every day, they would see him head down with the chair. He never told anyone that he was 'going for a swim.' His family and friends found out later and teased him, using that weak line of reasoning that holds that one thing is theory, and quite another practice. He contended that by learning how to swim and breathe perfectly out of the water, he would only have to do the same once in the water. And he was right. He was in his teens, but he had never so much as stuck his foot in the pool before, so when he finally jumped in, the family thought it was a suicide attempt. His father was about to dive in after him, when they realized, to their astonishment, that not only was he swimming and breathing perfectly, but incredibly fast and with impeccable style."

"Oh!" Píulix would squeal.

And Lot would add, "And the family also mentioned something quite curious: He appeared to be gliding over the water." This part always made a tremendous impression on Píulix.

"Over the water?"

"Yes, that's probably the reason he's so fast, because his bones are light, and this must give him some, how should I put it? . . . aerodynamic advantage. The thing is, he actually does give the impression that he's gliding over the water."

"Oh!" exclaimed Píulix.

"Or so I've been told," Lot would add. "Because I've never seen it."

Over and over Píulix would ask to hear the legend. And, inevitably, she wanted to confirm it for herself.

"Why doesn't *Papi* swim?"

"He doesn't feel like it."

"How long has it been since he went swimming?"

"Wow, couldn't say."

For a long time, when he lived at his ex-wife's house, he had swum every morning, because he had the pool to himself. And he would recall the nights he swam while sailing with friends as the best of his life. Other than that, he detested beaches and pools, as well as sunbathing. And he hadn't donned a pair of swim trunks since he was thirty-five.

"What if I ask him? Will he swim here?"

"I don't know. You can try."

After hearing the story once more, she headed for the water, snorkel in hand. She greeted two girls in French, with the self-assurance she had at the time. A little later, Lot, sunning nearby, heard her still speaking in French; it was the first time Píulix was using the language outside of the family (Lot spoke French to her for half an hour every morning while taking her to school). Píulix was saying, "*Mon papa flotte beaucoup, mais il ne nage jamais. Jamais!*" Lot opened one eye and watched her do her dolphin plunge and come right back up, insisting, "*Jamais!*" with that emphatic little hand gesture she always made when using the negative. Lot thought she saw the girls point their index fingers at their temples, but a moment later, intrigued, they asked, "*Pourquoi?*" Píulix was unable to provide an answer, even less so in French, which she had not yet mastered.

But later, she asked her father: "Why don't you ever swim?" She begged and pleaded. Lot could recall every millimeter of her father's tan, protective arms as he carried her into the water at a time when she was still scared of it, and she had occasionally told Cometa that he shouldn't deny Píulix a similar memory. That day, their daughter managed to extract the promise from him:

"I will someday—maybe on a deserted beach, in any event."

"More deserted than this?" Lot chimed in. "There's practically no one, and, after five, it's only us." And he acquiesced. Píulix was elated. A man of his word always keeps his word, even when he immediately regrets it. The following day, in Bonifaccio, Lot purchased the darkest, longest pair of board shorts she could find. Cometa was about to make a great sacrifice. His strange sense of modesty dictated that not a single gaze other than theirs should come to rest on his swimsuit-clad body. And, by God, if he was able to manage that, it was only because there wasn't a soul left on the beach.

Around six in the evening, on the green landscaped hill sloping down from the hotel to the beach, they spotted a figure slowly wending its way down the path through the flowers. It was him. Sunglasses on, wearing a shirt and the swimming trunks that reached below his knees, and carrying a towel around his arm in case he needed to cover up even more, despite temperatures that averaged above forty degrees Celsius. His was a perfect mix between the surly air of a hung-over Jack Nicholson and the hieratic bearing of a befuddled Jacques Tati. That's what he looked like when he asked them to hold up the towel as a screen while he took off his shirt, though there was no one on the horizon—it wouldn't do for some sardine to get the impression that he flaunted his body for just anyone. Píulix warned him that the water was very cold in the cove where they were, and it was certainly true; the contrast with the blistering air was so pronounced that everyone who went in got a jolt.

Not him. Undaunted, imperturbable, without even letting out an *owww*, he waded into the water. When it was up to his waist, he turned around and said, "I hope you'll leave me alone now," and he started swimming with such even momentum and flow that he really did seem to glide like a shark. He swam so fast that Lot, who felt that age had slowed her down, lost sight of him almost immediately. Píulix was delighted and reassured her, "Look how small he is—there, there—look how tiny he's become." Then, he turned around and swam back. He got out, suddenly exultant, and announced, "The last swim of my life! It was glorious, I feel like I'm new!"

He stayed on the beach for a while, and then agreed to go canoeing with them. Píulix sulked because she wanted to row and they wouldn't let her. A strong wind was blowing. They were getting out of the canoe, as the sun was setting, when Píulix cut her big toe on a seashell. It was nothing serious; not even a Band-Aid was needed. She just hopped around on one foot for a while. Not even Lot—who always carried her mental camera with her, ready to capture memories for the future—could imagine that the cut would acquire such value over time.

The mental photograph she kept of that summer was from Palombaggia. One radiant morning, they spotted a white sandy beach with crystal-clear waters. It was deserted, and Lot thought that at least one of them should take advantage of such breathtaking beauty, if only for half an hour, before continuing to their destination. Píulix, for instance, since she always had her bathing suit on. They stopped and she took off running with that snorkel she never left behind. Lot leaned against the car, but Cometa, ever vigilant, walked down to the water, just in case. Lot could see Píulix moving from right to left, like a tiny submarine with only the periscope showing, her snorkel, her bottom and her fins projecting above the surface of the water. Right to left she went. Left to right. Lot watched Cometa, with his back to her, as he watched their daughter. And then she thought: *Another one; I've captured another one. Another image to feed my longing.* She was right.

Since his illness, she had been acutely mindful that every summer could be the last. And yet, she didn't indulge a fixation on the longing that lay in the future. Increasingly, step by tiny step (she had a lot of catching up to do when it came to abandoning the future), the present took over.

In a different way, he too experienced infatuations of his own during their trips, but his were fleeting, he didn't hoard them, he enjoyed them for what they were—though with great intensity. He had one such experience that September. They spent two days in Ávila on their way to Cáceres. It was love at first sight. He was blown away by the town of El Barco de Ávila, though probably the kidney beans of El Barco had a lot to do with that. He experienced a fierce, mystical communion with the place; it started at the city walls of Ávila and reached its climax at El Barco. "I want to spend the rest of my life right here, in this town!" he announced in a lofty tone. Whenever she heard him express a wish—precisely because he never expressed any futurable wishes—Lot immediately began to rack her brain for ways to make it come true. Could they perhaps rent a house there for a while? Would it be feasible to transport the house from Buzy there? Perhaps they should sell it instead? What house, if it hadn't even been built yet? Exactly, so why not? Or perhaps they could alternate between Buzy and El Barco? This was the one occasion he had expressed a desire to be somewhere other than the usual, and she was determined to do everything in her power to make it a reality. Yes. Partially, of course, because, during "the rest of (their) lives" they would also be occupied with other things: Buzy, writing, work, their daughter. And, yes, they could probably find time to spend part of their year in El Barco, even if it wasn't the rest of their lives. The rest of one's life is quite a mouthful.

On the other hand, how easy it would all have been if she had known that the rest of his life consisted of exactly thirty-eight days.

B10

Vegetables

As if he were peeling an onion, Jakob Magnus removes layer upon layer of a woman's body. One after the other. "I want to know if one can find the soul," he says. He wants to locate the soul. In the end, however, he only finds bloodied flesh: "I searched for it, but didn't find it." This is what he states at the end of the confession that sent him to the gallows. Hans Henny Jahnn wrote *Pastor Ephraim Magnus* as the war of 1914 unfolded. The publishing house José Corti salvaged it from the shadows and gave new life to that wretched character who wanted to find a living soul and instead committed a heinous crime.

The body is probably not the right place to look for such things. The body belongs to life. A Mexican saying, "He continued peeling the onion until he discovered that the skin *was* the onion," aptly summarizes Jakob Magnus's search for the soul in a woman's body. Fine. Let's not peel. But, later, when life ends and with it the body, wherein dwells that which remains? The body is gone, but where does the powerful presence of the departed emanate from?

The spirits of loved ones often have a peculiar effect on survivors: The daughter who didn't resemble her mother in the least suddenly turns into her after the mother's death. Cometa is a case in point. As a boy and a young man, he was heir to his mother's Nordic beauty, but after his father's death he began to show a slight physical and gestural transformation: He morphed into a carbon copy of his father; his well-proportioned nose became imperceptibly more Jewish; his expressive, chestnut-colored eyes turned a Palestinian black; his graceful body became more Gypsy-like. Does this happen in a voluntary fashion, unconsciously? It matters little: It is what it is.

The presence of the departed is bestowed in certain aspects of the living, whether physical or psychic, sometimes in improbably powerful ways. So, when Picasso lost Matisse—the friend, the indulgent father figure, and the best interlocutor he had—he announced, "He bequeathed me his odalisques." But it was more than that. Picasso immediately began to merge with his friend's legacy as he continued their dialogue. Matisse's presence was evident in Picasso's paintings, and echoes of Matisse's last room at Hotel Regina could be seen in Picasso's new house. Transformations take place in the living who are left behind: Before, the presence of the other is resistant (because the other is alive). Afterward, the presence remains; it abandons its resistance and places itself at our disposal, and we incorporate it with such ease and dexterity that it is not surprising many people come to believe in the power of spirits, something I have no intention of disputing (*The Being has no law, everything is possible*).

I feel some of these strange transformations taking place in me. For instance, why do I, who used to get up around eight to read, now feel compelled to rise at six to write, as he did? And despite my resistance (because it interferes with my meticulous plans), I have to admit that it has become the best time for me to work, as it used to be for him. Without causing him any travel woes, we have taken him with us from Ireland to New England, from Tamaulipas to San Luis Potosí. We know he can't see the clear waters of Playa del Carmen with his own eyes, or the enchanted castles that old Mr. Macrokady told us about. But why then, when I'm in Jalisco in the autumn and I go for a walk by myself in Tlaquepaque (a neighborhood in Guadalajara) and I hear some mariachis I don't like, am I able to accurately detect, as if I were him, the musical flaws I couldn't pinpoint before, not even when he tried to explain them to me? Why then, in Ireland, do I feel the need to drink more Guinness, if not to compensate for the fact that he cannot?

My little southern star also senses things. For example, when she sits under the desk where he used to work, she feels good and comes up with good ideas. That's what she says. She has set up a little house with all the necessary implements: the farm, the horses, the tins, the watering troughs, and a hundred other things whose use only she knows. If someone admires the little house she's made, she gives them her speech about her father's presence and how he used to work at that desk, and the person (in the grip of the political correctness that has made death a taboo) is shocked, while my daughter continues to explain that many ideas come to her while sitting beneath the desk because she can feel that he is there (But, where?).

It is easy to see him in such places: watering the ivy at the house with the three doors, or sitting at his desk, writing (But . . . how about including the body with that?). Curiously, the body's presence (the gestures, stride, gaze, voice) is best captured in words, not photographs. Perhaps because we weren't good photographers, in the sense that it wasn't our intention to capture hidden meanings with our pictures. I'm very bad at taking pictures, and he hated posing for the camera. So the hundreds of photographs I took during the first few weeks of our relationship are, in the end, of little use. Talent is required for an image to be rich and remain fresh. The images we have are poor, with a few exceptions: a photograph of him at a bar in Davos. He's talking to me through the smoke, and he's all fired up. And another from that last summer, with Píulix sitting on his knees. He's kissing her hair and gazing into the distance, with a look somewhere between serene and terrified, a look that stares into the terrible abyss of nothingness—a look that faces totality, everything, all things, Borges's Aleph. He is two months away from death.

And, nevertheless, even these images end up wearing away. Only the words, the pages he wrote, are able to bring us joy, offer us new things, and allow us to access his thinking. The written word can be constantly revisited, relived: It is not a sculpted gravestone, or a monument, or the name of an avenue . . . it is living tissue that regenerates, that speaks to us differently each time.

His book often helps me. I have only to open it to any given page and I hear his soothing voice. Yesterday, I choose a page at random, and I hear him citing Deleuze. And I hear him assuring me that everything is still here, now:

If we experience such difficulty in conceiving of the survival of the past in oneself, it is because we believe that the past is no longer, that it has ceased to be. We confuse, then, the Being with the Being-in-the-present. However, the present is not; rather, it is pure becoming, always outside itself. It is not, but it acts upon. Its proper element is not that of being, but that which is active, or useful. Of the past, on the contrary, it must be said that it has ceased to act upon or be useful. But it has not ceased to be. Useless and inactive, impassive, it is, in the full sense of the term: It is confounded with being-in-itself. It must not be said that it "was," because it is the being-ness of being and the form in which being remains in-itself (in opposition to the present, the form in which being becomes consumed and located outside its being-ness). At the limit between the two, ordinary determinations are exchanged: Of the present, it must be said in each instant that "it was," and of the past, that "it is," that it is, eternally, since the beginning. Such is the difference in the nature of past and present.

For Píulix, these pages of his are a fortuitous gift. They don't speak of botany or quantum physics; they are not a novel or a story, or a diary, which would be similar to a still image. The book is him. Him and his reading, that is: he himself. Maybe that's why he never finished it. When his daughter reads it, she'll be able to say, and rightfully so, "I'm reading his mind." With much more solid information than I had when I tried to do the same, sitting at the bar at the Bebop, on that first day.

Posthumous writings, posthumous poetry, posthumous voice, posthumous sex. I would have never imagined there could be so much posthumous life. And, at the same time, I had never lived as fully in the present as I do now, or done so many things, established so many relationships. He has left us a rich presence. He clearly had a vocation for posthumousness. In his diary, I find the following (one of the three confessions I've mentioned—the first one, actually): He says he is starting the diary out of loneliness. He doesn't wish to lend any pathos to this word; he's referring to the loneliness of the writer, not a sad loneliness, but a confirmation of the irreducible singularity of the individual, of the impossibility of indiscriminate communication. He says that every human contact is, finally, a hand of fate that isn't very different from the message found in a bottle in the middle of the Pacific. He says writing is comparable to hurling such bottles into the ocean with little hope that anyone will ever find them. He says his true vocation is the spoken word, but the avenues for its expression are closing, one after the other. His friends don't listen to him with the mindful attention he would wish, "with a few glorious exceptions that cannot satiate (it is a question of quantity) my dialogical thirst." This, then, has forced him to seek refuge in writing, because he is, regrettably, unique and alone.

"I have finally confirmed that I am Unique—the unique cabbage, possibly—but nevertheless unique. On the other hand, it is absolutely true that I am Posthumous: I insist, perhaps the posthumous cabbage, but posthumous nonetheless."

Unquestionably so.

A fabric made of words is like an onion you never finish peeling. However many times you visit it there is still peeling to be done. You will never catch sight of the bloodied flesh. It contains infinite possibilities. It is the everlasting onion, the infinite onion—that which most resembles a slice of life. To us, his book will be the whole onion.

A, B . . .
And All the Letters

Once more, she started a book. He had been gone almost three years. Every day, at a certain point along the highway, she would spot a billboard that read: GET IT OUT OF YOUR SYSTEM: BUY IT. It was a sports car ad, and inevitably it gave her ideas. Ideas. But what she wanted could not be bought. She had had it and now she did not. Fine. She could live with that. She could process it: Lucky streaks always dry up at some point. But what wouldn't she have given to be able to refashion a Cometa for her daughter in that often-conjured, hypothetical kitchen! Píulix didn't have the chance to know him well enough, and, in the long run, that would be the only real injustice in this whole mess. Something had to be done. He was, of course, comfortable enough inside the heads of his survivors, which is, finally, as good a place to be as any. Still, he needed a bit more action.

Between the ages of five and seven, Píulix asked her father about her favorite fictional character a dozen times a day. "What would Asterix say if he saw this?" "What would he do now?" "Would he ask for a sip of magic potion?" "Would he be shouting?" There were no new Asterix books to pore over—she had read and reread them all over and over, again and again. The complete works (to her, incomplete) he brought home for her one day weren't enough. She wanted more. She wanted the characters in her head to have more of a life. Curiously, after Cometa's death, she started to pose the same kind of questions, except now, instead of asking about Asterix, she asked Lot about her father. A dozen times a day. Months went by, then years, and the questions didn't diminish. Píulix was begging for a character, begging Lot to construct a father—a father fashioned out of words.

They say explaining death to children is difficult when one is not religious. Lot and Píulix had no sense of religion at all, only a few solid guiding principles, nothing more. But they did have fiction, which served all the functions needed by the spirit: Píulix had been brought up in this belief. They were cheerful, authentic beliefs that didn't deceive anyone. It wasn't necessary to invent superstitions or a great ideological system when they knew that Quixote or Madame Bovary, Hans Castorp or Holden Caulfield were, in addition to immortal, more real than any of their living contemporaries had been. As a result, though they were not religious, death didn't affect them as much as it did atheists who only trust in the objects of external life, which they are able to see with their own eyes and touch with their own hands. Píulix used to say, "I have my father inside my head." Just as her father had had William Brown and his band of Outlaws. As she now had Asterix, Obelix, and her beloved Panoramix.

Lot had never stopped weaving words together from the time she first met Cometa. So it shouldn't be hard for her to turn him into a character; after all, he was already one when she first met him. Since he had been gone, Lot, resolute as always, had ventured out daily into the darkness with her thick WordNet. In theory, with so many millions of word combinations, pure life in motion, what wouldn't she be able to capture? In practice, not much: a movement of his wrist between a couple of adjectives, a twinkle in his eye dangling from a comma. Still, that is considerable when the body is missing. Every now and then, she would give a little puff between two adjectives and a tiny bit of Cometa dust would appear. She immersed herself in her mission of constructing a Cometa for Píulix. Had she not had a daughter for whom this gift was intended, however, she would almost certainly have done the same.

Rediscovering a slice of that life rested now on her skills. She couldn't complain for want of characters: Cometa had always had the makings of a character. It was more of a challenge for her to become one. But she couldn't leave him alone in the book; she had to accompany him. That shouldn't be too difficult. Especially now that she no longer believed in the boundaries between reality and fiction.

When she started the book about the two of them, the first thing she realized was that she no longer remembered what she was like before she met him. She made an effort. And she recalled a difficult woman. A young woman whose men always wilted. Her gaze had the cursed ability to project heat, a heat that withered everything, burnt everything: the cities where she lived, the landscapes she contemplated, the projects she undertook—the men she loved. To make matters worse, rather than concealing her disappointment, she would tell them in all frankness: "You seem wilted." She would engage in something once and feel as though she had done it a million times. She began to wonder if she would ever escape this curse.

And then, suddenly, a man who did not wilt! How was it possible? He was as fresh as the dawning of the world. The years went by and he would say: "I'm getting old," and it was true. But he always had a freshness that was like the beginning of the world. The years passed, and he continued to plow his fertile mind; he still thirsted for meaning, and, above all, he continued to display that immense, comforting tenderness, without which all the traits that comprised his character would have amounted to no more than mere anecdotes. When they added a child to their lives, she heard him use a conditional perfect verb tense for the first time. "I would never have thought," he said. Lot was already asleep that night, in the house with the three doors, but the conditional tense must have woken her up. They had arrived after a forty-hour trip from Hefei. Exhausted and bone-weary, they put the little cot in their room so the baby wouldn't be afraid that first night. "I would never have imagined that a happiness of *this kind* could exist," he said. She, who didn't find it strange at all (because all she had ever done in life was to imagine the varying degrees, colors, and nuances of happiness and unhappiness), awoke suddenly, in time to detect a furtive tear in his eye. He had spoken with great emotion. "You said it, you said it! You have finally used the conditional perfect tense!" she exclaimed. "Wrong. I didn't say: *If I had imagined that it existed* . . . I said *I would never have imagined*; it's a confirmation, not an illusion." *Yes, but he has uttered the words, "I would never have imagined." Aletheia, aletheia—he's fallen off his high horse*, she thought, already half asleep again. It was probably true that if he had opened his mouth it was because he thought she was asleep. Píulix was asleep too. All the sweet things that Cometa said to them, he uttered while they were sleeping. Either he was exceptionally cunning or he had acquired considerable experience with women: He did his best never to say anything that could be used against him.

The daughter had forced the mother to poke her head out of the warm cocoon she shared with Cometa. But only her head. That was enough. Nothing in the world could force her to abandon that shelter. And she lived in terror of losing it. The warm parental insides would contract every now and then, as though warning her that one day there would be a harrowing birth. As though warning that no nest, even one acquired through struggle and hardship, lasts forever. *One of these days*, the contractions seemed to be saying, *you will have to venture out into the world. You guard yourself from too many things in order to remain under my protection. Let down your guard.* The message was communicated without being voiced. In silent yet audible words—the words of parental contractions. And one morning, during that last week, Cometa voiced this same idea more clearly than ever before. Premonitions. Lot felt a shudder that morning; he had never spoken that way, with those words, with premonitory words.

A few days after those words, he died, slain by the spear (What's the matter, *amor*, what is it?).

Only that—Death.

First, who-knows-what artery exploded, then the lamp in his sister's bedroom, then everything else.

It happened in the autumn. The season had always been important in their lives. They were autumnal people. He was a November man. Not a summer man, impassive and frugal; or a spring man, impulsive like fireworks; or a winter man, a blanket-man, snuggly and affectionate. He was of the autumn, a proper November man: tender and abrupt, passionate and quiet, neither profoundly sad nor exultant in his joy. Like true poetry, he touched the chords of pain in the midst of our happiness, and those of happiness in our pain. He felt the presence of death in the most joyous gatherings, and that of rebirth in darkest night. She was also of the autumn. She had died and been reborn so many times . . . Her father had died in the autumn. Her first book was published in the autumn. They learned they would have a daughter in the autumn. Their daughter was born in November, as were they. Everything that was good, everything that was bad, had happened in the autumn. And now, the explosion. All the fragments swept aloft, like a gust of wind that scatters dry leaves.

For a long time, the fragments floated around her. Nothing was in its place. Things would never again be all in one place, in the same place; now she would be forced to wander about in order to collect them. Distressing. The suspended leaves— like shrapnel in slow motion—had dilated time. This was a long period that seemed to have no end. And for a while, she was content with feeling numb. For a few hours a day. And then, it wasn't enough. She wanted to be, once more, what do they call it . . . happy? Well then, happy. We're never satisfied, are we?

The fragments began to reassemble. Some came together. Others disappeared. Others became more important. Some were completely new pieces. But nearly everything, she had inherited from him. He had left her a legacy of bonds that could not have been better had it been tailor-made.

Almost three years had elapsed when she finished the book.

Almost three years have gone by, though it seems like many, many more. How strange. I imagined a pain that would last twenty years, forty perhaps. An interminable pain. After him, I thought there would be only hell. And yet. I didn't think that joy could be possible again. Or even contentment. And yet. Sometimes (this is a dream that appears from time to time, one that I've failed to mention) I have a nightmare: I dream that the pain hasn't started yet. Imagine that. Sometimes, I think: *It can't be that this is all there is to it.* But, certainly—and this is nothing new—bereavement is work and elaboration, activity and transformation. And I am addicted to transformative work. I can't understand why things have gone so well, and by well I mean that we have returned to the fold of happiness without having to renounce his presence. But I will never know what this time of mourning would have been like under different circumstances.

If, for instance, there had not been so many pages to plow. If, for instance, despite it all, I had not insisted on trusting in the power of words. If, for instance, I had not been surrounded by all of this undeserved affection. If, for instance, he had not bequeathed me friends, some of whom are more than friends. If, for instance, my daughter did not radiate so much light. If, for instance, serotonin reuptake inhibitors had not been invented. If, for instance, we had not thought so much about death that when it did arrive (that's the advantage for those of us who always imagine the worst), it was practically part of the family. If, for instance, my mourning had been contaminated by guilt, as it sometimes is. If, for instance, I had insisted on getting rid of his clothes.

But it's also more than possible that his personality had something to do with this, and with the gentle mourning he left me, light and considerate, like him. That would seem logical. It is only natural that a tiresome person will leave you a tiresome mourning, a cold person a frigid mourning, and a scoundrel an inconsequential mourning. Some deaths propel you forward, others pin your big toe to the ground so that you cannot move forward without them. Some deaths, on the other hand, leave us with a mourning as light and gentle as a feather. A load so easy to carry that you never want to let it go.

"It is possible to live without memory, but impossible to live without forgetting," goes the line by Dubuffet at the beginning of his book on oblivion. The only way I have found to balance memory and oblivion is to turn Cometa's presence into a second skin. It happens to me often, with him. *Where is he?* I think, not realizing that I am wearing him. Like your reading glasses. You look for them—you can't do without them—and suddenly you realize that you're wearing them around your neck. That is exactly it. A memory so present that it resembles oblivion.

ABOUT THE AUTHOR

IMMA MONSÓ (Lleida, 1959) is a Catalan fiction writer and contributor to the main Spanish and Catalan newspapers like *El País* and *La Vanguardia*. All her literary works have been translated into Spanish, and most of them to several languages. She has received numerous awards, such as the Premio Tigre Juan (1997), for her first novel *No se sap mai*, the Premio Ciutat de Barcelona (2004) for her collection of stories *Millor que no m'ho expliquis* and the Premio Ramon Llull (2012) for her last novel, *La dona veloç*.

On its first publication in Catalan language *A Man of His Word* won the Premi Maria Àngels Anglada, Premio Salambó and Premio Internacional Terenci Moix awards.

ABOUT THE TRANSLATORS

MARUXA RELAÑO, a dual citizen of the United States and Spain, is an English-language editor and translator, working primarily from Spanish and Catalan. From 2002 to 2010, she worked as a journalist for different news publications in New York City, including the *Wall Street Journal*, the *New York Daily News*, *Hoy Newspaper*, the *New York Sun* and *Newsday*. She holds a BA in journalism from the University of South Carolina and an MA in International Affairs from the New School. She currently lives in Barcelona.

MARTHA TENNENT is an English-language translator who works primarily from Catalan and Spanish. She was born in the United States, but has lived most of her life in Barcelona.

Her translation of Mercè Rodoreda's novel *Death in Spring* was long listed for the Best Translated Book Award in 2010. Her work has appeared in *Epiphany*, *Two Lines*, *Words Without Borders*, *A Public Space*, *World Literature Today*, *PEN America*, and *Review of Contemporary Fiction*. Her recent translations include the novels *Waltz* by Francesc Trabal and *The Siege in the Room: Three Novellas* by Miquel Bauçà.

CPSIA information can be obtained
at www.ICGtesting.com
Printed in the USA
FSOW02n1301121214
3842FS